New Graves at Great Norne

Also available in Perennial Mystery Library
by Henry Wade:

New Graves at
Great Norne

Henry Wade

PERENNIAL LIBRARY

Harper & Row, Publishers
New York, Cambridge, Philadelphia, San Francisco
London, Mexico City, São Paulo, Singapore, Sydney

CONTENTS

Contents

New Graves at Great Norne

CHAPTER I

Parochial

LIGHTS shone brightly through the big windows of the parish church of Great Norne, and through them, too, came the cheerful sound of voices in full song. The voluntary choir of St. Martha's was just completing its weekly practice; collectively they enjoyed letting themselves go on these Friday evenings, without restraint of Service, and the more so now that Summer Time was over and they had the bright lights to encourage them. To a listener in the churchyard the singing might even have appeared harmonious, because at that slight distance the reedy treble of Miss Emily Vinton, a semitone flat whatever the key, was swallowed up in the general choral effect.

For ten years the harassed organist had begged his Vicar to approach Miss Vinton on the subject of honourable retirement, but Mr. Torridge had not been able to screw himself up to the pitch of striking such a cruel blow. For the last fifty years, woman and girl, Emily had lifted her voice in this choir, and for most of that time she and her sister had been the mainstay on which succeeding choirmasters relied, but twelve years ago Beatrice had been struck down by paralysis, and Emily had never recovered her pitch since that tragic evening.

Punctually at seven o'clock the voices died away, the big south door swung open, and out clattered a crowd of small boys and large girls, followed more sedately by their elders, six women and four men. Last of all came the Vicar, in cassock and biretta, accompanied by his organist and choirmaster, and by a small elderly lady in coat and skirt of antique cut and hat of nineteenth-century design.

"Oh, Vicar, it was perfect to-night, I thought," exclaimed Miss Vinton as soon as she was over the threshold of the Early English porch. "Mr. Kersey took us along with such a swing; I felt inspired to sing my *very* best."

A stifled grunt from the organist was quickly merged into his: "Well, good night, Vicar; I must be getting to my supper. Good night, Miss Vinton."

"Good night, my dear Kersey. I thought Bunnett in F quite in our best form. Oh, by the way, isn't Freddy Porter's voice beginning to crack?"

"Yes, that's one that'll have to go," replied the organist darkly, and hurried away before he was tempted to enlarge his meaning.

The church lights had been turned out now and the crash of a heavy key told that the sexton, Josiah Chell, was locking the big door.

"And how is Miss Beatrice to-day?" asked the Vicar, anxious to get away, but unwilling to appear discourteous to his faithful supporter.

"Oh, the same as ever—so wonderful, so brave," exclaimed Miss Vinton, her thin voice trembling with loving sympathy.

"A good woman indeed, a worthy woman; she . . ."

"Worthy the Lamb to be slain," broke in a harsh voice behind them.

The Vicar started.

"Really, Josiah," he said, " you must restrain yourself. Your quotations are neither apt nor reverent."

Chell grunted. He knew that well enough, and took an impish delight in acting the elderly *enfant terrible*. Sextons were hard to come by, and he knew the strength of his position. The pay was not much, and he might as well get what fun he could out of his privilege.

" You'll let me see you home? " asked Mr. Torridge, hoping for the best.

" Oh, no, my dear Vicar. Thank you, but it is *quite* unnecessary. Nothing harmful could happen to me in dear Norne."

" No, I believe not; nor, indeed, anywhere, Miss Emily. Well, perhaps I should be going in. The Colonel is coming up to discuss the Church accounts. Good night, then, and thank you for all your help."

The Vicar sketched a gesture which might be a salute or a blessing and which Miss Emily accepted blissfully as the latter. He turned down the path which led past the chancel towards the Vicarage, while Miss Emily Vinton ambled along the main path to the lych-gate.

The Reverend Theobald Torridge had been Vicar of Great Norne for twenty-five years. As his Christian name suggested, he came of an ecclesiastical family which had not benefited by any appreciable infusion of profane blood. He was, in fact, narrow in outlook and interest, harsh in judgment of his fellow-men, though diplomatically gentle with those who thought and saw as he did. He was a tall, handsome man, now approaching seventy years of age, but his good looks were marred by a weak and obstinate mouth, which he firmly believed to be strong and sensitive. He was a disappointed man, in that promotion, which he had fully expected to receive, had passed him by; he had sought consolation in a rising scale of churchmanship—a fact which had brought grist to the mill of the two Nonconformist sects which had taken root in the parish shortly before his arrival. He was a good preacher, and could still fill two-thirds of his large church, but the congregation showed a growing proportion of older people; the young thought him pompous and an ass, their harsh and critical judgment missing his better points.

Entering the side door of his big Vicarage, Torridge found that his churchwarden, Colonel Robert Cherrington, was already awaiting him and not too pleased about it. Colonel Cherrington was a heavily built, choleric-looking man on the standard pattern of the Indian Army, in which he had made his honourable career. He was a year or two older than the Vicar, and regarded him as a promising youngster who had to be guided in the right way—which was Colonel Cherrington's way. He was a deeply religious man; his natural tendency in this direction had been turned to near-fanaticism by a tragedy in his married life that had embittered his outlook on his fellow-men. What the Vicar of Great Norne would have done without Colonel Cherrington's stalwart and formidable help only Theobald Torridge knew—and he only in part.

"Evening, Vicar," grunted the Colonel. "Thought we said seven o'clock."

"We did, Colonel, we did. *Mea maxima culpa*. I should have asked you to make it seven-fifteen; it always takes me a little time to say good night to my choir. Miss Emily . . ."

"Exactly. Always a woman in it when a man's late."

Theobald Torridge flushed at this base insinuation, but thought it wisest to leave the subject.

"So good of you to bring along the accounts, Colonel. They are on the right side, I trust?"

Colonel Cherrington dropped a substantial account-book on to the study table.

"Not too good last quarter. Collections falling off, expenses going up. That fellow Chell's not worth his money; an impudent dog, too, they tell me, though he hasn't tried his saucy tongue on me."

" I'm afraid, yes. But so difficult to replace. People don't seem to need the extra money nowadays."

" Spoon-fed, coddled, cradle to grave. The country's financial position was never worse, and nobody works. That son-in-law of mine, living on his wife's money, instead of earning his own. No conscience, no guts."

" Oh, but I thought Captain Hexman worked on the Stock Exchange."

Colonel Cherrington snorted.

" Half commission agent, or whatever they call it. Sounds like an inferior type of bookmaker to me. Cadging business from his friends is about what it amounts to. No work about it . . . and precious little money."

As it was evidently a sore subject with the Colonel, Torridge did not pursue it. Cherrington was commonly believed to be a rich man, but there had been rumours lately that all was not quite so rosy in that quarter as it used to be. Indeed, few people living on so-called fixed incomes—pensions, invested capital, and so on—had failed to feel the pinch since 1929.

For a quarter of an hour the two men went through the church's quarterly accounts. Then Colonel Cherrington began to feel the need of his pre-dinner sherry, and knowing that he would get none—none drinkable, at any rate—in this house, rose to take his leave.

" Mrs. Torridge well, I hope," he asked, or rather stated.

" Rather poorly, Colonel; rather poorly."

Knowing that his visitor would not want to listen to a record of feminine ailments, the Vicar switched to a subject more congenial to the old soldier.

" Do you think this Munich settlement will mean peace, Colonel? The Prime Minister seems very confident, but somehow . . ."

" Peace? Good God, no. Neither peace nor honour. We've sacrificed a valuable ally. The Czechs can fight, and they meant to fight; they've got a magnificent armament works at Skoda, they could have held the Germans up till the French Army could reach them. Not only that, but the Russians might well have come in, too. I don't trust the Russian Government, but the people are fighters, when they've got weapons. The Reds have kept very quiet about their army, but they're proud of it, and they didn't make it for nothing. If we'd called that fellow's bluff we might have had peace; as it is, he'll go on from one grab to another, and we've thrown away two valuable allies and lost our standing in the world into the bargain. But none of our statesmen have courage now. Only Lloyd George; he'd got that, radical as he was, but he's too old. And Churchill; he's a fighter, and he was right about India, but no one will listen to him."

This tirade lasted till the Colonel had shrugged himself into his overcoat and was making for the front door.

" May I let you out by the garden gate, Colonel? " said the Vicar; " it will save you a hundred yards or so."

The evening had grown colder during the last half-hour, as October evenings do after the warmest days. The moon had risen too, a three-quarter moon, but it was often obscured by drifting clouds, and the rising wind sighed through the old trees that surrounded the Vicarage.

In spite of the cold, Torridge walked to the gate leading from his garden to the churchyard, and looked lovingly at his great church and its surroundings. He loved it at all times, but never more than by moonlight, which accentuated its massive strength and added beauty to the old yew trees that surrounded it. Now the drifting clouds seemed to make the church move, too, the tower appearing to sweep over towards the watcher with an effect that

was both thrilling and terrifying. Torridge felt a little
shiver pass through him, a shiver that might be physical
or nervous.

The moon was shining now upon a far corner of the
churchyard, illuminating a small white cross that stood
by itself, close up against the dark yews. That would be
Ellen Barton's grave.

The Vicar stood contemplating the scene in a mood of
sentimental melancholy. He hoped to lie in that corner
himself one day. It had not been filled because of a wave
of popular hostility to the idea of lying near a suicide—the
sort of unreasoning superstition that so often swayed
country people. But now it was almost the only empty
space left in the old graveyard. People were changing
their minds about it now. They did not like the new
addition, outside the old boundary; it seemed less holy
ground, consecrated as it had been. But he had been
firm; he was keeping that corner now for himself and
for one or two of the elect. The Squire, of course, would
lie in the family vault; but Colonel Cherrington had
pegged out a claim, and so had Faundyce and Willison,
and others had a right to consideration who had not yet
taken the step of talking to him about it.

Barton, no doubt, would some day join his wife in her
uneasy grave; Barton was a grim, hard man, cold as ice,
but he was a Christian, and though he never spoke of the
subject, Torridge felt that he had forgiven poor Ellen the
sin for which she had paid so dearly.

During the Vicar's melancholy reverie a heavy cloud
had rolled over the moon, darkening the whole scene.
Now it passed on, releasing the bright moonlight. But
the scene was strangely different. For a moment Torridge was puzzled; then his heart gave a bound as he
realised that though moonlight flooded the corner, the

white cross was no longer visible. A shadow seemed to cover it, a shadow that moved and revealed itself as a dark figure, with the glimmer of a white face.

It was only a momentary glimpse before another heavy cloud blotted out the view. When it cleared all was as it had been at first. There was no figure now.

CHAPTER II

Nothing Happens Here

GREAT NORNE had once been a flourishing little port, in the days before railways drew a large part of the profit away from the coast-wise carrying trade; before, too, the small independent fishing-boats had been practically driven out of business by the mechanised fleets from Yarmouth and other big ports. In the early nineteenth century it had attained its peak population of over five thousand, but it was now down below three, and numbers were slowly but steadily falling.

The harbour lay a little way back from the sea, being approached by a wide creek which in the days of prosperity had been kept well dredged, but was now silting up, so that only vessels of very light draught could use it. Coast-wise trade was a mere trickle, but a score or so of fishing-boats still made spasmodic efforts to earn a livelihood for their masters, and in the summer a short visitor season brought useful money to the owners of the few heavy petrol-driven launches that took loads of cheerful trippers a little distance out to sea and along the coast for a few shillings.

What saved Great Norne from complete stagnation was the fact that it had no near neighbours of comparable size. It was the shopping town for a dozen villages, and it was also the market town for an area of some fifty square miles. Motor-cars and cattle-boxes were carrying the more go-ahead farmers to the bigger market town of Snottisham, twenty miles inland, but there were still enough of the smaller men to bring useful business to Great Norne, and this had encouraged two of the Big Five Banks to build branches in the town, during their building boom after the Great War. Neither of these, however, had been able to compete successfully with the old East Coast Bank, to which the conservative people of these parts still clung faithfully, in spite of its antiquated methods and manuscript pass-books.

A single-line railway had its terminus at the town, and a narrow, tortuous coastal road ran through it, but a modern motor road had by-passed it by several miles— a fact to which the inhabitants attributed their enviably low mortality rate. Aircraft were still a rare sight, though there were rumours of one or two large aerodromes being made farther inland.

Altogether, though they realised that they were out of the way and behind the times, the people of Great Norne were contented with their lot, proud of their old town and its stately church, and ready to regard as an inferior being any ' foreigner ' who had not been so fortunate as to be born within their parish bounds, or at least within the confines of their county.

     •   •   •   •

Market Ordinary at the ' Royal George ' was the social feature of the week in Great Norne. Market business was not of such volume as to prevent anyone from spending an hour over this ritual luncheon, preceded usually by half an hour for short or long drinks in the spacious lounge with its modern corner bar.

On a Tuesday early in November three prosperous-looking farmers were sitting on one of the comfortable sofas, with a very small table holding three whiskies in front of them. Two were local men—Fred Pollitt and Jeff Lorimer—both in their late forties and making a modest living out of three-hundred-acre farms. The third was a visitor, no less a person than county-famed John Houghton, of Snottisham, a farmer and breeder on the thousand-acre scale, with a four-figure income deriving more from the breeding than the growing side of his business. He was paying a long-promised visit to his old yeomanry friend, Pollitt, and had gratified local opinion by looking in on the market and buying a few young beasts at a generous figure.

" Yes, you've got a nice little market here, Fred," said Mr. Houghton. " Too small a scale, of course, to get you far, but there were some nice beasts there."

" It's your Snottisham market that's dropped our scale, Mr. Houghton," said Lorimer. " The bigger men go there now, and it don't help us one bit."

" I suppose that's so. You know, I think it's your roads that's half the trouble. Narrow and winding, they're not fit to move stock on in these days of motor traffic. And naturally, men who can run to motor transport for their stock prefer to use a bigger market."

" Well, whose fault's that ? " asked Fred Pollitt warmly. " Your darned County Council. You won't spend a penny on our roads, and take our money just the same."

Fred was a big man, of bucolic appearance, and his temper was inclined to flare up at slight provocation, especially when he had got a glass or two of whisky inside him.

" Not yours, Fred, nor yet mine," retorted Houghton with a chuckle. " Government did us a good turn when they de-rated farm buildings. The little we pay on the house don't hurt us."

" Maybe no," grumbled his friend. " But you don't give us a fair deal here, none the less. Look at that old timber bridge over Gaggle Brook. Come the rains and Gaggle's a torrent ; that old bridge ain't safe, and you know it. Put up temporary in Queen Victoria's day and still there . . . but won't be much longer, I reckon, 'cause Gaggle'll have her down."

"Ah, yes," said Houghton. "I heard tell of that old bridge in Highways Committee. On the Holt road, ain't it?"

"Yes, a mile out," said Lorimer. "I come over it when I'm for town, and I tell you I don't fancy it—not when there's a flood coming down. Why, last . . ."

A burst of loud laughter from the bar interrupted his remark. The three farmers looked across to see what was the cause of the merriment.

Among the legginged farmers leaning against the bar there was a youngish man of different type. Fawn cord trousers, a dark blue shirt, and a riding-jacket of check tweed set off his light, slim figure to advantage. He had dark hair and a small, thin moustache, and was unquestionably handsome in a rather rakish style. He was grinning down at a short, grey-haired man, whose flushed face and watery eyes were now crinkled with merriment; it was he whose shout of laughter had disturbed the sedate atmosphere of the lounge.

"Who's young spark?" asked Houghton.

Fred Pollitt leaned closer to mutter in his ear.

"That's Captain Hexman—old Colonel Cherrington's son-in-law," he said. "Quite a card, he is; generally got a good tale to tell, not always fit for the ladies."

"And the old chap with him?"

"Not so much older than you nor me, John. That's Bert Gannett. You know him. He was in the Yeomanry with us in Palestine."

Houghton stared at the subject of his question.

"Good God! Gannett," he said in a low voice. "I'd never have known him. What's he done to himself?"

Fred Pollitt shrugged his heavy shoulders.

" The old trouble," he said; " can't keep his elbow down.   Personally I think it was that sock on the head he got at Gaza that done the mischief.   When he come out of hospital in Cairo he got on the loose with the Aussies, going the rounds and that like.   His head wasn't strong enough to stand it."

" Rotten luck," said Houghton.   " I never knew him intimate, but I'd have said he was a steady chap, with something to him."

" He was that.   What's more, he was in a fair way to be one of the big men round here.   Owned the Manor Farm —his father had bought it from Squire before the war— was on the District Council, and such-like.   But people wouldn't stand for his drinking, and he got chucked off one thing after another.   His girl gave him the chuck, too;   might have pulled him round if she'd stuck to him. Of course, he's still got the Manor, but he lives there like a pig, only an old labourer's wife to look after him, and the land gone to ruin;   in a shocking state it is."

Another burst of laughter came from the bar.   Captain Hexman was evidently trying to detach himself from the maudlin Gannett, who was patting him on the arm and trying to persuade him to ' have another '.

" Not to-day, Gannett.   I must be off to lunch. Won't do to keep the Colonel waiting."

" Do the old mucker good.   Your pardon, Cap'n; shouldn't say that.   You come along to my place one evening.   Got something there, I have—nice drop of something that does you good.   Any evening you fancy; I'm always there.   No competition for Bert Gannett's company these days.   Kindness to come and have a yarn with me."

" Of course I'll come;   delighted.   So long now. Morning, Mrs. Winch.   Morning, everybody."

With a wave of the hand, George Hexman strode towards the entrance, but paused to have a word with Fred Pollitt. He leant down to him and murmured:

"Old Gannett's two over the eight this morning, I'm afraid. Daresay you'll keep an eye on him."

"I generally do that, market days," said Pollitt drily. "You know Mr. Houghton? Big man on the N.F.U., County Council, and all that. Come to show us how to do things in Norne."

The two men shook hands.

"Don't pay any attention to him, Captain Hexman," said the visitor. "He's jealous 'cause I outbid him for a pair of heifers he thought he was going to get on the cheap. You've got a nice market here, I've been telling them."

"*I* haven't," laughed Hexman. "I'm only a foreigner, as they call anyone who wasn't born in the place. But I agree, it's a good market, and Great Norne's a place to be fond of. But I must be getting on. Glad to have met you, Mr. Houghton. Morning, Pollitt; morning, Lorimer."

"Seems an affable sort of chap," said Houghton, when the soldier was out of earshot.

"Oh, yes, he's that all right. Bit too affable, some of them thinks. Personally I like him; gives himself no airs and always got a cheery word."

"Can't think how a young chap can kick his heels about doing nothing," said the quiet Lorimer.

"He's not in the Army now, then?" asked Houghton.

"No, retired when he married the Colonel's daughter. I fancy the old Colonel's not too pleased about it. He's not so well off as he used to be, they do say. Probably doesn't see why he should keep the Captain in luxury."

"And I don't blame him," said Lorimer. "The young fellow does a bit in London at times—Stock Exchange or something—but it can't be steady work because he's down here so much. Bit of a parasite, I'd call him."

Unconscious of the verbal autopsy to which he was being subjected, Captain George Hexman was meanwhile striding down the High Street towards Monks Holme, the old house on the eastern outskirts of the town which was the home of Colonel Cherrington. What he was conscious of was the fact that he had had perhaps two whiskies too many and that his wife would certainly have something to say about it. Still, for the moment the effect was agreeable and his heart was enlarged unto his fellow men. So much so that he stopped to greet the first person whom he met upon his homeward way. This was Richard Barton, the principal builder of the town, a sturdy, thick-set man of about fifty, dark, handsome, but with an expression so coldly ·grim that under normal conditions Hexman would have thought twice about casting a fly over him. However, those two extra whiskies. . . .

"Morning, Mr. Barton. You on your way to the ' George '? "

The builder did not check his stride, but raised his hand to his bowler hat, said: " Good-morning, sir," and continued on his way.

A flush of angry colour deepened the existing tint on Hexman's face. He stared after Barton, and did not at first notice a small car that had drawn up at the kerb beside him. A young man put his head out of the window.

"Morning, George. That was a fairly short talk you had with Barton."

"Surly——," muttered Hexman. "Oh, hullo, doc; I didn't see you. What's the matter with that chap? "

Dr. Stopp extracted himself from his minute car and held out a packet of cigarettes. He was short and square, with an aggressive jaw and alert grey eyes.

" Nature of the beast, I should think," he said. " I've never yet seen him smile. As a matter of fact, now I come to think of it, I believe he did have something to sour him years before I came here; in fact, I know he did. Wife had an affair with a young sailor, and when Barton found out, she did herself in."

" Bit overdoing it, what? Was he a local fisherman? "

" No, a naval rating, I believe."

" Ah, ' every nice girl ' and all that."

" Exactly. She seems to have taken it too literally—and too seriously. But it was umpteen years ago. You'd have thought he might have got over it by now."

" Probably has. Just didn't like the look of Captain George Hexman, I expect."

" That might well be. As I say, though, I've never seen him smile. But he's so damned healthy that I don't know him as well as I should like to."

" Lot of ghouls you fellows are. I suppose you prefer a sick man to a sound one."

" Well, a doctor must live."

" Not necessarily. I believe we should do better without you—stop fussing about ourselves."

" I shouldn't think you did much of that, George. Anyway, when are we going to have another round? I want to try that new putter of Dixon's."

" I don't suppose I shall be here much longer," said Hexman gloomily. " The old man's always getting at me to go and do some work. There's simply nothing doing on the Stock Exchange; all this war talk."

" I should have thought you'd welcome that. Bit of fun for a soldier. It beats me why you hang about in a dead-alive place like this. Nothing ever happens here. People are just born, live about a hundred years till their arteries are practically ossified, and then die."

" Not a doctor's paradise, certainly," said Hexman with a grin. " But why do you stay here if you don't like the place? "

" Because I can't afford to get out yet. My dad bought me a quarter share partnership with Faundyce, with a reversion of the practice when the old boy dies. I don't see any reason to suppose he'll do that for another twenty years."

George Hexman inhaled deeply and let the smoke trickle out through his nose.

" What's the good of being a doctor if you can't regulate a little thing like that? " he said.

CHAPTER III

In the Mist

A HEAVY mist lay over the town and harbour of Great Norne. Whether it was sea mist or November fog or a combination of the two only an expert could say, but it had been there ever since dusk the previous evening, and had covered everything with a skin of clammy dampness more depressing than rain. But the natives of the East coast were accustomed to it, and did not let it interfere much with the normal routine of their lives.

Certainly old Silas Penticle paid little attention to it as he wandered round the harbour, carrying out the simple duties for which he was paid. Silas had been a fisherman and a member of the lifeboat crew, but had sustained a compound fracture of the thigh in the course of rescue work. At his age—he was over sixty—the mend was of doubtful security, and he was compelled to give up the sea and descend to the humble status of a long-shore-man; but the Town Council, in recognition of his gallant service, had invented a harbour job for him, in order to have an excuse for providing him with an honourable livelihood. His duties consisted of little more than keeping the quay clear of obstructions, controlling its use in the unlikely event of their being excessive competition for its accommodation, and discouraging children from falling over the edge or committing acts of damage or immodesty in the presence of visitors.

Early on this misty morning Silas was hobbling slowly along the edge of the quay, quite unconscious of any risk of falling over himself. He was sucking at an ancient briar pipe, and every now and then he would pause to spit over the edge. Silas's hearing was still acute, and he could hear the gob hit the water after an appreciable interval—an indication, had he needed one, that the tide was low.

Presently he came to the top of the flight of steps that led down to the water, and stood there contemplating the soles of a pair of boots that presented themselves surprisingly about the level of the third step. The boots were attached to black-trousered legs, but the rest of what was presumably a human form was obscured by the mist. Slowly and deliberately old Penticle lowered himself tread by tread until he could see the whole of the body, which lay on its back, head downward, on the steps. When he could see the face he paused, slowly withdrew the pipe from his mouth, and spat again.

" By ——," he exclaimed; " if it ain't t'old vicar."

The oath was of a rich profanity that would no doubt have caused distress to the Reverend Theobald Torridge if he had heard it. But he did not, and never would again hear either blessing or cursing.

Silas Penticle knew nothing about *rigor mortis*, but in the course of his long contest with the sea he had seen enough of death to realise that this rigid figure was not only dead, but had been dead for some hours. The fact that caught his attention at once, because it impinged upon his own duties, was that the legs were caught up in a tangle of rope, one end of which was attached to a bollard on the quay. It was this, no doubt, that had prevented the body from slipping farther down the steps, possibly even into the water; as it was, the head was above the normal level of high tide.

Automatically Silas disengaged the rope from the legs and coiled it near the bollard. The body, being rigid, and having a shoulder wedged against the wall of the steps, did not move. The longshoreman bent down to see if he could discover the actual cause of death, though it seemed certain that this must be due to a fractured skull or a broken neck. He put a hand under the head to lift it, and as he bent down to look he became aware of a faint odour that seemed familiar to him. Lowering himself another couple of steps, he put his own face close to that of the dead man, and at once his nose owned to the scent of whisky.

" Well I'll be ——."

Once again it was as well that the reverend gentleman could not hear.

But the smell on the lips was very faint indeed, and Silas did not think that it would have reached him had he not bent right down to it. Moving his hands over the body, he heard a faint clink from the skirt of the black coat, and there he found the smell of whisky again. Putting his hand into a pocket, he extracted several pieces of glass that seemed to be fragments of a broken bottle or flask.

Silas knew that the Vicar was in the habit of visiting the Men's Club, which stood on one side of the harbour, on certain evenings in the month; he had first imagined that Mr. Torridge had lost his way in the mist, tripped over the bollard or the coil of rope, and crashed down on to the steps. But now it seemed that there might be another explanation of the wandering footsteps. However, that was nothing of old Silas's business, and it occurred to him that it was about time he got hold of a doctor or a policeman. Hoisting himself up to quay level, he hobbled off towards the town, and presently was in collision with a small boy who came dashing round the corner of the nearest house. Just managing to retain his balance, Penticle grabbed the small boy by the arm.

" Watch your steering, you little varmint," he exclaimed angrily. " You'll sink someone one o' these days."

The panting boy muttered an apology and tugged to free himself from the old man's grip.

" And now you can do something useful. Cut along up to the police station and tell 'em there's a dead man on the quay."

The small boy gasped, his eyes popping with excitement.

" Coo! A stiff? How did he croak? "

" Never you mind. Run along and do what I tells you. And mind, hold your gab about it."

But the small boy was quite incapable of holding his gab, and long before lawful authority could arrive a small crowd had begun to collect on the quay. Old Penticle stood at the head of the steps and kept them away from the body; though he was unable to prevent them from looking down over the side of the quay, the mist was still too thick for them to identify the body, over which Silas had thrown his own oilskin.

After a time the ponderous steps of the law were heard approaching, and presently a Police Inspector appeared, accompanied by a constable bearing a folded stretcher over his shoulder. The crowd was quickly driven back to a respectful distance, and while the Inspector questioned Penticle, the constable patrolled like a sheep-dog, keeping the flock from encroaching.

Before long a car appeared and a tubby, elderly man, with a red face, grey whiskers and scrubby grey moustache, got out of it. This was Dr. James Faundyce, who was not only the leading practitioner of Great Norne, but one of its most respected citizens.

Inspector Heskell soon put him in possession of the few facts which he himself knew and, after a quick examination, Dr. Faundyce directed him to have the body conveyed to the mortuary of the Cottage Hospital.

"I'll make a full examination there," he said, "but there's no doubt about it; a fractured base due to a fall on the edge of the steps. There will be no need for a full autopsy; no need to distress Mrs. Torridge too much. Poor lady! this will be a terrible shock to her. A sad tragedy indeed. No doubt he lost his way in the fog. Visiting a sick parishioner, in all probability."

"The reverend gentleman made a practice of looking in at the Men's Club every Thursday," said Inspector Heskell, "I will inquire, of course, whether he was there last night. Could you form an opinion as to how long he has been dead, doctor?"

Dr. Faundyce shook his head.

"Not to within an hour or two," he said. "There are many considerations which would affect the estimate. Not less than ten or twelve hours, I should say."

"That would take us to eight or ten last night—just about the time he would be at the Club. Not that it can matter, sir; the poor gentleman is dead, and that's an end to it."

"Exactly. By the way, was there any report of his being missing? One would have expected Mrs. Torridge to notify you when her husband did not return."

"Not a word, sir."

"Curious. You have not, of course, had time to inform the poor lady of his death?"

"Not yet, sir. I only got here a few minutes before you."

"Then I will do it myself. She is a delicate woman, and must be spared shock as much as that is humanly possible."

"Thank you, sir. I will inform the Chief Constable;

he will wish to know. And, of course, the Coroner; there will have to be an inquest."

" No doubt there will. A mere formality in such a case."

By this time a second police constable had appeared, and the body of Theobald Torridge, shrouded in a grey blanket, was borne away. Penticle, having been warned not to disclose the identity of the deceased, enjoyed withstanding a siege by the curious. If the public-houses had been open no doubt he would have been subject to irresistible temptation, but, as it was, he had no difficulty in maintaining a dignified and mysterious silence.

Dr. Faundyce drove away on his melancholy mission, wishing that he had had time to fortify himself with breakfast. He found that Mrs. Torridge was still in bed and asleep. The maid told him that her mistress had had a severe sick headache on the previous evening, had gone to bed early and taken a sleeping draught. That, no doubt, thought the doctor, accounted for the fact that her husband's failure to return home the previous night had not been reported. The maid told him that she herself always went to bed before ten o'clock and had been unaware of the Vicar's absence. She had thought it curious that he was not, in accordance with his custom, in his study by eight o'clock this morning; it was not part of her duty to call her master and mistress, as Mrs. Torridge did not think it nice for her to see a gentleman in bed.

Dr. Faundyce decided that the kindest thing was to wake the poor lady and break the news to her before she discovered her husband's absence and started to rack herself with doubts and fears. When he entered her room he found her just returning to consciousness, but she had hardly shaken off the effects of the sleeping draught, and had evidently not yet realised that the pillow beside her was undented.

Gently as the doctor did his sad duty, the news was an overwhelming shock to Mrs. Torridge. As he had told Inspector Heskell, she was a delicate woman, not only in health but in character, and had not the moral fortitude to stand up to such a catastrophe. It was half an hour before Faundyce could leave her, and he promised to send his wife up to be with her. In the meantime he urged her to take some nourishment—advice which he felt sure would not be followed.

Mrs. Torridge had told him, as he expected, that she had been asleep before the time of her husband's expected return, so that she had had no cause for anxiety overnight. This the doctor reported to Inspector Heskell, who informed him that the Vicar had not been at the Club the previous night. His absence had been attributed to the fog. Clearly the accident had happened as he was on his way there. Doctor and police-officer agreed that now that the widow had been informed, the news of the Vicar's death might be generally released.

.   .   .   .   .

That evening, in the public bar of the 'Silver Herring', Silas Penticle came into his own. Although the identity of the corpse was no longer a secret, such an unwonted event as a sudden death in Great Norne was the subject of avid curiosity, among all classes and creeds, so that a full house of the inn's regulars assembled at the earliest possible hour—because Silas, being a tactician of Nelsonian calibre, had been saving his ammunition until he could discharge it with the greatest benefit to himself. He was a faithful and regular customer of the 'Silver Herring', and nobody had the slightest doubt that he would be found at his post on this auspicious evening.

The meeting—for it was scarcely less—was so well and punctually attended by regulars that it was impossible to accommodate all the casuals who sought to hear old Silas's story—a fact which caused untold remorse to the host, Jasper Blossom, who watched with bitter agony as his pot-boy pushed out into the night one after another of the potential customers for whom there was no room.

Blossom was by nature a cheerful soul, who enjoyed the sound of his own voice. In the proper tradition of inn-keepers, he was large, rubicund and commanding, the possessor of a temper he normally kept under reasonable control. Thirty-five years previously he and Mrs. Blossom had been unable to resist the temptation to call their first-born daughter Rose, and that warm-hearted lady was now presiding in full bloom—if not actually full-blown—behind the bar, still richly pluckable, though as yet unplucked. Rose enjoyed a full house, with plenty of noise, and her eyes sparkled as she exchanged words of merriment and seemly jest with her many admirers across the counter.

The clientele of the ' Silver Herring ' consisted almost entirely of fishermen and farm labourers, with such odds and ends as mixed naturally with that stratum of society. Among these latter were Eb Creech, a carpenter who worked for Richard Barton, Crooky Blake, an odd-job man, and Josiah Chell, sexton of St. Martha's. Creech, well on in the sixties, was one of the most respected characters in Great Norne; he was a strong Chapel man, and took particular exception to Josiah Chell, whom he regarded as light-tongued and irreverent. Eb himself was a man of almost impenetrable silence; an opinion or a statement of fact had to be dragged from him, but when it came it was generally worth waiting for.

Blake, on the other hand, had a ready and amusing tongue; though he generally sat by himself in the darkest corner of the bar, he was on good terms with the other

customers, in spite of being a ' foreigner ' and no native
of Great Norne. He had, in fact, come south after the
industrial slump of 1930, wandering from place to place,
trying his hand at any job of work that he could find.   In
Great Norne he had started as a labourer under the Town
Council, but after a year had created for himself an
entirely original job as ' outside porter ', which consisted
of a barrow and himself to push it; in a surprisingly short
time a lot of tradesmen and private individuals had found
it useful to have their small errands and carryings done
in this way, for Blake was handy and reliable, even though,
when off duty at night, he was occasionally found asleep
in his barrow with an aroma of gin permeating the air
around him. His nickname of ' Crooky ' was due not to
any defect of character but to a badly deformed shoulder,
which did not, however, appear to handicap him in his
work. His age was difficult to determine; his grizzled
hair and rather gnarled appearance suggested that he was
over fifty, but he might have been considerably younger.

As soon as the public bar was full to capacity and all
were served with drink, Jasper Blossom called on Silas
Penticle to tell his tale. He told it with a deliberation
that took time, so that, though there was not much meat
in it, several replenishments of his tankard, at the charge
of eager neighbours, were necessary before he had done
justice to the occasion. In telling his story to the police
he had made no mention of the smell of whisky or the
broken flask, leaving them to find those details for themselves; being a godly as well as a kindly man, he had not
intended to reveal the sordid secret now, but a seventh
pint, laced with brandy—the contribution of ' the house '
—proved too much for his discretion, and out it all
came.

Inevitably there was a clatter of excitement and

laughter. Everyone had assumed that the accident had
been due to the fog, but now a richer explanation had been
provided. Younger members of Silas's audience attempted to illustrate their views by drunken staggerings,
but there just was not room in the place to do it with any
breadth of realism. Uncertainty of leg control· was not,
of course, unknown to most of Jasper Blossom's customers,
but it was a rare thing to see one of the gentry afflicted in
that way, and that such a thing should happen to a minister of the cloth passed all experience and expectation.

" Th' old rascal," exclaimed Ben Hard, one of the
senior fishermen. " Preachering to us folks about the sins
of the spirits and then taking them on the quiet hisself."

" Yes, and you, too, Josiah Chell," echoed another
grinning salt. " You holy men setting yourselves up
above the rest of us, and all the time you're no better nor
what we are."

Josiah, seated on a low, backless bench near the fire,
drained his tankard and set it down on the floor.

" I never sets myself up nowhere," he said. " I sets
myself down in the lowest seats in the feast-room and
waits for a gentleman to say to me: ' Friend, come up
higher and have a pint with me.' "

The sexton's special sense of humour was not always
well received by simple folk who had been brought up to
read their Bible even if they did not attend church.
There was a short silence after his retort, and then Blossom
started a discussion on why the Vicar should have been
on the quay at all.

" On his way to Men's Club, Thu'sday night," muttered old Silas, thickly.

" Odd he should have drunk that amount before going
to the Club," mused Rose.

" More likely he was coming away from Club," suggested Crooky Blake from his corner. " Hard drinking lot, they tell me, at the Club."

There was a general chuckle at this, as the Men's Club specialised in tea and soft drinks.

" I don't reckon the drop o' whisky had nought to do with it," said Ben Hard. " 'Twas a thick night, and he just lost his way and fell over something."

" Ah, it's you careless sailor-men leaving your tangles of rope about to draw decent folks to their death."

Silas Penticle, coming slowly to the surface through a daze of beer, brandy and shag, eyed Crooky inquiringly for a time, while the rattle of banter and speculation continued on all sides.

"What was that about rope?" asked Silas slowly. " Who said aught about rope? "

The ' outside porter ' scratched his ill-shaven cheek.

"Why, I reckon someone did," he said. " What's it matter, anyway? "

Penticle relapsed into muttering incoherence and Blake rose to his feet and tapped out his pipe at the big fireplace.

" And what do you think of it all, Eb Creech? " he asked the silent carpenter.

Eb slowly cogitated this question and then delivered his opinion.

" I think the poor gentleman's dead," he said, " and I don't see aught to laff at."

Embarrassed recognition of this fact seemed to spread through the company.

" I'm with you there," said Crooky. " 'Tis a sad night for God-fearing folk, and I'll go sober to my bed."

CHAPTER IV

A Bell Rings

THE inquest on the Reverend Theobald Torridge passed off uneventfully, to the disappointment of those uncharitable spirits who had hoped for a bit of fun. No mention was made of whisky or broken flask either by the police or by Dr. Faundyce, and as Penticle had not mentioned it to the police when they first appeared on the scene, he could not very well do so now, even if he had wanted to.

One juryman, in the know, did venture to ask Dr. Faundyce whether he had found anything unusual in the stomach. The doctor glowered at him and replied that he had not opened the stomach. Death was clearly due to a fractured base of the skull, as he had said in his evidence; there was no point in causing unnecessary distress by an exploratory autopsy.

The Coroner was not a Great Norne man, but he was in the tradition of old Carnaby, whom he had recently succeeded—a family solicitor who would go a long way to avoid ' distressing ' the gentle-folk to whom he looked for the major part of his business.

The inquisitive juryman was silenced and a verdict of accidental death recorded.

Whether Dr. James Faundyce had in fact looked farther than he had stated, or whether his nose had told him what the more sensitive organ of old Silas had recorded, only Dr. Faundyce could say. And he said nothing. It was hardly likely that the police could have failed to notice the broken bits of glass in the pocket of the Rev. Theobald's coat. But why stir up mud? There was no question of any crime here. It was an accident that might have happened to anybody, and the thick mist was quite enough to account for it. Let the reverend gentleman rest in peace.

Even as it was, the sudden violent death of their Vicar was a terrible shock to the faithful. By those who liked him Theobald Torridge had been greatly admired, even reverenced. He had been their minister for twenty-five years, and though for a time he had been thought to be narrow-minded and too stern in his judgment, this feeling had gradually evaporated, partly, no doubt, because people got accustomed to him and partly because he himself had mellowed with the passing years.

To Beatrice and Emily Vinton he had always been the object of respectful admiration, and with the younger sister this was carried to the extent of blind adoration. Beatrice, the elder, was made of sterner stuff. Whatever she felt, she did not carry her heart upon her sleeve. She gave the whole of her spare time not needed for the running of her house and household to parish work; in fact, she played the part of unpaid lay curate—in the absence of the real article—and did a great deal of what was not done by the Vicar's ailing and feeble-spirited wife.

It had been a shattering blow to Theobald Torridge when Miss Vinton was struck down by paralysis. At first it had been thought that she could not possibly live, let alone recover, but Beatrice was a woman of indomitable spirit, and she had refused to die; when she knew that she would live, but that she would never speak or walk again, she refused to despair. She had the use of her eyes and ears and, to a limited extent, of her hands. Before long she was once more controlling her house, sitting upright in a straight-backed chair, and slowly inscribing orders and directions on a wax pad. This ingenious device enabled her, when the message had been read, to obliterate it by lifting the sheet of prepared paper, on which she could then write again. It avoided the untidiness which would have resulted from lead pencil and ordinary paper, and untidiness, next to cowardice, untruth and ungodliness, was what Beatrice Vinton most deplored.

This tragedy had occurred in 1926, and since then Emily Vinton had done her best to take her sister's place in the parish, but she was a bird of very different feather. With all the devotion, all the earnest intent, all the selflessness of her sister, she had none of her ability. As Torridge, in a moment of exasperation, expressed it to his churchwarden, she was a ' ditherer ', and it was not long before he felt he would gladly do without her help at all. It was one of the inscrutable acts of Providence that this blow should have fallen upon the wrong sister; that was Theobald's secret thought, though he never expressed it, even to his wife.

For all her piety, Emily Vinton liked to be what she called gay. She enjoyed visiting her friends and receiving them at ' The Chestnuts ', though the latter event could not happen often, as visits tired Beatrice and she would only have to her house the really intimate friends who knew how to talk to her without causing her fatigue.

Chief among these were the Beynards. Norris Beynard was the local Squire, though he made no attempt to play the traditional Squire's part. He was a thin, stooping man, nearly sixty years of age, a scholar and philosopher, quiet, retiring, almost a recluse. Although deeply interested in the history of Great Norne and its people, he took no part in its present life, feeling himself out of tune with its pace and stridency. Not many people would have connected those words with the placid tempo of this forgotten East-coast town, but Beynard preferred to live entirely in the past and in his own thoughts, relying on his sister Catherine, five years younger than himself, to run his household and even the greater part of the affairs of his small estate.

He was on friendly terms with the Vintons, greatly admiring the courage of Beatrice and mildly amused by the twittering sociability of her sister Emily. His principal male friend had been his solicitor, Howard Carnaby, with whom he played chess and discussed local lore, but Howard Carnaby had died in 1936, and his nephew Cyril was a man of very different type, the modern, flamboyant product of the post-war years which Beynard most disliked.

Nor did he like either the late Vicar or his church-warden, Colonel Cherrington, though he attended church with reasonable regularity and subscribed generously to church funds. He thought them both lacking in the real spirit of Christianity, men of pride rather than humility, harsh where they should be forbearing. But the Squire kept these thoughts to himself, and would not have dreamed of hurting the devoted Miss Vintons by any word of criticism of their idol.

Curiously enough, the man to whom Norris Beynard had paid most attention in recent years was Richard Barton, the man to whom Dr. Stopp and Captain Hexman had applied the word ' surly '. The Squire had felt great sympathy with him over the tragedy of his married life, which, he thought, had been badly mishandled by the good people of the town. Barton was certainly morose in his relations with the general run of his neighbours, but he had responded, after a doubtful start, to Beynard's sympathy, and had formed a habit of going to the Manor sometimes in the winter evenings, to play chess and even to discuss philosophy, a subject that seemed to appeal to his unhappy spirit.

His visits were not welcome, however, to Catherine Beynard, to whom he appeared as he did to most people, surly, self-centred, and even ill-mannered. She thought him a boor, and felt sure that he himself had been to blame for the worst of the troubles that had befallen him. She was too good a sister to try to disturb her brother's friendship with the man, but she did nothing to encourage it.

Catherine Beynard was a short, stocky woman with no grace of figure or beauty of face to attract men, even when she was young and presumptive heiress to her bachelor brother, but she had kindness of heart and contentment with her lot, and those were qualities that made for happiness. She was deeply attached, not only to her brother, but to the old Manor House that was their home. The dwindling income of a small landed proprietor made very difficult the task of keeping the Manor as it should, in her view, be kept, but she ran the estate and the house and household with a skill that made the old Beynard home a comfortable, as well as a beautiful place in which to live.

Into these placid homes—the homes of Beynards, Vintons and their like—the profane story that had circulated in the bar of the ' Silver Herring ' did not penetrate. It reached Monks Holme, because George Hexman brought it there; he had heard it from Albert Gannett, and Gannett had got it from its place of origin. Alone among the farmers Gannett was an occasional visitor to the ' Silver Herring ', where he was treated with the respect due to his former position and the unspoken sympathy which these decent men felt for one who had fallen on unhappy days. Hexman, too, felt some sympathy for a man whose trouble was largely due to war service, and did not rebuff him as he would normally have done an unmannerly sot. The story of the Vicar's assumed fall from grace was not particularly funny, but it was funnier than most things to be heard in this dead-alive place. So he took it home and retailed it to his wife, who received it with chilling disbelief and absolutely forbade him to say anything about it to her father.

" I can't think why you have to gossip in a bar with a lot of maudlin farmers," said Winifred Hexman. " If you must drink in the middle of the day, why can't you do it with Cyril Carnaby, or even that common little Dr. Stopp? He does at least know when he's had enough."

" Cyril, eh? " said Hexman, seeking the best defence in counter-attack. " When did you get on those terms? "

To his surprise, his shot seemed to go home. His wife blushed and looked annoyed.

" Why on earth not? " she asked. " I've known Cyril Carnaby for years and his uncle before him. They're one of the oldest families in Norne."

" Uncle was, no doubt, but not Master Cyril," retorted her husband. " He's only been in the place a little over a year."

" He was here as a boy; spent his summer holidays here. I often saw him then, and before he was sent to a solicitor's office in London."

" Boy meets girl? I see. I shall have to keep an eye on that bright lad."

George Hexman was the type of man who liked to amuse himself with other women and expected his wife to be interested only in him, so that even the slightest suggestion of the contrary ruffled him.

Winifred Hexman was a good-looking, even a handsome woman, with thick, dark hair, a fresh complexion and long eyelashes. Her looks were rather spoilt by a naturally sullen expression, which ten years of life married to George had done nothing to modify.

In this little passage of words each had attained to his immediate object, Winifred deflecting her husband from a story which she knew would greatly upset her father, and George deflecting Winifred from criticism of his social habits. But they had not made themselves any happier.

Although his little bit of scandal had had such a damping reception at Monks Holme, George Hexman could not drop it altogether. So he took it along to his crony, Dr. Frederick Stopp, who gave it an enthusiastic reception as one slight spark of humour in a boring world. Over their whiskies the two men worked it up into something quite artistic, but when, a day or two later, Stopp tried to pump his partner, Dr. Faundyce, on the subject, he was so severely snubbed that he saw the wisdom, from the professional point of view, of letting the thing drop. The joke had already run its course in the lower strata of society, and very soon even the Vicar's death was forgotten by all but the faithful, and life in Great Norne resumed its even, uneventful course. The last leaves fell from the trees, the last autumn furrows were ploughed, Trinity faded into Advent, and on Christmas Eve a telephone bell interrupted Inspector Heskell in his pre-bedtime yawn.

Smothering both yawn and curse Heskell took off the receiver.

" Great Norne Police Station. Inspector Heskell."

Over the wire a man's voice said sharply:

" Please come round to Monks Holme; Colonel Cherrington has shot himself."

CHAPTER V

Two Small Points

INSPECTOR HESKELL stood in the middle of Colonel Cherrington's study and tried to think. Thinking was not his strong point; he would carry out his orders promptly, thoroughly, efficiently; he was trustworthy, conscientious, but he had no initiative. A violent death like this was almost entirely outside his experience—even the simple accident to the Vicar had found him not too sure of himself—and he was uncomfortably afraid that he might make some bloomer which would interfere with his eventual chance, slight enough in any case, of promotion to Superintendent.

He was aware, of course, of the obvious DONT's in a case like this. Don't move the body. Don't move anything else. Don't touch anything. Don't tell anybody anything. Don't let anyone leave the premises. One or two equally foolproof DO's he had promptly attended to. He had summoned Dr. Faundyce, notified Headquarters, posted P. C. Flaish at the front door to discourage the curious. What puzzled him most was whether or not he should ask anyone any questions, strike while the iron was hot, while facts were still fresh in people's minds; that seemed right enough, the first police officer on the scene should ascertain the facts. But was it enough? Ought he to try some clever questions that might trap someone into contradicting himself?

But why should anyone contradict himself? The facts were simple enough, and had been given to him by Captain Hexman directly he arrived. The Captain had been upstairs in his dressing-room, just beginning to undress for bed, when he heard a loud bang that sounded to his trained ear like a revolver shot. He had rushed downstairs and into the study, where he had found his father-in-law lying dead on the floor, with a wound in his right temple and a still-smoking service revolver on the floor beside him. Well, so he was, dead enough, that was obvious, and the revolver still there—not actually in his hand, but just beside it. And the smell of gunpowder still in the room.

Inspector Heskell sniffed vigorously, just to confirm his first impression. Yes, the smell of gunpowder—not so strong perhaps as when he had first arrived a quarter of an hour ago, but quite unmistakable. *Sniff.* Yes, the smell of gunpowder . . . the smell of . . . something else, even more familiar. *Sniff.* Burnt paper; that was it.

Heskell stepped across to the fireplace and, stooping down, identified a considerable bundle of black, flaky ashes, obviously the remains of papers recently burnt. One or two scraps not completely burnt, one at least with a few words of writing visible on it. Heskell's hand went out, and was quickly drawn back. DON'T touch anything. He straightened his back, walked deliberately to the middle of the room and started to think again.

Captain Hexman had told all he knew, which was little enough. Mrs. Hexman had said much the same—Mrs. Hexman looking a bit of all right in a dark-green dressing-gown over mauve silk—he thought—pyjamas. A good-looker that. Dark hair done in two long plaits. Why did these women wear pyjamas? He liked. . . . He wasn't here to think about that. Mrs. Hexman had been on the point of getting into bed when she heard . . . and so on, same as her husband, omitting the bit about its sounding like a revolver shot. Getting into bed. Would it be a double bed, like his and Annie's? He'd heard that these upper-class people slept in separate, single beds. What on earth was the point of getting married if . . . Switch off.

Two maids—Heskell glanced at his note-book—Dorothy Trott and Fanny Smith—had heard the bang, but had not come downstairs. Dorothy—aged about thirty, he supposed—had gone into Fanny's (eighteen) room, just to see she was all right, and there had stayed till rung for, being in their nightgowns and not wishing to get mixed up in any bangs. Nothing to be got there.

And here was the doctor.

Dr. Faundyce was looking worried, as well he might, the Colonel being a friend of his as well as a patient. Heskell was glad he had come; the doctor would relieve him of the necessity of thinking any more, so far as the body was concerned. And in a case of suicide what else mattered?

" I'm sorry to have been so long, Inspector," said Dr. Faundyce. " I was in bed, as I was up all last night with Mrs. Hook's baby—didn't save it either; time she stopped. What time did it happen, exactly? "

Heskell consulted his note-book again.

" Eleven-twenty, sir, Captain Hexman puts the time at. It was eleven twenty-eight when the call reached me."

Dr. Faundyce was kneeling beside the body, and did not seem interested in the answer to his own question. His sensitive fingers felt round the black hole in the dead man's temple. He lifted the head, grunted, and put it down again in exactly the same position. Opening the waistcoat and shirt, he put his hand over Colonel Cherrington's heart and, after a pause, withdrew it, carefully refastening the clothing. Taking a small steel mirror from his breast-pocket he held it to the dead man's lips; there was, there could be, no dimming of the polished surface.

"Instantaneous, of course," he murmured, as he rose to his feet. "Someone coming from Headquarters?"

"Yes, sir. Super's coming. I expect he'll bring Inspector Joss with him."

"Joss? Who's he? Don't think I've heard of him."

"Detective-Inspector Joss, sir," replied Heskell shortly.

"Oh yes, I remember. The Chief Constable has started a detective branch, hasn't he? I did hear about it, but I forgot. Very enterprising and up-to-date. What sort of a man is Joss?"

"I hardly know him. He was a youngish Sergeant when he was promoted to this job."

Dr. Faundyce sensed disapproval behind his companion's correct but unenthusiastic words.

"Hendon College, eh? One of Lord Trenchard's bright boys?"

"Well, not exactly that, sir," replied Heskell, whose mind was fair, for all its narrowness. "He has been through the College; but he's a County man, come up through the ranks. I feel sure he's a very able officer, sir."

Dr. Faundyce's interest in Inspector Joss was already apparently waning. He was looking down at the dead man, with a frown on his usually cheerful face. The high colour had already faded from Colonel Cherrington's cheeks, leaving a network of tiny purple veins still showing against the grey background.

"Can't make it out," muttered Faundyce. "Last man I'd have expected to take his own life. Soldier, high sense of duty, deeply religious man. You don't know what motive he can have had, do you, Inspector?"

Heskell stiffened.

"Not my duty to inquire into motive, sir," he answered. "Superintendent Kneller will no doubt go into that."

But he was worried. He hadn't thought about motive.

Of course, there must have been one.   Ought he to have
asked questions about it?   The son-in-law, the daughter—
they might know something.   Ought he to have questioned them at once?   They might be putting their heads
together to cook up something to save the old man's face.
That is, if there was any shady reason for his taking his
own life.   A man didn't do that for nothing.   Perhaps . . .

The sound of a car pulling up outside the house interrupted the Inspector's ponderous thoughts.   A minute
later the door of the study opened and in walked a stolid,
soldierly looking Superintendent in uniform, with greying
hair and a benevolent expression.   He was followed by a
younger man in plain clothes, dark, alert and clean-
shaven.   There was a glimpse of two other plain-clothes
men in the hall before the door closed.

" Good evening, doctor.   Very sorry to hear about this.
Evening, Heskell.   You know Inspector Joss? "

Dr. Faundyce shook the Detective-Inspector by the
hand; Heskell merely nodded.

" Dead, I suppose? " inquired the Superintendent, with
a glance at the still body on the floor.

" Instantaneous," answered the doctor.   " Of course,
I must have the body for an autopsy, but the facts are as
you see them."

" Exactly, doctor.   We shall have to take some photographs and have a look round.   After that the ambulance
will take it wherever you like.   Have you got a mortuary
here? "

" Yes, at the Cottage Hospital.   I will let you have a
report to-morrow evening.   Do you want anything more
now? "

Superintendent Kneller hesitated a moment.

" Perhaps better to wait till the Chief comes, doctor, if
you wouldn't mind.   He shouldn't be long."

Dr. Faundyce nodded, and Kneller turned to the local Inspector.

" Now, Heskell, tell me what you know about this."

Heskell told his chief all that he knew, and was thankful not to have to answer any searching questions. He mentioned the burnt paper in the grate, and Inspector Joss went over there, knelt down, and began to poke very gingerly at the ashes.

" Better leave all this till the Chief comes," said Superintendent Kneller. " I'll have a word with Captain Hexman while we're waiting. You ask him any questions, Heskell? Apart from what you told me? "

" No, sir. I thought that should wait for you."

Kneller grunted. Heskell, of course, had no initiative; it was probably as well that he had not tried his hand at interrogation.

In the hall two young men were standing, looking like greyhounds ready to be slipped. They were Detective-Constable Gilbert and Detective-Constable Morris. Together with a Sergeant and a clerk they constituted the whole of the County's Detective Branch, under Detective-Inspector Joss. Gilbert was the photographer, with an expensive toy still almost virgin except for practice work; Morris was trained to find and identify finger-prints, with the help of Gilbert and his camera.

" Better wait till the Chief's had a look round," said Superintendent Kneller. " He'll be here any time. After he's satisfied you can go in and do your stuff."

" Yes, sir. Thank you, sir."

" You haven't seen anything of Captain Hexman, I suppose."

Gilbert nodded towards a door, slightly open, on the far side of the hall. Superintendent Kneller pushed it open and walked into what was evidently the dining-room.

In front of the fire, in which a few ashes still smoked feebly, Colonel Cherrington's son-in-law was sitting, a tumbler of whisky in his hand. He was in evening dress—a double-breasted smoking-jacket and black tie. He rose to his feet as the Superintendent entered. Kneller thought the young man looked greatly shaken, which was only natural.

" I'm Superintendent Kneller, sir. I heard you were in here, and I wanted to express my deep sympathy with you and your wife. The Chief Constable will be here any time now, and I know he will want to do the same."

" Thank you, Superintendent," said Hexman. " It has been a most awful shock, as you can imagine."

He motioned the Superintendent to a chair and held out a cigarette-case.

" Can I offer you a drink? "

Kneller shook his head.

" Not now, thank you, sir. I'm afraid I must ask you a question or two. Inspector Heskell has given me your account of what actually happened; I needn't go into that again—not now, anyhow. What I should like to know is whether you can give me any idea of why the Colonel should have done this—taken his own life."

Hexman shifted uneasily in his chair.

" That's exactly what I've been asking myself," he said, drawing deeply at his cigarette. " I simply can't give you a reason—not a real reason, an adequate reason. Of course, he had been getting very worried the last few months—but, then, who hasn't? We can all see there's a war coming, and we're all feeling the pinch in one way or another. My father-in-law was bothered about his financial position, about the financial position of the country, too. He has, I believe, had one or two setbacks lately, but I don't believe there was anything seriously wrong—nothing to drive him to such a step as this."

" Had he made any drastic cuts in his mode of living? "

" No, nothing to speak of. I must admit that he has had one or two cuts at me and my wife about extravagance. It makes me feel pretty bad, in view of what's happened, because I'm afraid I wasn't very responsive. He was nagging at me about getting a regular job. Well, I do work, on the Stock Exchange; I admit it's rather a part-time job; but, then, things are so quiet now, with everybody nervous about a war starting. But I'm afraid I did annoy the old chap by not taking him seriously enough."

" I shouldn't worry yourself too much about that, sir," replied Kneller. " It couldn't have annoyed him enough to make him shoot himself. You don't, I suppose, know . . . it's a difficult thing to ask . . . there wasn't any other cause of worry that you knew of? His health, for instance; that often upsets a man's balance more than one realises at the time."

Hexman shook his head.

" Absolutely fit, I should have said. Touch of liver occasionally—the usual thing with an I.A. soldier—but nothing to upset him."

" There couldn't have been . . .? Oh, well, the doctors will tell me that. But, you'll excuse me, sir; I must ask you this. Colonel Cherrington was a widower, I know; could he have got entangled in any way with a woman? There's often a woman at the bottom of a suicide."

George Hexman stared.

" The Colonel? A woman? "

He gave a short laugh.

" He hasn't looked at a woman for thirty years, or something like it. His wife ran away from him, you know, with a brother officer. He's hated women ever since—and that's not putting it too strongly. I sometimes wondered whether he didn't hate his own daughter. He was polite enough, kind and generous in a cold sort of way, but not one scrap of what I'd call real affection."

" That's very sad, sir," said Kneller quietly. " No doubt that washes out that idea. And your wife, sir; I don't suppose she would know any more than you do, but, just as a matter of form, I'm bound to ask her some time."

" I'm afraid I told her to go to bed, Superintendent. She was a good deal upset, naturally; I told her to take a couple of aspirins and have a good sleep."

" Very wise, sir. I'll take an opportunity in the morning."

He rose to his feet.

" I think I heard the Chief Constable arrive a few minutes ago. May I tell him you'll be in here? He won't keep you long, I know. Oh, and by the way, sir, I shall put a constable on duty outside for a time. You won't want to be bothered with people—Press and so on— making inquiries and snooping round. You know what they are when something's happened out of the ordinary run, especially in a quiet place like this."

George Hexman thanked him, and the Superintendent returned to the study, where, as he expected, he found the Chief Constable talking to Dr. Faundyce.

Major John Statford had served in the Indian Army and the Indian Police, before being appointed to his present post. He had known Colonel Cherrington very slightly in India, but, being twelve or thirteen years younger, his knowledge of him was superficial, though in recent years the two men had had occasional friendly gossips on their past careers. Like many I.A. officers, Statford was very thin, with a dry, weather-beaten skin.

His grey eyes had a searching quality that could be very disconcerting, but there was often a humorous twinkle in them, and he was very well liked by his Force and by the people of the County who came in contact with him.

"What on earth did the old man do this for?" the Chief Constable asked, as soon as Kneller had closed the door behind him. "Have you got anything?"

The Superintendent shook his head.

"Not out of the son-in-law, sir," he said. "A bit worried about money, state of the country and so on. Health good. No woman in the case—at least, so Captain Hexman says."

"And he's about right, I should say. He tell you about the wife? I didn't know her, but I always heard it knocked him right out when she went off. Some people console themselves, some don't—and those are the ones who often crack in the end. If there's a woman in this case I think it'll be the one who left him twenty-five years ago."

Kneller looked sceptical, but did not argue the point.

"The Captain's in the dining-room, sir," he said. "I told him I felt sure you would want to have a word with him."

"Of course, of course. And that gets me out of the way," said the Chief Constable with a grin. "No, don't bother to come; I'll find him."

"And do you want me any more now?" asked Dr. Faundyce, who had been stifling yawns in the background for the last ten minutes.

"My dear doctor, I'm so sorry. Inexcusable of me. You don't want Dr. Faundyce any more, Kneller? No, by all means fall out, doctor. You've fixed up about to-morrow? Good. Good night, and many thanks."

"Would you allow Inspector Heskell to go, too, sir?"

asked the Superintendent. "He'll have a lot to do to-morrow, and I should like him to get a bit of sleep."

Major Statford realised that Kneller was ridding himself of a 'stuffed shirt' with his own inimitable tact. With equal tact he removed himself, and left the Superintendent free to get on with his inquiry.

As soon as the door closed, Kneller turned to Inspector Joss, who had been standing quietly in a corner while the polite talk was going on.

"Got anything, Joss?"

"Just a little, sir. There was paper burnt in the grate. One or two scraps are legible, and . . ."

"Just a minute. Gilbert and Morris haven't had a chance to do their stuff, I suppose? No, I told them to wait till the Chief had had a look round. Let's have them in now and get them out of the way before we start talking."

The two young detectives were soon at work, Gilbert with his camera, Morris with powder and insufflator. It was routine work, for which they had been trained, and there was no need to tell them what to do. The two seniors retired to a corner to be out of the way, and Kneller told Joss, in a quiet voice, what he had learned from Captain Hexman. While they were still talking the Chief Constable came in again and shut the door behind him. At a sign from Kneller the two detective-constables effaced themselves.

"I'm just going, Kneller," said Major Statford. "But what did you make of Captain Hexman?"

"A good deal upset, sir. Blaming himself—unnecessarily, I thought."

"Seemed to me almost rattled."

"Very natural, isn't it, sir? A great shock."

The Chief Constable pursed his thin lips.

" Is it? " he asked. " That's the polite thing to say, of course; but come down to brass tacks. The old Colonel can't have had much in common with this young waster— if I'm any judge, that's what Cherrington would have called him. I don't believe they had any great affection for each other, and, from his own account, Hexman was being hunted by his father-in-law. Now father-in-law is dead and his not inconsiderable fortune will come, pre- sumably, to Mrs. Hexman. Why should Hexman worry?"

" Just the shock, sir," said Kneller doggedly.

Major Statford looked hard at him and then laughed.

" Brer Fox ain't saying nuffin to-night, is he? But per- haps you don't know that simple tale, Kneller; Joss certainly doesn't."

" Oh, yes, sir; I was born and bred in a briar patch, all right. But I really haven't got down to this case yet. There's nothing I can usefully say . . . at present."

" How right you are. And I'm only hindering you from getting down to it. You'll look in at my office in the morning? Good. Good night, then. Good night, Joss."

The Chief Constable disappeared, and as soon as the two constables had finished their jobs they were told to take the car, get back to Headquarters and start developing.

" And don't forget to send the car back. Have we finished with the body, Joss? "

" Just one minute, sir. Something I'd like to show you."

" Right. Gilbert, tell Sergeant Oliver I'll give him a call when we're ready for him to collect. The ambulance is there, of course? "

" Yes, sir; it's here all right."

As soon as they were alone Superintendent Kneller locked the door.

" Now, Joss. He shot himself, I suppose? "

" Looks like it, sir."

Kneller's thick eyebrows lifted a little.

" But you don't think he did? "

" I wouldn't go as far as that, sir. Not at all. It's just that there's a small point—perhaps two small points— that are a bit odd."

" Lack of motive, eh? "

" Oh, the motive's here, sir."

" The deuce it is. What is it? "

The detective opened a drawer of the writing-table and took out a sheet of pink blotting-paper. On it lay two scraps of yellowish paper with charred edges.

" I put them out of the way while those young fellows were operating. Those scraps were among the ashes in the fireplace, sir; the rest was too far gone to show anything."

Several words were visible on the largest piece; Kneller stretched out his hand to pick it up, but his subordinate checked him.

" Excuse me, sir. There may be a finger-print on that. I've only touched it with the forceps. I thought I wouldn't have Morris test it till I'd shown it to you."

" Eh? What are you getting at? "

Without waiting for an answer Kneller put on a pair of spectacles and bent down to examine the scraps of paper.

Unless you pay up . . . make public all I . . . last chance.

The Superintendent whistled.

" Blackmail, eh? "

" Perhaps, sir."

Kneller looked sharply at the detective.

" Obvious, isn't it? "

" That's just it, sir. Looks a bit too obvious to me. If the Colonel was being blackmailed and either couldn't pay up or decided to shoot himself rather than face the risk of exposure, he naturally would destroy all the evidence that there was something to expose."

" And that's just what he's done."

" Not exactly, sir.   I've had a look round this room and the drawers of his writing-table.   He's quite obviously a careful, tidy man; thorough—that's what I'd make him out to be.   And yet, when he's going to commit suicide to avoid exposure, and when he sets out to burn the evidence, whatever it may be, he leaves unburnt just the very scrap of paper that shows that there was something to expose. Not in character, I'd say, sir."

Superintendent Kneller nodded his head slowly.

" I get you.   This is a serious matter, what you're suggesting, Joss.   It amounts to a plant.   It'll need very careful looking into, because if you're right . . . well, you can see what it means.   What was the other point? "

Joss returned to the drawer and extracted the lid of a narrow cardboard box, inverted.   On it was lying the broken remains of a pair of tortoiseshell spectacles.

" Those were under the body, sir."

" Broken when he fell, I suppose."

" Must have been, sir, but it's a very complete smash. I'm not quite clear why they should have been so shattered. You see, sir "—Joss used his forceps to lift scraps of tortoiseshell—" both lenses shivered—in fact not much of them left in the frame, the frame itself broken in three places, and the left arm broken."

" Yes.   Well, what of it? "

" The point that strikes me, sir, is that the right arm is · not broken."

" Eh?   What's odd about that? "

Inspector Joss stepped across to the body and knelt down.

"The wound, sir; in the middle of the right temple, exactly where that right arm of the spectacles would have been. If he was wearing them when he shot himself, why didn't the bullet smash that arm? Or if not that—if he pushed it out of the way—wouldn't there be some sign of blood or smell of powder on them? There is neither. And if he had taken them off, why should they be lying broken under his body?"

CHAPTER VI

Quiet Corner

THE congregation of St. Martha's were in anything but a seasonable spirit this Christmas morning. Some were unhappy, all were more or less excited, and there was little thought of the birth that that day celebrated; it was death that was in the air.

The Vicar, who had been inducted only a fortnight ago, was greatly put out by this shocking tragedy, news of which had reached him only half an hour before the service was due to begin. His sermon, so carefully prepared for this first great festival in his new cure, was now, he realised, out of tune with the mood of his congregation. It was a gratifyingly full congregation, but he wondered how many of them were there to pick up the latest gossip about their churchwarden's suicide. And how was he to refer to that? He could hardly ignore the death of a man who had been Vicar's Churchwarden and the main lay pillar of St. Martha's for so many years. But suicide! The man had taken his own life; self-murder was a sin, punishable by law if the attempt failed, and punishable by the Church, at least in stricter days, by the denial of interment in consecrated ground.

It was a problem that the Reverend John Berrifield found quite outside his experience. He was an elderly man, coming from a quiet parish on the far side of the county. The living of Great Norne, in the gift of the Bishop of the diocese, was his reward for faithful service which, he realised now only too well, had not been of a sort to prepare him for sudden emergencies. Not only was the problem a most difficult one, but the whole tragedy was **a** shock to him. He had met Colonel Cherrington once or twice at Diocesan Conferences, and had respected him; he had known his own predecessor even better, and these two sudden deaths, even though the first had been an accident, were deeply disturbing.

Somehow Mr. Berrifield got through his trying ordeal, he hoped with not too great discredit, and dismissed the congregation to return to their dinners or to stay and gossip in the churchyard as they would; he himself had no intention of joining them in the latter unseemly pastime.

The People's Churchwarden, an elderly ironmonger named Coote, joined him in the vestry and attempted to draw him into a discreet discussion of the event; but Berrifield responded frigidly, and the little man, after counting the collection, took himself off in no Christian mood of respect for his minister.

In the churchyard, while several parties lingered talking in the main path and round the lych-gate, one little group had moved round to the north side of the church. Norris Beynard and his sister had found Miss Emily Vinton in the porch in a state of evident distress. She was recovering a home-made wreath of holly which she had deposited there before the service and which, she told them, she was intending to place upon the ' dear Vicar's ' grave—by which, of course, she meant the Reverend Theobald Torridge. The Beynards could see that she was agitated, and even excitable; they thought it would relieve her to have someone to talk to, so they walked round with her towards the corner of the churchyard where the late Vicar lay. As soon as the rest of the congregation were hidden by the great bulk of the church, Emily Vinton burst into tears.

" Oh, isn't it dreadful! " she exclaimed, when she could speak coherently. " First dear Mr. Torridge, and now the

Colonel. What shall we do without them? What will
become of St. Martha's? This new creature—how could
he say . . .? What did he mean . . .? Nothing will
ever be the same again. I don't know how I shall break
it to Beatrice. I haven't told her yet. Minnie told me
when I went in to speak about luncheon. Suicide! Isn't
it awful! Do you think it can be true? I am sure it was
an accident. The dear Colonel, such a good man—not
sociable, of course, and he hardly said two words to me
when we met, but such a *good* man. I just can't believe
that he would take his own life. I just can't believe
it . . ."

The Beynards let the babbling stream run on, knowing
that it was the way relief would most easily come to the
hysterical little lady. They were fond of her, and were
ready to put up with her silliness in a way that younger
people, or people of the greater world, would not have
found possible. The Squire himself was shocked by
Cherrington's death. He had always regarded suicide,
if it was done to escape trouble, as the act of a coward,
and he found it difficult to place the austere and upright
Colonel in that category. Like Emily Vinton, he was not
yet prepared wholly to believe the common rumour that
had circulated with lightning speed through the town,
and even out to the Manor House in the breakfast hours of
that Christmas Day. There could be no doubting the fact
of the death, nor the death by revolver shot, but it was too
early to accept self-murder as the only explanation.

The Beynards did their best to comfort Emily Vinton
with gentle words. They stood beside her while she
deposited her little tribute on the narrow grass mound
which alone, so far, marked the late Vicar's resting-place;
while, too, she stood with closed eyes and clasped hands
at the foot of the grave asking for mercy which would

surely be given. Her face was happier when she looked up at them at the end of her prayer.

"May they both rest in peace," she said in a quiet voice.

Norris Beynard, who was always embarrassed by emotion, said that he had not realised that there was still room for burial in the old churchyard; he had thought that all new burials had now to take place in the extension.

"This is a pleasant, quiet corner," he said. "If I hadn't got the old family sarcophagus to go to, I shouldn't mind lying here."

"None will lie quiet here," said a harsh voice behind them.

All three turned quickly, and saw that the sexton had come up unnoticed.

"Oh, Josiah, how you startled me," said Miss Vinton. "I didn't hear you come."

"The footstep of Death is in the land," said Chell. "None can tell where his tread will be heard next."

"That will do, Chell," said Beynard sharply. He could feel Emily Vinton's hand trembling on his arm. "I was wondering who this remaining patch of ground was reserved for. Is Colonel Cherrington likely to be buried here, do you know?"

"Likely enough, since Emily Barton's buried here, a suicide, too. By rights he should lie at the cross-roads with a stake through his gizzard."

"Oh, Josiah, you are an old ghoul," said Catherine Beynard cheerfully. "I'm not going to stay here and listen to you. Come along, Miss Vinton; we've got the car outside the gate; you've got cold standing here; we'll drive you home."

Normally Emily Vinton would have briskly declined

the offer, as she prided herself on her vigour and inde-
pendence. But now she felt shaken and frightened, and
she meekly accepted, clinging to Catherine's arm as the
three walked past the church towards the lych-gate.

Josiah Chell watched them go, with a sardonic smile
on his face. Then he turned to look down at the new
grave and the space of bare grass beside it.

"Ay, the Colonel'll lie beside ye, old rascal," he
muttered. "And there's room for a two-three more;
room for a two-three more."

CHAPTER VII

Reconnaissance

" I SEE your point," said Major Statford.

For half an hour he had been listening to Superintendent Kneller's report of his interview with Captain Hexman and his subsequent discussion with Detective-Inspector Joss, culminating in the suspicion that the shooting of Colonel Cherrington might not have been his own act.

" After you had reached that point, did you have any further talk with Captain Hexman? "

" No, sir. I considered doing so, but came to the conclusion that I ought to consult you first. If I do question him further, it will have to be something a bit more awkward than last night's; with the Captain's position and so on, I thought it best to ask for your authority."

The Chief Constable nodded.

" I quite see that it will be awkward, but it's got to be done," he said. " If he's got anything to hide it won't do any harm to have let him down easy last night—lull him into a sense of false security. But, of course, that's jumping a very long way ahead; we don't know yet that there has been any foul play, let alone that he's responsible for it."

" Certainly not; sir, but one's bound to look at him first. On the spot and likely to benefit . . . and all that."

" Exactly. ' Opportunity and motive ', as the Detective Branch would say. By the way, where is Joss? "

" He stayed at the house last night, sir. He wasn't going to risk anyone getting into that room and doing anything that might want doing."

Major Statford laughed.

" Keen chap, eh? We can give him marks for that, eh, Kneller? "

" I give him a lot of marks, sir. This is the first time I've really seen him in action, and he seems to me keen, intelligent and tactful."

This was jam to the Chief Constable, who had not been at all sure how the Divisional Superintendents would take his innovation—the Detective Branch. But he was not going to let his enthusiasm for it lead him astray.

" If this turns out to be a murder case, Kneller," he said, " it will be a nasty case, and probably a very tricky one. I'm not at all sure we ought not to call in the Yard. Murder is something rather outside our experience. Except for one or two baby cases and that poor daft chap, Huzzell, and his girl, there hasn't been a murder case in the county for forty years or so—anyhow, before any of us were in the Force. I know you won't think I'm slighting you by speaking like this; a murder investigation is a highly specialised job, and we are none of us really trained for it."

" You don't think Inspector Joss, sir . . .? He's been through Hendon, and he's got some good young detective-constables with him."

" I think they are, and I'm glad you think so, too. But what they know at present is all theoretical; they've had no practical experience of serious crime. I'll keep an open mind about it for the time being, but if we do decide to call in the Yard we don't want to do it on a cold scent."

Superintendent Kneller nodded.

" I expect you're right, sir. How would it be if I went back now, had another look round with Joss, and put some searching questions to Captain Hexman? On what

I get you might feel able to decide what to do about the Yard."

" That's exactly what I was going to suggest. If you'll give me a ring at my house when you get back, I'll come across. I can't do any good here in the meantime, and Christmas Day is Christmas Day, when you've got a family. I hate spoiling yours and Joss's, but I'm afraid it can't be helped."

Kneller hated it, too. He went along to his house to explain things to his wife, and ten minutes later was on his way back to Great Norne. He found that Inspector Joss had miraculously breakfasted and shaved without leaving his post, and he suspected that the good-looking young detective had already established friendly relations with the late Colonel's female staff.

" Any more bright ideas come to you in the night, Joss? By the way, I suppose nobody tried to come in? "

" Not that I know of, sir. And I don't think they knew I was here until I rang the bell this morning. That seems to have given the girls a bit of a shock, when they saw the study bell indicator down; they thought it was the old man's ghost ringing."

" Did they answer it? "

" They came as far as the hall, and I heard them twittering, so I opened the door . . . and that nearly gave them fits. But they cheered up when they saw it was only me."

Superintendent Kneller grinned.

" I'll bet they did. And what about the ideas? "

" There is just one thing, sir. I can't quite interpret the position of the body."

Joss pointed to a chalk outline on the carpet, drawn by himself before the body was removed the previous evening.

" The feet are close to the chair and the chair is pushed

back a little way. The body is well clear of the chair and fairly straight out, as you see, sir. Now, what position was the Colonel in before he shot himself or was shot? Take suicide, first. Was he sitting when he fired the shot? If so, if he was in the normal position of someone sitting at a writing-table, would the body have straightened out on the floor like that? Wouldn't it have slumped forward on the table? Alternatively, he may have stood up to shoot himself, which is perhaps what a soldier would be more likely to do. In that case I think the body would have fallen much as one saw it. I've experimented myself a bit, and that seems a natural way to fall if one is on one's feet."

"That's probably what he was. Where's your difficulty, Joss?"

"The difficulty comes when one looks at the other alternative. Murder, sir. Take the sitting position first, though it doesn't look the likely one. The desk faces the door; the Colonel would have been bound to see anyone who came in. Surely he would have made some effort to defend himself—shouted or something? He wouldn't have just sat still and waited to be shot."

"There are two answers to that, Joss. Either he knew the person who came in—the murderer—and so wasn't afraid of being shot, or else the murderer was hidden in the room before the Colonel came in."

"As regards the last, sir, I doubt if that would be possible. There's really nowhere to hide, except behind the curtains; they were drawn and, as you can see, they lie very flat against the window. Look, sir."

Joss slipped behind one of the curtains and flattened himself as much as he could; even so his figure was clearly outlined.

"The maids think the Colonel was in here an hour

before he shot himself, as they assume he did. He had been out to a British Legion Christmas Eve dinner, and they heard him come in at about a quarter past ten. They are pretty sure he came in here, and it was his custom to sit in here in the evening till well after eleven. It doesn't seem possible that the murderer could have stood behind that curtain, or hidden behind any bit of furniture, for an hour without being spotted."

"It certainly doesn't seem likely, Joss. So that points to the known person. And he could have wandered round behind the Colonel's chair and shot him as he sat."

"He could, sir. But I don't believe the Colonel was sitting when he was shot . . . for the reasons I gave, the position of the body as we found it."

"The body might have been moved after it fell."

Joss's face fell.

"It might, sir. I didn't think of that. But why?"

"I don't know. Anyway, what does it matter if he was standing? The argument is the same; the known person wandered round behind him and shot him as he stood."

Inspector Joss still looked uncertain.

"That's what I can't quite visualise, sir. The Colonel is a tall man—six foot at least, I should say. Not at all easy to shoot in the temple when he was standing up. Especially if the murderer is a shorter man. One mustn't jump to conclusions, but the most obvious ' known person ' isn't much above the five nine mark."

"I agree. We must find out from the doctor whether the bullet was rising in the head. In any case, it seems extraordinary that he shouldn't have seen out of the corner of his eye what was going to happen. The muzzle of the revolver must have been quite close, because there was powder-blackening. There are puzzles here, Joss. You are quite right."

After a little more discussion the two police officers decided that the time had come to question Captain Hexman and the other occupants of the house more closely about the events of the previous night. Superintendent Kneller rang the bell, and when the maid, Fanny, appeared, asked if Captain Hexman would see him for a few minutes. Before very long the Captain himself appeared; he was looking rather drawn, but his manner was calm.

" All right for me to come in here? " he asked. " I gather that there was a sentry on last night."

" Just a matter of form, sir, till we have had time to go through papers and so on."

Captain Hexman glanced quickly round the study, raised his eyebrows slightly at sight of the chalk outline on the carpet, but made no comment on that.

" I expect you'll find everything in order," he said; " my father-in-law was a very methodical man."

" That's always a help, sir. Now I must ask you one or two questions about what happened last night. I understand that the Colonel was out part of the evening; could you tell me about that, sir? "

" Yes, we were both out. We went to the British Legion dinner; they always have one here on Christmas Eve. I'm not a member of this branch, but they very kindly invited me to their dinner. It was the usual thing —I don't suppose you want a recapitulation of the speeches; we managed to get away about ten and came straight back. The Colonel came in here, as he always does in the evening after dinner, and I went up to the drawing-room, where my wife was."

" And did you see the Colonel again last night? "

" Not till I found him dead."

" You didn't come down again to the ground floor? "

" No. Oh yes, I did, though. Just came down to the

dining-room and got myself a drink. I went up to the drawing-room again and then to bed."

" And when you came down for your drink, sir, you didn't see anyone about on this floor?"

Hexman stared at the Superintendent.

" Why do you ask that? " he asked.

" You didn't see anyone, sir? " repeated Kneller, ignoring the question.

Hexman shrugged his shoulders.

" I didn't. There was no one to see. The Colonel was in here. The maids go to bed soon after ten, I believe. My wife had gone up, too, before I came down for my drink."

" And you heard nothing unusual, sir? "

" Nothing at all."

" What about locking up, sir? Who does that? "

" The maids do that before they go to bed. Colonel Cherrington always tried the front door to make sure it was locked; I've noticed him do that often."

" Windows? "

" Shutters on the ground floor; the maids close them when they draw the curtains. I wish you'd tell me what all this is about."

" Just routine, sir. Now, you went up to bed yourself at what time? "

Hexman thought for a moment or two.

" Must have been a little after eleven—say ten past. I'd taken off my jacket and I was just taking off my shoes— I think I'd got one off and one unlaced—when I heard the shot. That was eleven-twenty; I know, because I looked at my watch."

" Why did you do that, sir? "

" Look at my watch? Oh, I don't know; automatic, I suppose; matter of military training."

" And then? "

" Then I came downstairs and found . . . well, you know."

" How quickly did you come downstairs, sir? Was there any pause? Any interval of time? "

" I suppose there was a little. When I first heard the shot it startled me; I think I listened for a moment. Then I came to the conclusion it was a revolver shot, and that was a bit of a jerk, as you can imagine. I realised I must come down and find out what had happened. I put on my shoe again and my jacket—that's automatic, too, I think, especially the shoe part—and ran down the stairs."

" And how long would it have been, sir, between your hearing the shot and getting down here? Five minutes? "

" Oh, no; not as much as that. I should have said a minute; two at the outside."

" And did anyone see you come down, sir? "

George Hexman was no fool. He saw the import of that question at once.

" There's something behind all this," he said sharply. " I should like to know what you're getting at, Superintendent."

" As I told you, sir, these are just routine questions," replied Kneller blandly. " No doubt your wife saw you come down."

" No, she didn't. She was in bed, or just getting into bed, I think she said; I was in my dressing-room. I don't suppose anyone saw me come down."

" That's quite all right, sir. And as soon as you saw the Colonel's body you realised he was dead? "

" I did. Bullet in the brain is apt to cause death, they tell me."

" Quite, sir. You didn't move him? "

" No. Rule One; I know that one. I rang straight through to the police station."

" And you didn't move anything in here? Books, papers, anything like that? "

" Rule Two. We've all been brought up on those, Superintendent. I touched nothing."

" Didn't stir the fire, or anything automatic like that, sir? "

Again Hexman stared.

" I touched nothing, Superintendent," he repeated.

" Then that's quite clear, sir, thank you. Now, just a word or two about the Colonel's affairs. I think you told me he was worried about money matters; can you enlarge on that, sir? What sort of money worries? "

Hexman shrugged his shoulders.

" The usual thing, I suppose. Income going down, expenditure going up."

" That's rather vague, sir. Was he actually in debt? Overdrawn? That sort of thing."

" I wouldn't know. He didn't confide in me."

" Then you wouldn't know if he had had any definite loss of money? A large sum, say."

Hexman hesitated. For a moment Kneller thought he had seen a glint of disquiet in the dark eyes.

" He had had one setback on the Stock Exchange," he said. " Some Mexican Oil shares went wrong. He'd bought rather a block of them."

" Would that have been on your advice, sir? "

The soldier-stockbroker gave a wry grin.

" As a matter of fact it was. Bit of damn bad luck. I thought I was on a winner there, and that it would do me a good turn to put my father-in-law on to them. He hadn't got much of an opinion of me as a stockbroker . . .

and naturally these things going wrong didn't improve his opinion. He was pretty sick."

" That was bad luck, sir. Was that quite recently? "

" No, it wasn't. A year or more ago."

" And did you put him on to anything else after that? "

" He didn't give me a chance."

" Was it a large sum he lost over the Mexican shares? "

" Something between five and six thousand he dropped; I forget the exact figure."

" And that would have embarrassed him? "

" Well, nobody likes losing five thousand pounds. But I don't believe really it was more than he could afford."

" Well, I daresay I can find out more about that, sir. Now, about this revolver; did you know he had got one? "

" Oh, yes, I knew that. I'd seen him clean it. As a matter of fact I should say everyone in the house had seen him clean it one time or another."

" And you knew where he kept it? "

Hexman's eyes narrowed.

" Yes, Superintendent," he said quietly. " I knew where he kept it. He kept it in the top right-hand drawer of his writing-table."

" Thank you, sir," said Kneller brightly. " Then I think that's about all. You don't happen to know about his will, I suppose? Who his money goes to and all that? "

" No. I've never seen his will. It wouldn't be unnatural if he left his money to his only daughter—only child. But I don't know. I'm not expecting you to believe me, of course."

Superintendent Kneller laughed.

" Oh come, sir; why shouldn't I believe you? Now,

I'd like to ask Mrs. Hexman one or two questions. Perhaps you would prefer to be present when I do that?"

"If they're the same sort of questions—routine questions—that you've asked me, I certainly should. Shall I fetch her?"

"Please don't trouble, sir; Inspector Joss will do that."

Joss knew the drill for the next movement. The Super would question the wife, and he himself would watch the husband. It was a stock catch; nine husbands out of ten couldn't resist the temptation to try to give a hint to their wives as to how they were to answer. That, of course, was why Captain Hexman was not being given a chance to have a word with her beforehand.

Mrs. Hexman was washing china in the pantry when Joss found her. She was wearing a grey coat and skirt, and though her face was pale, she had put some colour on her lips and finger-nails. Joss thought her a handsome but not particularly agreeable-looking woman. However, she was pleasant enough to him, and made no difficulty about accepting Superintendent Kneller's invitation—'fly into parlour', with the Super in the role of spider, thought Joss.

She did not look at her husband as she took the seat which Kneller offered to her, nor did she appear to notice the sinister outline on the floor.

"I didn't have an opportunity of offering you my condolences last night, madam," said the Superintendent. "I'm afraid this has been a tragic shock for you."

"It certainly has. I'm sorry about last night—not seeing you. I mean. My husband thought I had better go to bed. I expect you want to know why this happened."

"Co-operative," thought Joss. "Perhaps too co-co-operative."

" If you could suggest any reason . . .? "

" I've tried very hard to think of one. I can't. It seems quite pointless . . . and quite unlike him."

" Would you have said he was in his usual spirits? "

" Oh, yes. I haven't noticed any change in him. He wasn't in high spirits, if you mean that."

" Was he . . . you will forgive my asking you such a personal question . . . was he normally a happy man? "

Winifred Hexman shook her head.

" I couldn't call him that. I don't think he was ever happy after my mother left him. I believe my husband told you about that."

" Yes, he did just mention it, Mrs. Hexman. I understand it was a long time ago. Do you know anything about it? "

" No, nothing really. I was only two at the time."

" Was it . . .? You'll forgive me, I hope. Was it a case of another man? "

" Yes."

" Do you know who? "

" No, I don't. He never told me anything about it. When I was quite small I did once ask him. He shut me up, and I never asked him again. I never asked anyone. It seemed better to let it be forgotten."

Superintendent Kneller thought it a miracle that no kind friend had ever gossiped to the girl about this spicy scandal, but perhaps she had been as shutting-up as her father. No doubt he would be able, if the Chief Constable thought it advisable, to get the information from some other source.

" And about his health; would you say it was good? "

" Oh yes, quite. He never had any real illness. Some rheumatism, till he had his teeth out. One or two of the things people have when they are getting older. But nothing to worry him, I'm sure."

" And no business or other worries that you know of? "

" He never said anything about it. There was a bit of trouble a year or so ago. George could tell you more about that."

She looked at her husband for the first time, and smiled.

George Hexman grinned back. Inspector Joss thought, though, that the grin concealed some anxiety.

" There is just one point I must ask you about. Did your father receive any letter recently that appeared to upset him? "

Winifred showed some surprise at the question, but shook her head.

" No, I haven't noticed anything like that."

Kneller held out a scrap of charred paper. There was no writing visible on it—the writing was on the other side.

" This rather yellowish paper—have you noticed a letter like that . . . or an envelope? "

Winifred Hexman leaned forward to look at it carefully, as did her husband.

" No. But, then, I didn't particularly look at the letters he had; there were quite a few generally."

" And you, sir? "

" No. He might have had it. I haven't noticed it. Is there something special about it? "

Superintendent Kneller took no notice of the question, but put the scrap of paper back in the envelope from which he had taken it.

" Then about last night. Did you see your father after he got back from the British Legion dinner? "

" No. I was in the drawing-room. He went straight to . .'. he came straight in here. He always did after dinner; I didn't usually see him again till next morning."

" You know he did that last night? "

" Yes. At least . . ."

She glanced quickly at her husband, but George Hexman was looking straight in front of him.

" George told me he did. I don't really know . . . from my own knowledge."

" Thank you, madam. Now, when you heard the shot . . . you were in bed? "

" I was just getting into bed."

" And your husband? He was with you? "

Joss, whose eyes had strayed for a moment from their proper objective, saw a sudden look of disquiet appear on Mrs. Hexman's face. Again she glanced at her husband, but got no answering look from him.

" No, he was in his dressing-room."

" You know that . . . from your own knowledge? "

" Oh yes, I heard him moving about . . . undressing."

" You heard him, but you didn't actually see him? "

" No, I didn't actually see him, but . . . who else could it have been? "

" Exactly, Mrs. Hexman. And after the shot, you heard him go downstairs? "

" Yes I did. I heard his door open and then his footsteps running downstairs."

" And how long after the shot did you hear that? "

Winifred Hexman did not answer, but turned towards her husband.

" George. Why are they asking me these questions? " she asked sharply.

A slow, bitter smile appeared on Hexman's face.

" They think I shot the old man," he said quietly.

CHAPTER VIII

Mr. Carnaby Talks

A SHORT train dragged itself slowly and cautiously into the terminus station of Great Norne. It was two o'clock on the afternoon of the Tuesday following Boxing Day, and there was a fair load of passengers, mostly people who had been away on short Christmas visits.

In the station yard Crooky Blake was waiting hopefully with his barrow. It was a home-made barrow, a cross between the garden and railway varieties, with a high front on which was painted the inscription C. BLAKE, OUTSIDE PORTER, in letters which had once been white on blue, but were now grey on slate. Blake was waiting hopefully because there should be people with suit-cases on the train and there was no taxi-cab service in Great Norne. Anyone who wanted a hireling car had to ring up Noah's or Pearson's garage, unless they had ordered a car beforehand. To-day Noah's car was waiting, but Crooky knew that it had been ordered by young Mr. Carnaby, who never patronised the outside porter; there should be others who were ready to use their feet to save a few shillings but were not young or strong enough to hump luggage.

So Crooky sat on the side of his barrow, sucking a disreputable briar pipe, his keen grey eyes searching the stream of passengers now flowing out through the door of the booking-office. Here was that young Carnaby, tall, good-looker, pushing his way out and into Noah's car, not offering a lift to anybody. And here Mr. and Mrs. Jeddon from the Co-op; they would likely . . . no, seemingly they had no luggage. Tews, the draper, carrying a small case.

" Porter for you, Mr. Tews? "

" No, thank you, Blake. No weight in this."

Mean old cuss. A bob or two wouldn't have hurt him.

The stream was thinning to a trickle. A thick-set, sturdy man came out, carrying a substantial bag. Blake did not accost him, but his face had hardened. He did not like Mr. Builder Barton, who had not only never employed him, but had never a civil word to spare.

Two old women with nothing to carry, a young fellow and his girl, carrying each other's hand, and that was the lot. A wash-out. Not a bob, not a tizzy. Crooky sucked angrily at a pipe as empty as the train.

Then another man came out—a stranger, a thinnish man of middle age, clean-shaven and a Londoner's pale face. He carried a suit-case and looked about him as he came out into the yard. Blake stepped forward, a finger to his grimy peaked cap, but as he did so a dark car passed him and drew up close to his intended customer. Out of the car emerged a large figure in a blue uniform with a crown on the shoulder. Blake saw policeman and Londoner shake hands and heard a mutter of words, which he could not distinguish. The traveller went back into the booking-office, but emerged again after a minute, entered the car and was driven away.

Blake watched the departing car with a speculative look on his weather-beaten face. He knew, of course, all there was to be known about the old Colonel's death, and had already seen Superintendent Kneller about the town. Who was this newcomer? Another policeman? A busy? The Yard? If so, the County police must have smelt a rat of some kind.

There was a glitter of excitement in Crooky's eyes as he

picked up the handles of his unwanted barrow. Likely
he'd hear something at the ' Herring ' to-night that'd give
everyone a morsel to chew on. He gave his cumbersome
barrow a push . . . and saw another man emerge from
the booking-office—a younger, healthier-looking man
than the last, but still, in the eyes of the East Coast
countryman, a town-dweller. Carrying a bag, too, and
no car about this time. Blake pushed his barrow up to
the newcomer and reached for the bag.

" Outside porter, sir. I'll take that along for you."

It was a statement, rather than an invitation.

A quick frown passed over the face of Detective-Sergeant Plett. This was not what he had intended. He
had, on the orders of his chief, waited till the station seemed
clear, so that his arrival in the town should pass unnoticed.

But Plett's brain worked quickly. He was noticed now,
so he might as well make the most of it. This quaint old
character looked just the type to be full of local gossip,
and might produce something useful. But was he old?
No, probably on the right side of fifty, but knocked about
by a rough life, by the look of him. It was part of Plett's
training to size up men he came in contact with, and he
was quick at the job now.

" You're just the man I wanted," he said cheerfully.
" Where's the place for me to put up? I'm down here to
look into the chances of starting a little business—electrical
engineer. You can give me a tip or two as to what there
is in the town now. But first, where do I stop? Is there
a Commercial? "

Blake scratched his coarse, not over-clean hair.

" Yes," he said slowly; " there's the ' Railway '." He
jerked his thumb towards a small, gloomy-looking building
just outside the entrance to the station yard. He wouldn't
get much for a carry of a hundred and fifty yards. " Calls

itself Family and Commercial. But you wouldn't fancy that, sir. Kep' by a widow woman that's seen better days, sour old squint. A mean, poor table, and waters the beer."

Plett laughed.

" Doesn't sound a bed of roses. What do you suggest? "

" There's the ' Royal George ', sir, in the Market Square. Best hotel in the town. Patronised by all the best. Market ordinary—on to-day, sir. All the farmers, some of the tradesmen, as is not too mean to stand theirselves a drink, you'll meet 'em all there, sir."

" Sounds a bit above my cut. I'm not in the money, yet. Isn't there a smaller place? "

" Well, there ain't really much choice, sir. Not in what you might call the hotel line. There's the ' George ' and the ' Railway ', and the rest is mostly a matter of pubs— drinking-houses you might call them."

"Then I suppose it will have to be the ' George '," said Sergeant Plett, " because I certainly don't fancy your description of the ' Railway '. But I'd like to get round a bit and meet other people besides well-to-do farmers and shop-keepers. Where do you have your own glass as a rule? "

"' Silver Herring ', sir, down by the harbour. Fisherfolk, mostly. Odds and ends like myself, labourers and such like. Not much good to you, sir, if you're looking for business."

" Don't you believe it," said Plett heartily. " The more people one meets, the more chance of an opening. Besides, I bet you have more fun at the ' Silver Herring ' than the nobs do at the ' George '."

The outside porter grinned, showing a mouthful of stained and broken teeth.

" Bit more free and easy, perhaps," he said. " You're

like to hear what's going there. The lads do like to wag their tongues."

This was an opportunity not to be missed, though the detective had not intended to appear inquisitive at this early stage.

" Well, we all like to hear the news," he said. " Though I suppose life's a bit quiet here, isn't it? "

" It is and all. But you're in luck there, sir. There's a rare twitter on now, because we've had a suicide— Christmas Eve it was. And one of the nobs at that. Colonel Cherrington; perhaps you'd have heard of him, sir."

Plett shook his head.

" What did he do it for? " he asked.

"Ah, there's many'd like to know that," said Crooky, with a knowing leer. " He didn't shoot himself for nothing, the old Colonel, I'll be bound. I do reckon there's a skeleton in that cupboard somewhere, but I expect they'll keep it all dark."

This conversation had taken place as the two men made their way from the station to the Market Square, Plett walking on the pavement and the porter trundling his barrow in the roadway close to the kerb. It was only ten minutes' walk, and the detective was soon registering his name at the office of the ' Royal George ', though he did not disclose his professional identity. His florin to Blake had been accompanied by an invitation to join him in a pint at the ' Silver Herring ' that evening, which Crooky cheerfully accepted.

. . . . .

In the meantime Superintendent Kneller was making the acquaintance of Chief Inspector Horace Myrtle, C.I.D. He had begun by apologising for keeping the Chief Inspector waiting, explaining that he had not wanted

to attract attention by being seen at the station by too
many people.

" That's quite all right, sir," said Myrtle. " I thought
it a perfect bit of timing."

" Never mind about the ' sir ', not while we're alone
together, anyway," said Kneller. " I reckon that a
Scotland Yard Chief Inspector is a bigger noise than a
County Super, though I don't suppose all my colleagues
would agree with me. By ourselves we'll be ' Kneller '
and ' Myrtle ', if that that suits you."

" Suits me fine. The less formality the better when
one's working on a case, I always think. The A.C. told
me your Chief wasn't quite sure whether this was suicide
or murder faked to look like it."

" That's so. I'll give you the facts, as far as we've got
them."

The two officers were by this time closeted in Inspector
Heskell's tiny office at the police station. Kneller went
carefully through the story, giving the C.I.D. man a clear
picture of the background of Colonel Cherrington's life,
so far as he knew it, as well as the details directly connected with the death, and the result of the inquiries made
by himself and Inspector Joss. Myrtle listened attentively,
only asking a question when a point was not quite clear to
to him.

" I don't say that it's certain that the Colonel was
murdered," concluded Kneller, " but I wouldn't like to
swear he wasn't. That scrap of paper looks fishy to me ;
the wording looks a fake, and it's hard to believe he
wouldn't have seen it was all properly burned. Nobody
had seen a letter on that yellowish paper ; I questioned
the maids about that, too, and you know they look pretty
close at what comes in the post, just out of curiosity. It
doesn't follow, of course, that there was no such letter,

because it may have come in an ordinary envelope. I couldn't show the writing, because I didn't want anyone to see the words."

" No, you're handicapped there," said Myrtle. " What did you make of the Hexmans when you questioned them? Was their manner suspicious? "

Kneller hesitated.

" They were both pretty quick in spotting what I was getting at," he replied; " but, then, they're intelligent people. One could say they both acted a bit suspiciously —their manner, I mean, and a look or two—but, then, wouldn't most people do that when their nerves are on on edge, whether they're guilty or innocent? "

" I think you're right there, Kneller. I don't put much weight on appearance. Now suppose this was murder; you're bound to look close at the son-in-law, but I gather that you had other possibilities in mind. For instance, you asked him if he had seen anyone about. Of course, if it's true that he ran downstairs within a minute, or two minutes, of the shot being fired there wasn't much time for anyone to make a get-away. Did the maids say anything about that, by the way? "

" Nothing very definite. They heard him run down, but I couldn't pin them to a time. The younger one— Fanny—seems the brighter of the two; I think she'd have come down herself if the cook hadn't come in and pretended to take care of her. Fanny put it at not much more than a minute. But, then, a lot can happen in a minute."

" It can indeed. But what about doors and windows? If anyone got away, something would have to be open— a door or a window. What about that? "

Kneller nodded.

" Hexman said he found the front door locked and

bolted when he went to open it to admit Heskell—that's the Station Inspector here—who was the first police officer on the scene. After that, of course, it was being constantly opened and shut to let people in or out. I don't think anyone could have got out that way after Heskell arrived. Joss and I had a look round the house after we'd begun to suspect murder, but I'll admit it wasn't a very thorough search, because we didn't go into the Hexmans' rooms or the maids'. We didn't find anyone. The back door was locked—there's no bolt—and the ground-floor windows shuttered. The other windows were shut, but I didn't think to look at the catches. I'm afraid that was a slip; I ought to have."

"Well, you were in a difficult position at that stage, Super. A bit early to be really snoopy."

This, of course, was the sort of point on which the County police always let one down, thought Myrtle. But he knew that he was lucky to be called in as quickly as he had been; generally it was a week-old scent that he was asked to follow.

"If anyone was hidden in the house I suppose his best chance of getting away was before your Inspector—Heskell, is it?—arrived."

"I'd say so. Hexman and his wife would be in the study, pretty well taken up with the Colonel, and the maids up in their rooms. But if anyone did get away, then I don't think it was from the ground floor."

After a little more discussion the two officers drove to Monks Holme, and Myrtle made a quick inspection of the study. Then he asked to be introduced to Captain and Mrs. Hexman, suggesting that his interview with them should be in the dining-room.

Superintendent Kneller explained to the Hexmans that the Chief Constable was not yet fully satisfied that Colonel

Cherrington had died by his own hand, and that Chief Inspector Myrtle of New Scotland Yard had come down to help clear up the point. Kneller then took his leave, saying that he had much routine work to attend to.

Myrtle could see that husband and wife were in a highly strung and nervous condition, but that was only natural in view of the fact that they thought—or pretended to think—that Captain Hexman was suspected of having shot his father-in-law. The detective did not intend, at this first interview, to go into detail or cross-examine them in any way; his idea was to form his own broad general picture of the scene and characters of this problem, as he had often found himself to have been misled by the picture painted for him by someone else. He tried, therefore, to relax the tension by asking only about Colonel Cherrington's life and interests in recent years. The only question of detail that he asked was whether it was usual for the Colonel to work or write after dinner, particularly as late as eleven o'clock.

" Why, no, Chief Inspector," said George Hexman. " I should say it was most unusual. He did most of his work and his letter-writing in the mornings, or after tea in winter-time. After dinner he generally read the paper or a book; sometimes, I think, he just went to sleep. I think he was usually tired by that time and didn't feel like working."

" That's rather what one would expect in an elderly man," said Myrtle. " And after a tiring affair like a British Legion dinner one would expect him to leave letter-writing till next morning—unless, of course, he had some special reason for it. I just wanted to get confirmation of what I expected would be his normal routine."

By this time it was well past four o'clock, and Myrtle had

an appointment at five. The detective was not a man who
believed in a short day's work, and if he wanted to make an
inquiry he had no hesitation in inconveniencing other
people. He had therefore asked Superintendent Kneller
to arrange for him to see the family solicitor, though he
realised that in the country five might be regarded as a
bit late in the day. Not only that, but when the Hexmans invited him to have a cup of tea he accepted, thinking that this opportunity of getting to know his characters
under relaxed conditions was worth the price of a little
irritation for Mr. Carnaby.

However, it was only a quarter past five when Inspector
Heskell's car deposited him at the solicitor's office. It was
a small, dingy house, but Mr. Carnaby's own room was
large and comfortable. The walls were panelled, a cheerful fire burnt in the open hearth, and a pot of hyacinths
stood on a side table. Mr. Cyril Carnaby himself was
anything but the dried-up stick which tradition seems to
expect in solicitors. He was tall, good-looking in a rather
flamboyant way, and looked nearer thirty than forty.
He wore a dark blue, double-breasted suit, with a white
flower in his button-hole. He rose from his chair when
Myrtle was ushered in, and walked forward to greet him
with outstretched hand.

"Very glad to see you, Chief Inspector," he said heartily.
"It was intelligent of the Chief Constable to get you down
so quickly."

"You thought the case needed looking into, sir?" asked
Myrtle.

Carnaby waved his visitor to a chair and held out a slim
silver cigarette-case.

"Suicide always does, I think," he said. "Especially
with a man like Colonel Cherrington. There was nothing
neurotic about him. I've got no special reason for

thinking that it was anything but suicide, but I'm bound to say I find it very difficult to understand."

Myrtle knew that the solicitor would realise that Scotland Yard would not have been called in unless something more than suicide was suspected.

" That's one of the reasons why I wanted to see you as soon as possible, sir," he said, " and I hope you will take that as my excuse for calling at such a late hour; I only got down at two o'clock, and I have had to hear the Superintendent's story and see Captain and Mrs. Hexman. They had already told Superintendent Kneller that they knew of no real reason for suicide; just a bit of worry about money, but not enough to cause such a drastic step as that. But you are his solicitor, sir; you may know something that they don't."

Carnaby inspected his well-polished finger-nails.

" Perhaps I do," he said, " though it doesn't amount to a reason for self-destruction; not, that is, with a man like the Colonel. I know that I could sit on my dignity and withhold information of a confidential nature, Chief Inspector, unless you got an order of the Court, but I'm not going to. George Hexman probably told you that Colonel Cherrington had lost an uncomfortably large sum of money in Mexican Oil shares that he put him on to. What Hexman probably doesn't know is that that wasn't the end of it. The Colonel didn't like losing that money, and he thought he had only lost it because George was a fool, and that someone would get it back for him. So he went to a firm of brokers—not the ones George is with—and, to cut the story short, in the last year he has not only not recovered his five thousand that George dropped for him, but he has lost the best part of another fifteen thousand."

Chief Inspector Myrtle pursed up his lips in a silent whistle.

" And how has he taken that, sir? "

" Like the man he is—or was. On the chin, without blinking an eyelid, though it must have been a terrific punishment for a man who is not a gambler. When I say ' not a gambler ' I mean by nature. Of course, he has been gambling, but I doubt if he'd have called it by that name. Extraordinary how these stern religious men can kid themselves. They're quite capable of having a red-hot affair with a woman and pretending it's something good and noble, no relation to the seventh commandment."

" You don't think there's anything like that in this case, sir? " asked Myrtle quickly.

" No, I certainly don't. You know the story about his wife leaving him? You do. Well, I honestly don't believe, from what I've seen and from what my uncle told me, that he's ever looked at a woman since. He seems to have cut them right out of his life."

" And yet . . . well, sir, about these losses of his. Did anyone know about them? "

"Willison would presumably know; that's his Bank Manager. But I don't believe anyone else did. He never told me; I only know because the broker happens to be a friend of mine and he told me one day after a City dinner —which he certainly oughtn't to have done. I've told no one else, and I'm telling you, now, Chief Inspector, in confidence. I hope you won't have to divulge it, because I had great respect for the old man, and I shouldn't like anything to get about that might be thought in any way a slur on him."

" I quite understand that, sir. Probably no one else need know, but it's a valuable piece of information. It makes one think."

It did indeed. Chief Inspector Myrtle was thinking

that if by chance Captain George Hexman had discovered—as well he might, from a fellow stockbroker whose tongue responded to liquid treatment—that his father-in-law was gambling away the family fortune, he might well have thought that the sooner a stop was put to it the better.

CHAPTER IX

Inside or Outside

THE Coroner's inquest was due to be held on Wednesday morning, but Chief Inspector Myrtle had no intention of attending it. The body would be identified, and then Superintendent Kneller would ask for an adjournment; in view of the confidential information which would have been given him beforehand, the Coroner would certainly grant this. The whole affair would not last long, but as the entire household of Monks Holme had been summoned to attend as witnesses, Myrtle saw a heaven-sent chance of a thorough and uninterrupted inspection of the house. He had arranged with Superintendent Kneller that Detective-Inspector Joss should help him in his search; his own subordinate, Detective-Sergeant Plett, was not yet to be identified as a police officer; for the moment he was better employed gathering gossip in his guise of electrical engineer.

Before starting work in the house, Myrtle had paid a call upon Mr. Willison, manager of the East Coast Bank. Willison was far more true to type than Carnaby had been, but he was not the less forthcoming. Myrtle gathered that the old Bank allowed far more discretion to its managers than did the Big Five; certainly he had seldom met a manager who produced the required information with so little fuss. Colonel Cherrington's balance, it appeared, was in credit, as it always had been, but this had only been made possible by his selling securities to make good his losses on the Stock Exchange. The capital still remaining to the estate was not far short of a hundred thousand pounds, but even so the loss of twenty thousand in a year must have been a formidable shock, and Myrtle was in no wise deflected from his opinion that it constituted a very definite possible motive for early elimination of the gambler. As he had discovered from the family solicitor that Mrs. Hexman was the sole legatee, there was no doubt as to who was most likely to feel this incentive.

Myrtle liked the look of the young County detective who was to work with him. Joss was clearly keen and intelligent, without pushing himself forward. He had explained his difficulty about the position of the body when he first found himself alone with the C.I.D. man. Now, since there was half an hour before the house would be empty, Myrtle returned to the point.

" You're right to keep the two possibilities distinct, Joss," he said; " it's the only way to be clear. If this was suicide, then I see no great difficulty. The Colonel stood up to shoot himself, and that position is a perfectly possible one for him to have fallen into. As regards the glasses, he might have pushed them out of the way of his barrel, or taken them off and held them in his left hand, and so fell on them and smashed them when he dropped. That's possible, though what does rather puzzle me is their being so very badly smashed. One explanation of that is that he dropped them before firing the shot and trod on them. We'll keep that in mind."

" I hadn't thought of that, sir," said Joss ruefully. " It's a very simple explanation."

" It's a possible one, anyhow. But if this is murder— as we have grounds for suspecting—then both the position of the body and the condition of the spectacles take on a very different aspect. I agree with you in not believing that the murderer was hidden in the room for an hour at least before firing his shot. And I don't believe he could have come in by the door while Colonel Cherrington was sitting at the writing-table, facing the door. And that leads to the further point that if this was not suicide, it is most unlikely that the Colonel would have been at his writing-table. Captain Hexman himself says that the old man didn't write or work after dinner; he read the paper or went to sleep. Now, where did he do that, Joss?"

The two detectives looked round the study. It was not a large room, and there was only one comfortable arm-chair in it. That stood on the opposite side of the fire from the writing-table; it had a standard lamp at one side of it and its back to the door.

"Stands out a mile, doesn't it?" said Myrtle. "The old man comes back tired from that dinner, sinks into the armchair with a book or a paper, probably falls . . . book or a paper . . . was there one, Joss?"

Joss shook his head.

"Not when I came, sir. Sure I should have noticed it. Heskell was here first, and he swears he moved nothing."

"And yet surely he'd have had one? One doesn't sit down deliberately to sleep. It was his habit to read. No doubt the murderer—if there was a murderer—put the book away so as not to upset the idea of suicide."

Myrtle looked round the room. On a side-table were a number of periodicals and a newspaper. The detective picked up the paper and looked at it; it was *The Times* for 24 December, 1938, the day Colonel Cherrington died.

"It's been read. It's not what you'd call a virgin," said Myrtle. "But no doubt earlier in the day . . . Ah! Aha! Look at that!"

He had unfolded the newspaper and opened it. The right-hand side was deeply torn to more than half its depth. Myrtle's eyes sparkled.

"That's good enough for us, Joss, though perhaps not

for a jury. That paper was torn by the spasmodic action of the hands when he was struck."

" Struck, sir? "

" Yes, of course. Think, man. If Cherrington was murdered those papers were burned before he was shot; otherwise there would have been no time; directly the shot was fired there could only be a minute or two before someone appeared on the scene. No, it's a certainty that the old man was knocked out—sand-bagged, probably— when he was reading or dozing in that chair. Even if he was asleep the shock would probably have made his arms jerk and tear the paper. We're warming up, Joss; we're warming up."

" You think the murderer folded up the paper and put it on the table, sir? Why didn't he burn it? Then we shouldn't have known it had been torn."

" Too risky. Some intelligent person might have noticed that there was no copy of *The Times*, which was always read by the Colonel in the evening."

" And the spectacles, sir? You said that if it was murder their condition . . ."

" Yes, yes, don't you see? It may have been the murderer that trod on them. Get down on the floor, man, and do a Sherlock Holmes stunt; start near this chair. He was shot in the right temple, so that's where he was hit; the glasses would have jerked to the left."

Joss was flat on his stomach before the C.I.D. man had stopped speaking. He had taken a small electric torch from his pocket and, with his nose only an inch or two from the floor, he hunted over the carpet, moving the beam slowly from side to side. In a very short time his eyes caught a tiny glitter, another . . .

" Here it is, sir," he exclaimed eagerly. " Broken glass, tiny scraps in the pile of the carpet."

" Yes, he'd have picked up everything normally visible to the eye. Obviously he had not noticed the spectacles, and trod on them. He couldn't leave them there, by the armchair, because they wouldn't have fitted in with the suicide. He couldn't get rid of them altogether because, as with *The Times*, somebody might have noticed their absence and started wondering. So he had to shove them under the body and hope the police would think they were broken in the fall. Quite a lot of policemen would have thought that, Joss; full marks to you, my lad, for spotting that point."

Joss blushed with pride. To be praised by a C.I.D. Chief Inspector was something that didn't often come the way of a County detective. Still, he realised that it was not he who had followed his own point to its logical conclusion; it was the experienced C.I.D. man who had done that—a sobering thought.

" Do you think it points to the Captain, sir? " he asked.

" Not necessarily. It points very definitely to murder, and that's a big step forward. The son-in-law is obviously first suspect, because it would have been so easy for him, and he had the motive; but we mustn't shut our minds to other possibilities."

He looked at his watch.

" Hell, it's nearly half-past eleven. They may be back any time now. We must drop this, Joss, and search the house while we've got it to ourselves."

As time was limited, Myrtle decided to leave the ground floor; with locked doors and shuttered windows, it was most unlikely that an intruder could have got in or out that way—leaving everything closed behind him, as it apparently was. The first floor was much the most likely place to look; farther up would have been more difficult, and the maids were there all the time after the shot was fired. There seemed no point in looking in Mrs. Hexman's bedroom or in Captain Hexman's dressing-room, assuming that they had nothing to do with the killing; no intruder would have chosen to enter the house by one of those, and if they were guilty—well, there was no need to look for an intruder. '

Besides the bedroom and dressing-room used by the Hexmans there were two other bedrooms on the first floor. One of these was Colonel Cherrington's—a small, austere room, furnished rather like a Barrack quarter; Myrtle thought that its bleakness provided a definite clue to the dead man's character. The other bedroom on the floor was a small room at the back of the house, close to the backstairs; it was evidently used as a dump, and there was a good deal of dust about. A careful examination showed that there was evidence of at least possible intrusion in the recent past; the latch of the window was not fastened and was in any case rather loose; it would have been no difficult matter to push it back from the outside, and there were even slight marks on latch and woodwork that might have been made by a knife-blade inserted between the sashes.

Myrtle examined the sill carefully, but could see no sign of recent scratches on this, nor were there marks on the outer brickwork below the window. On the other hand, there was a very convenient coal-shed just below the window, and it was clear that here was a possible line of entry and exit.

" The dust round this window has been disturbed recently, sir," said Joss, " but that's about the only place where it has been disturbed; there's a lot of it about. Beginning to look like an outside job, sir."

Chief Inspector Myrtle smiled.

"Perhaps that's what it's meant to look like," he said.

"You mean . . . a faked entrance, sir?"

"Exactly. If this room had been searched immediately after the shooting one would put some weight on this evidence; as it is, anyone in the house has had plenty of time to cook this."

Joss looked crestfallen.

"I shouldn't let it worry you," said the C.I.D. man. "I don't see how you could have worked out all these possibilities on that first night. In any case, the faking might have been done—most probably would have been done—*before* the shooting. All one can say is that here is a possible line of entry and exit for an outsider; so far there is no proof of such entry."

Joss was grateful for this tempering of his self-reproach, but he knew that he ought to have searched the house at once. Rather difficult, though, with Superintendent Kneller in charge of the case.

"I quite see the possibility of someone coming in this way, sir," he said. "If he watched things carefully no doubt he would have a pretty good chance of getting down to the ground floor and along to the study without anyone seeing him, though there would be a risk of a door suddenly opening. But how did he get away after the shot? If this was an outside job, then one must accept the Captain's evidence that there was only about a minute's pause before he ran downstairs; why didn't he see the man?"

Myrtle nodded.

"That's well argued," he said. "Come downstairs and we'll talk it over in the study. I don't much want people to know what we have been looking at."

The two men went down the backstairs and through into

the hall. As they passed the front stairs on their way to the study Myrtle checked.

"Just go outside the front door for a minute and see if there is any sign of anyone coming."

Obediently the County detective opened the door, walked across to the gate and looked up and down the road; a boy on a bicycle and an elderly lady making slow progress down the footpath were the only people in sight. Joss returned to the house and found the hall empty, so he went into the study. The study was empty, too. He presumed that Chief Inspector Myrtle was having a look round elsewhere, so decided to wait for him.

Then he heard his name called. He went back into the hall, but it was still empty. Again he heard his name called, and this time from close beside him. Looking quickly round, he realised that under the front stairs there was a built-in cupboard; pulling open the door, he saw the Scotland Yard man on his knees inside, flashing a torch round the dark interior.

"This might be the answer to your intelligent inquiry," said Myrtle, crawling out and then rising to dust his knees. "Looks like an answer to prayer, that cupboard, from a murderer's point of view. I don't quite see anyone running upstairs, either back or front, after firing the shot; such a risk of meeting someone coming down. But he could pop in here and then wait till the coast was clear."

"Pretty risky, wouldn't it be, sir?"

"Murder's a risky business, Joss. If it wasn't, there would be a lot more of it. But if this was an outside job the murderer is a cool customer and one who knew what he was doing. It's a planned job. But as a matter of fact, the risk is not so great as it appears at first sight. Assuming that this *is* an outside job, what happens? Everyone assumes that the Colonel shot himself; it is the obvious assumption. The son-in-law runs downstairs, finds the old man dead, thinks it is suicide, rings up the police, almost certainly stays in the study; he wouldn't start hunting under the stairs for a murderer. If the wife comes down, she goes into the study with her husband."

" The maids might hang about in the hall, sir."

" They might, but it's more likely that they stay upstairs, as they did, or are sent upstairs, either to dress or to go back to bed. That's the moment for this cool customer to slip out, up the backstairs, and out through the window. But suppose the maids do wait about in the hall, or the Captain for that matter; that's just too bad, and the poor chap has to stay in his kennel, feeling damned uncomfortable and rather cross. The police arrive and go into the study. Perhaps there's another opportunity to slip out, perhaps not. More police arrive—the nobs from Headquarters this time, including the Chief Constable. The hall is full of people, no getting out now. But does anyone look in the cupboard? *Did* anyone look in the cupboard, Joss? "

Joss stared at the Chief Inspector.

" Good God, sir; do you mean he was here all the time? "

" He may have been. I don't know . . . nor do you, because you didn't look. And why should you look? Everyone is still assuming suicide; it's a thousand to one that everyone assumes suicide . . . until an intelligent young detective has got the study to himself and has time to look round and do a bit of thinking. And then he has to talk things over with his chief, and by that time the crowd has cleared away and it would be damned unlucky if our cool customer hadn't an opportunity to

slip out . . . perhaps straight out through the front
door."

Joss slowly nodded his head, feeling a little less culpable.

"And still that intelligent young detective didn't look
inside the cupboard, or search the house," he said ruefully.

"No, he didn't. And perhaps he ought to have.
But how many murder cases have you investigated,
Joss? "

"This is my first, sir. My first serious case of any
kind."

"Exactly. It takes a lot of experience, young fellow,
to take all the right steps at the right time. That's
where Scotland Yard earns its pay. We don't set
up to have better brains than anyone else, but we
have accumulated years of experience behind us, as
well as one of the most thorough routine organisations
in the world. And even so we make mistakes, we forget
things, we leave things undone that . . . you know.
Before we've cleared this case up, Joss, you'll see me
making some howling blunder or other, and you're perfectly welcome to point it out to me, because one's
learning all the time at this job, and if one isn't, one's no
good."

Joss listened respectfully to this dissertation. He
couldn't quite see himself pointing out mistakes to Chief
Inspector Myrtle, C.I.D.

"Did you find anything in that cupboard, sir? " he
asked. "Anything to support the outsider theory? "

Myrtle laughed.

"I wish I could say I found some of the dust that was
disturbed in the bedroom; that's what old Sherlock would
have found. There's a good old jumble in there—
baskets, golf-bags, guns, cardboard boxes, all the usual
junk. There's room for a man to hide there and no proof

that someone did—not that I could find, anyhow, though
I'd like you to try your hand at it.   What we've got this
morning, Joss, is some evidence that this *might* have been
an outside job; we've certainly no evidence that it was
not an inside one.   What we've got to look for now is
motive for the outsider."

CHAPTER X

No Smoke without Fire

JASPER BLOSSOM presided over a full house at the
'Silver Herring' on the evening following the inquest.
Any unusual happening in Great Norne brought grist to
Jasper's till, and an inquest was a happening of the rarest
vintage, especially when it concerned a townsman of such
distinction as Colonel Cherrington. Everyone had views
to express and questions to ask, and the fact that few were
in a position to give an authoritative answer to these
questions in no way diminished the pleasure of asking
them. Although the word 'murder' had not been
mentioned at the inquest, it was in the air to-night; no
reader of the Sunday 'cheaps'—and patrons of the 'Silver
Herring' read little else—could fail to know that an
adjournment meant that someone was smelling a rat. It
was the nature and identity of the rat that formed the
centre of discussion.

Ben Hard, fisherman and self-appointed foreman of this
Grand Jury, was of opinion that death was not due to gun-
shot wound at all, but to poisoning, or possibly strangula-
tion. When asked what grounds he had for this idea he
replied that he had no special grounds, but that he reckoned
it would turn out to have been something like that, no one
outside the household having heard any shooting.

"And who do you reckon poisoned him?" asked his
friend Caleb Wittle.

Ben pondered the question.

"I won't say as I've gone as far as to lay a name to him
as poisoned the gentleman," he replied, adding as a bright
afterthought: "Maybe he poisoned hisself."

94

" Ah, and maybe he strangled hisself," suggested a humorist, amid general laughter.

" Well, if it was poison you wouldn't have far to look," said Rose Blossom.

" Someone in the house? Aye, that's the most likely."

" A well-to-do man, the Colonel. What he can't take away with him will be bound to go to someone else."

" Ah, that's right," said Josiah Chell, nodding over his tankard. " He brought nothing into this world and it's a certain thing he can't take nothing out. And the worms'll soon devour his vile body."

" Oh, Mr. Chell, what horrid things you do say," exclaimed Rose. " Give me the creeps you do."

" It's the worms that creeps," said the sexton with a grin. " You should see them scuttling up when I digs a new grave."

" That'll do, old mouldy," cut in Jasper, who was afraid that Josiah's ghoulish humour might spoil men's thirst. " What's this I heard about a man come down by train yesterday that the Superintendent met at the station? Would he be from the Yard? "

This fresh topic quickly whipped up interest again and called for further libations of beer. Though no one could give official confirmation of the idea, it was generally agreed thât what little had been seen of the newcomer did strongly suggest a Scotland Yard 'tec.

It would perhaps be more accurate to say that no one did give official confirmation, because Detective-Sergeant Plett could have done so had he wished. He was sitting quietly at one of the marble-topped tables, with the silent Eb Creech beside him, listening with considerable interest to the ebb and flow of discussion. Nobody paid much attention to him, but by reason of a generous distribution of pints on the previous evening he was accepted as being

not unworthy of the company. He had expected that the
porter, Blake, would touch him for a further drink, but
Crooky, though he had given him a friendly nod on
arrival, was not a cadger, and had settled into his own
corner, to contribute an occasional word and consume a
generous quantity of beer at his own expense.

Plett tried to draw his neighbour into the discussion,
but Eb Creech was in his most silent mood and was not to
be drawn. He did go so far, in reply to Plett's explanation
of his own business in the town, as to say that he did not
see any need for any more electricians in Great Norne, as
his own employer, Mr. Barton, kept a couple of tidy
fellows in that line himself. It was not a reply that
encouraged much development of the theme.

Discussion soon swung back to the Colonel himself and
to his son-in-law. The stern old man had been respected
in Great Norne, though he had done nothing to make
himself liked. As Deputy Chairman of the local Bench
he was known to have been responsible, on more than one
occasion, for stiffening a sentence which the Squire, as
Chairman, was proposing to inflict. There was some
recollection, too, of his having been harshly critical of
Richard Barton's wife over her affair with the young sailor,
but this had been understandable in view of the tragedy of
his own married life, the story of which was generally, if
rather vaguely known.

His son-in-law, on the other hand, was popular without
being respected. He put on no airs, had a friendly word
for everyone he met, and was generous in the matter of
tips and occasional drinks. The absence of respect was
due to the fact that he was looked on as rather a waster,
who was content to live on his wife's money, or at any
rate on her father's.

" Don't keep the style he used to, though," said Ben

Hard. "That noisy little motey car he used to traipse about in; lot o' power in that I used to reckon, and that's gone these two years."

"Sports car, that was; thirty or forty horse-power, I should say," said Jasper Blossom.

"Yes, he gave me a ride in it once," said Rose. "Fast as the wind it was."

"Ah, you wouldn't want to go too fast with the Captain, I reckon," said Josiah, shaking his head disapprovingly. "That's the way many a girl's taken the wrong turning."

"Not this girl hasn't," said Rose, tossing her head. "You want to keep a civil tongue in your head, Mr. Chell, or you may get a thick ear one of these days."

"That's right, Rosie; you dot him one if he sauces you," said Ben. "Anyway, the Captain's got a pretty girl of his own as lawful wife. But I do allow a bit more money in his own pocket might not come amiss. Not that I want to be thought to say that the Captain would go so far as to put the old man out of the way."

"I don't hold with all this talk of murdering," interposed Crooky Blake, who had been silent for some time. "There's no manner of doubt that the old gentleman put himself away. And for why? Because he's got something to hide what he didn't want come out into the light of day. There must be something to 'count for his making away with himself; there's never smoke without fire somewhere. Mark my word, there's a skeleton in that cupboard, a skeleton in that cupboard."

"There'll be a skeleton in the churchyard soon enough, anyway," cut in the sexton with a grin.

Blake shook his head, but did no more than mutter to himself, staring into his empty tankard, which Plett calculated to be the third, if not the fourth of its kind. After a time he rose to his feet and made his way rather unsteadily to the end of the bar counter. Sergeant Plett, who had been listening to the two fishermen on his other side, felt a nudge in his ribs, and saw that Eb Creech was actually grinning. Following the direction indicated by a jerk of the carpenter's thumb, he saw the outside porter receive from Blossom a flat bottle containing a colourless liquid, in return for which he slid two or three pieces of silver on to the counter.

" Gin, eh? " Plett whispered.

Creech, still chuckling gently, nodded.

" On the Q.T.," he said.

Blake made his way slowly to the door, nobody in the crowded room paying much attention to his exit. Attention was now centred upon a small man in the uniform of a postman who was propounding a new and attractive theory.

" You all talk as if it was the Captain that the money went to, but it ain't, not by nature; it's the Captain's wife that'll get it."

" Same thing, isn't it, Charlie? " asked the landlord.

" Not on your life it ain't. Might have some other use for it, she might," said Charlie Trott darkly.

" What are you hinting at, then? " " Cough it up Charlie." " You been reading her letters, you old rascal? "

A chorus of eager inquiry, as of hounds owning to a new line, flickered round the taproom.

" I goes my rounds and I keeps my eyes open," declared the postman. " Stands to reason a handsome young woman's not content with one man alone. Ask Miss Rose."

" Who is it, then? " " Come on, you know something." " Put a name to him."

But Charlie Trott, having started the fresh hare, was not going to commit himself any farther. That was no hindrance to his listeners, however. The law of slander not being any worry to the fishermen and labourers of Great Norne, there was a general canvassing of candidates for the scandalous rôle indicated by postman Charlie. The names of Cyril Carnaby, Dr. Fred Stopp, Gerry Winch—son of the landlord of the ' Royal George '—figured most prominently in the market, the handsome young lawyer commanding the shortest price; but there were many runners in the imagined field, and it was not long before the general run of conversation was moving from the slanderous to the lewd, and Jasper Blossom decided that the time had come to spare his daughter's blushes.

The time had also come for Detective-Sergeant Plett to fade away, though the evening was yet young. He had an assignation with his chief at the police-station, where he had orders to report each evening at eight o'clock, to tell his own story and to receive his orders.

It was a cold night, and after the overcrowded and unventilated bar, Plett felt the chill strike quickly into his bones. He would have liked to step out quickly, but he had some difficulty in seeing his way. There was no moon, and the darkness was almost impenetrable after the bright glitter of electric light. The detective stood for a minute or two to accustom his eyes to the change. Presently he became aware of the dim outline of nearby houses; in the distance he could see a flicker of bright light, perhaps a car-lamp or a coutch-fire.

Plett did not want to start walking till he could really see where he was going. The ' Silver Herring ' was close to the harbour, and he was not too sure of his way; he did not want to go stepping off the quay into cold water or slimy mud; Blake, in his retail of local gossip, had told him the story of the late Vicar's accident.

However, he could not keep the Chief Inspector waiting, and he had lingered over-long listening to Trott's theory and the rather pointless imaginings that it had given rise to. He could make out a star or two now, and as soon as he had identified the pole star he knew his general direction and started off with some confidence.

It was rough going, because the local penny did not bring many pounds to the rates. Plett stubbed his toes badly twice and had bumped into a post and a wheel-barrow before he got his night-eyes. It was the wheel-barrow that really startled him, not only because it was obstructing what he believed to be the highway, but because it made a noise—a noise that sounded strangely like a groan. Startled, Plett pulled out his torch and switched it on; the light showed him a huddled figure lying on the barrow.

But it also converted the groan into a raucous snore, and the detective laughed as he realised that he was witnessing the final stage in the potations of his friend Blake. A strong smell of gin confirmed the evidence of his eyes, which presently showed him the flat bottle which he had seen pass from Jasper Blossom's hands and which now lay in Crooky's lap—empty.

' On the Q.T.,' as Eb Creech had said, was evidently the porter's idea of the end of a perfect evening.

Plett wasted no more time on this profane spectacle, but hurried on to his assignation. He reached the police-station just as the clock on the Town Hall, souvenir of Victoria's second jubilee, finished striking the hour. Inside, the brightly lit charge-room contained quite a little array of police officers, uniformed and otherwise. The large, soldierly figure of Superintendent Kneller was planted in front of the fireplace, absorbing most of the warmth that came from it. Sitting on the corner of the table, which occupied the centre of the room, was Chief Inspector Myrtle, and beside him stood Detective-Inspector Joss, scanning a note-book. With his back to the room, Inspector Heskell stood at the window, looking out into the night, whilst respectfully in one corner Police-Constable Peter Flaish shifted his considerable weight from one weary foot to the other.

It was evident that some sort of conference was going on. After a quick glance at his entry no one paid any attention to Sergeant Plett. Chief Inspector Myrtle held, so to speak, the floor of the house, though he was the only one seated.

" So you see, sir," he said, addressing Superintendent Kneller formally now as his superior officer, " we've come to a fork in the road. The main road still seems to me to point to an inside job, because motive and opportunity are obvious, and in my experience the obvious solution is generally the right one. But there is a possible side road; we've come across sufficient evidence to show us that this might have been done by an outsider, though at the moment there is nothing at all to indicate what outsider or what motive. I think we've got to follow both roads, and that means division of forces."

" What do you suggest? " asked Superintendent Kneller.

" Well, sir, I think we must find out more about the son-in-law. His work, such as it is, lies in London, and I think I should look into that myself, and also into his general life when he's up there. I understand that he either stays at his Club or, if his wife is with him, they go to a small hotel in Mayfair. From what I know of Mayfair hotels that's an expensive business, however small they are, and some inquiries there should give us a line on the Captain's financial position."

"Yes, I agree that that's an important factor," said Kneller. "Now what about the outsider?"

"That's where I think the County Constabulary can do more than I could, in the first place, sir. You are fortunate and go-ahead enough to have a detective branch of your own, and from what I've seen of it a very efficient one. I should like Inspector Joss here to take charge of that inquiry, at any rate till I get back from London. If someone else had a reason for killing Colonel Cherrington there surely must be some evidence of it; *somebody* must know something, though I'm bound to say that so far no one has volunteered any information. I think Joss might have a talk with the family solicitor, Mr. Carnaby, and the doctor, and one or two other people who knew the Colonel well; you and he will have a better idea as to who they are than I should. I'll have a word with Captain and Mrs. Hexman myself in the morning before I go. It won't do any harm to let them see we are on another line—might make them careless, if there's anything for them to be careless about. And then there's Sergeant Plett here; I suggest that he should work under Inspector Joss while I'm away, if Joss thinks he might be useful."

He looked inquiringly at Joss, who had shown evident signs of gratification at the responsible rôle which was being allotted to him.

"I shall be very glad to have Sergeant Plett's help, sir," he said. "I understand he's already working on some line, but I'm not very clear what it is."

"Not on any definite line. I thought it would be a good plan to have an open ear in the town that wasn't recognised as a policeman's. Plett has given out that he's an electrical engineer on the look out for opening a little business on his own; he's staying at the 'Royal George', and getting round to have a talk and a gossip with as many people as he can. Been drawing the pub coverts, too, haven't you, Plett? "

" Only one so far, sir. Thought I should get to hear more if I was familiar; they wouldn't be likely to talk much in front of a complete stranger. I was at a little place down by the harbour last night and to-night—the ' Silver Herring '."

" And did they . . . that seems familiar ground to you, eh, constable? "

This remark was addressed to Police-Constable Flaish, on whose open countenance a broad grin had appeared. Finding himself the centre of interest, Flaish passed the back of a large hand across his mouth—perhaps an automatic association of ideas.

" Well, sir, I has a glass or two there myself sometimes— when I'm off duty, of course."

" And what sort of people are the patrons? Reliable? Imaginative? Truthful? "

Flaish's grin broadened.

" Plenty of imagination, sir, when they've got a drop or two. Fishermen, mostly. One or two farm labourers, a postman, a craftsman or two, that like of fellow. The sexton up at St. Martha's, he's a regular."

" And have you listened to their imaginings since Colonel Cherrington was shot? "

" No, sir," said Flaish righteously. " I thought it wiser to keep away while this case was sub-juicy, so to speak."

Chief Inspector Myrtle concealed a smile.

" Perhaps you were wise," he said. " But tell me, before I ask Sergeant Plett what he has picked up, would you pay much attention to anything you heard at the ' Silver Herring '? Are they on the whole a steady, reliable lot, or, to put it frankly, are they a lot of damned liars?"

Flaish pondered this conundrum.

"On the whole I'd say they was a steady lot, sir, though they likes to hear their own tongues wag. There's one or two I wouldn't give much attention to, but on the whole I'd say they might know something and it would be worth looking into."

"Thank you, constable; that's a useful opinion. Now, Plett, have you heard anything that might help us? Anything, especially, that might point down the side road —to an outsider?"

Sergeant Plett shook his head.

"I don't think so, sir. The talk this evening has been about the Colonel and his family. Some still think he shot himself, some suspect murder—not from anything they know themselves but simply because the inquest has been adjourned and because the Yard has been called in."

"Oh, they know that, do they? I wonder how that got around so quick. I've only talked to the solicitor and the Bank manager and to Captain and Mrs. Hexman. One wouldn't expect any of them to talk."

Superintendent Kneller smiled.

"No need for anyone to talk," he said. "No doubt someone saw me meet you at the station or taking you here or to the house. Quite enough for intelligent folk to put two and two together; we're country bumpkins, but we're not all boneheads."

Myrtle had the grace to blush.

"Sorry, sir. I suppose it was obvious. They were bound to know soon, anyhow. So you got nothing useful, Plett?"

Plett hesitated.

"The only line that seemed to me at all out of the

obvious, sir, was a suggestion made by the postman; Trott, I think his name is. He had an idea that it might not be Captain Hexman who would benefit from his father-in-law's death. He thinks Mrs. Hexman is . . . interested in someone else."

Myrtle straightened his back.

" Eh? That might be interesting. Does anyone here know about that? "

Nobody spoke. Superintendent Kneller glanced across at Inspector Heskell, who for some time had been fidgeting about by the window, obviously not paying much attention to what was going on in the charge-room.

" Do you know anything about that, Heskell? " the Superintendent asked sharply.

Heskell turned round.

" I beg your pardon, sir. I'm afraid I . . . there's some sort of fire over beyond the town. I thought it might be a bonfire, but it's late in the year for burning leaves or rubbish, and it's getting bigger. Looks like it might be a haystack. I think if I might be excused, sir, I ought to go and have a look."

The telephone bell trilled sharply. Heskell walked across to it and picked up the receiver.

" Eh? The Manor? Manor House or Manor Farm? Have the Brigade got it? Right."

Heskell slammed down the receiver and turned to his Chief.

" There's a fire at the Manor Farm, sir," he said. " Exchange have notified the Fire Brigade. I must get over, sir, if I may."

CHAPTER XI

After the Flames

"WHOSE farm is that?" asked Superintendent Kneller.

"Mr. Gannett's, sir."

"Oh, that's the man who . . .?"

A slight lift of the elbow indicated Kneller's meaning. Inspector Heskell nodded.

"He might not be . . . very quick at putting a fire out, sir."

"Exactly. Well, if the Brigade's there they'll do all they can. No need for me to appear. I'll be getting along home. We've said all we need about our case at the moment, eh, Chief Inspector?"

"Yes, sir, I think so. I'll report directly I get back from London. I'll get along now and eat your supper, Heskell, and get early to bed."

Chief Inspector Myrtle was staying at Heskell's house.

"What about you, Joss?" asked Superintendent Kneller. "You'll come with me, I suppose."

"I think if you don't mind, sir . . . there was a farm fire the other side of Snottisham a couple of months ago; arson for insurance it turned out to be; I'll go along with Mr. Heskell, I think, and have a look round at the Manor Farm."

"Ah, yes, perhaps you're right. If this chap Gannett has gone to seed a bit he may be in financial trouble and want to find a way out. Though I believe he used to be a very decent fellow."

"Come on, Joss, for the Lord's sake, if you're coming," muttered Inspector Heskell. "I ought to have been there ten minutes ago. Flaish, you must stay here, but rout out Bridger and send him up to Manor Farm on his motor-cycle. We may need a messenger if the telephone's not working. Send Batt along, too, if you can find him; he's off to-night."

.   .   .   .   .

As the two Police Inspectors drove up to the Manor Farm they could see that the fire had taken a firm hold, though the streams of water from two hoses were beginning to get it under control. Heskell went up to the Chief officer of the Fire Brigade—Fire Captain Banner—and asked him if he wanted any help from the police.

" Only to keep people from going in. They'll loot if you don't watch them."

Heskell nodded.

" I'll see to that," he said. " Where's Mr. Gannett? "

" Haven't seen him. Haven't seen anyone except an old woman. Seems a boy on a bicycle gave the alarm; had the sense to pop into Ulick's and telephone from there. I rang Snottisham. They should be here soon. We'll have it out before long if the water lasts."

Heskell and Joss made a quick tour of the farm-buildings. Only the farmhouse was alight, and as there was no wind there appeared to be a good chance that the fire would not spread. It was too early to start looking about in the house, though fireman were at work inside. Police-Constable Bridger appeared on his motor-bicycle, and was posted at the back of the farm to keep the growing crowd of onlookers at a proper distance, whilst Heskell did the same himself in front, until he was relieved by the appearance of a second constable who, with a rueful grin, explained that he had been run to earth at the pictures.

" I wonder what started this fire," said Joss. " There's a telephone line going in, but I don't see any sign of an electric-light cable, so a short isn't likely."

"Well, if there's anything in your idea of arson there could be plenty of ways of starting it," said Heskell drily.

"Beg pardon, sir," said a woman's voice behind them.

Looking round, the two police officers saw an elderly woman, bent with rheumatism and poorly dressed. She seemed to be some seventy years old.

"I'm worried about the master," she said. "I've not seen him about, and he's usually to home come eight o'clock."

"Who are you, mother?" asked Inspector Heskell briskly.

"Pettitt's the name—Jane Pettitt. My Bob worked for Mr. Gannett, and his father before him till he was took; ten years ago that'll be come February. Mr. Gannett was very good to me—let me stay on in the cottage, though it's tied and the only one lived in now near the farm; the others is gone to pieces, but the master he kept my cottage in trim. I've done for him ever since my man went— ten years, as I say. There's no one else to look after him now, though there used to be two or more before the war, when his mother was alive. I want to know where he is; you don't think he can be inside, do you, mister?"

The old woman's anxious face peered up at Heskell, its rugged lines picked out and deepened by the flickering light of the flames.

"No reason to think that, mother. We'll be able to get in soon to have a look round; the fire's dying down now. You don't know how it started, I suppose?"

Jane Pettitt shook her head.

"I was away to my gran'daugther's," she said. "I always goes Wednesdays and spends the evening with them. Fred brings me back. You could have knocked me over with a feather when I see the flames, come we left

Daisy's. I've been that worried about Mr. Gannett, and no one would tell me aught."

" Where is your house, Mrs. Pettitt? " asked Joss.

She pointed to a dimly seen building beyond the light of the fire.

" It's no but there," she said.

" Then you go along in and get yourself a cup of tea. We'll come and tell you directly Mr. Gannett comes."

Shaking her head dolefully, the old lady hobbled off, and was barely out of sight when a fireman came up to the police-officers.

" There's a body inside, Inspector," he said. " We've just come to it, under a lot of timber. In the kitchen it is, where the fire looks to have started."

Heskell and Joss exchanged glances.

" Not much chance of the telephone working now," said Heskell. " I'll slip round to the back and send Bridger for the doctor and the ambulance. You go in if you like, Joss."

Joss followed the fireman into the house. There was little flame left now, and what light there was came from the powerful electric torches of the firemen. Part of the upper floor and of the roof had fallen in, and it was only with difficulty that Joss could make his way to the kitchen. Here the fire had evidently been at its height; the floor was covered with charred timber and blackened plaster, whilst a glimmer of stars could be seen through the floor above and the roof. In the centre of the room the floor had been partly cleared, and it was possible to distinguish the remains of a heavy deal table. On the floor beside the table lay a huddled form, so badly burnt that it was difficult to distinguish as a man.

The Fire Captain pointed to the remains of a brass lamp which lay beside the body and the collapsed table.

"What I expected," he said. "Look, there's glass about. That's the remains of a bottle; whisky, or I'm a Dutchman. Knocked the lamp over, without a doubt. There's no electric light in the house, though there is a telephone."

"Why did you expect it?" asked the detective.

The fireman shrugged his shoulders.

"You're a stranger here, though I know who you are," he answered. "We all know that Mr. Gannett used to spend his evenings in here with a bottle, not to put too fine a point on it. Directly I heard of the fire I guessed what we should find and where we should find it. As soon as the flames were out I started to look, and here it is."

"Bad business," said Inspector Heskell, who had just joined the group in the kitchen. "Better leave the body till the doctor comes; he shouldn't be long. There can't be any doubt but what he's dead."

No; there could be no doubt of that. Joss had tried to turn the body over on its back, but it seemed to be welded into a solid block. He had had one glimpse of the face, and had turned quickly away, but he knew that he would not soon forget the charred, featureless mask that that glimpse had shown him.

"Can't do much more to-night," said the Fire Captain. "I'll leave a couple of men here just to make sure it doesn't break out again. No doubt one or two of you fellows will be here, too, Inspector?"

Heskell nodded.

"Yes, we'll keep an eye on things. There's plenty in the house not damaged and, as you say, there are folks that aren't too particular what they lay their hands on."

It was not long before Dr. Stopp appeared and gave his formal verdict. The body was lifted carefully on to a stretcher and carried to the ambulance which would take

it to the Hospital mortuary. Dr. Stopp promised to make
a thorough examination of it in the morning.

"I'll come up again as soon as it's light," said Heskell.
"I shall have to make a report, and one can't see properly
now. I don't suppose you'll want to come, eh, Joss?
Chap wouldn't deliberately set alight to his farm and stay
inside it. Tight as an owl and knocked the lamp over,
as Banner said. Too drunk to get out of the way, I
suppose."

Joss made no comment, but thought it might be interesting to come back and have a look round by daylight.

· · · · ·

It was barely eight o'clock on the following morning
when the two Inspectors returned to the Manor Farm.
The light was still none too good, but the earliness of the
hour was likely to give them time to make their inspection
before the idle curious came on the scene.

There was not much more to be seen, but it was more
than ever clear that the fire had started where the body of
Gannett had been found. Damage to the rest of the
house was superficial, though there had been enough
woodwork and material burnt to cause a good flare-up.
But in the kitchen, and especially in the centre of it round
the table, there had been a very strong blaze. Besides
the kitchen table there were the remains—the limited and
deeply charred remains—of at least two chairs and
a good deal of other wooden debris not easy to identify.
Probably the damage would have been even greater if the
floor had been wood instead of stone-flagged, though the
carpet or rugs had added to the fuel.

Inspector Joss was interested in what he saw, though he
made no comment to his companion, who was busy writing
up his note-book. The detective poked about the room.

and found one curious freak, which so often occurs in a
fire. A large dresser against the wall next to the range
had escaped almost unscathed, possibly because the collapsing floor above had protected it. On the dresser was
an array of bottles, full and empty, and glasses, most of
them unwashed. Joss eyed these with interest, and then,
telling Heskell that he was going back to get some breakfast, made his way to the police-station and its telephone.

As a result of a guarded conversation with Superintendent Kneller at Headquarters, Joss betook himself to a
cross-roads on the outskirts of the town, and about twenty
minutes later was joined there by a police car containing
the Superintendent and the two detective-constables,
Gilbert and Morris, with their respective boxes of tricks.

" Better get inside and tell me what all this is about,"
said Kneller dourly.

Joss obeyed, and in ten minutes had given a short
account of the fire at Manor Farm and what he had seen
there on the previous night and this morning.

" Well, the man's burnt himself to death. That's all
very sad, but why are you so interested? You've got
some idea in your mind, I take it? "

Kneller paused and looked sharply at his subordinate.

" You think it's suicide, eh? Something to do with the
Colonel? "

Joss shook his head.

" I don't think it was suicide, sir," he said quietly. " I
think Gannett was murdered."

Kneller stared at him, while Joss could see his two young
men in the back of the car beginning to simmer with
excitement.

" What makes you think that? "

" The very fact of his being burnt, sir. I don't believe
that a man, however drunk, could fail to get out of the

way of flame from an upset lamp; it's not like a woman with flimsy clothes, and even then the victim always runs some distance; she doesn't collapse on top of the lamp. But there's more than that, sir. The body is terribly burnt, the face is unrecognisable. There's a lot of charred timber and other material all round the body; looks as if there had been a regular funeral pyre. I can't help thinking that paraffin was used and stuff piled up round the body."

Superintendent Kneller sniffed.

" Sounds melodramatic to me. We'll have to look into it, of course, but I shall take a bit of convincing."

Superintendent Kneller had not been too well pleased at being summoned from Headquarters this morning. The Cherrington case had already taken up a great deal of his time, and he was behindhand with his routine work, and feared it might spread into his week-end, which, in a County Constabulary, was still sacred. He was a conscientious officer, and had not hesitated to respond to Joss's call, but he wanted to be sure that his time was not being wasted.

" What about Heskell? " he asked. " Does he agree with this theory of yours? "

" I haven't spoken to him about it, sir. I don't think it struck him that there was anything suspicious, and I didn't want to start talk if there was nothing in it."

" Talk? " exclaimed Kneller sharply. " Are you suggesting that one of my officers would go blabbing about the town? Chief Inspector Myrtle was hinting at the same thing last night."

Joss flushed.

" No, sir, no. I didn't mean that for a minute. I . . . well, I'll only make it worse if I say any more. It was a very silly remark to make, sir. I'm very sorry, I'm sure."

" And what about Chief Inspector Myrtle? Have you told him? Or has he gone already? "

" He'll be gone by now, sir. His train left at 9.5. I daresay I could have caught him, sir, but I didn't try."

Joss knew that he was on delicate ground. He had already incurred one rebuke and did not want a second, but he went doggedly on.

" I've got very little definite to tell him, sir. I wanted to make sure. You see, sir, he gave us a job to do here while he followed his London line. I thought the County might slip one over on him."

To his relief he saw Superintendent Kneller's face break into a slow grin.

" Something in that, perhaps. Well, let's go and have a look."

Fortunately, by this time the Fire Captain—Banner— had finished his own inspection and gone back to the town. Still more fortunately, he had not disturbed the dresser and its glasses, in which Joss was particularly interested. There was no one now at the farm but one fireman, on the watch for a possible recrudescence, and P.C. Batt, engaged in keeping the curious at a distance.

Superintendent Kneller made a most thorough inspection of the kitchen and had a good look over the whole house. He agreed with Joss that there was a suspicious amount of combustible matter round the spot where the body had been found and also that the fire must have been ferociously hot there; it did, he thought, look suspiciously as if paraffin or petrol might have been used to inflame it.

" Doesn't wipe out suicide, you know, Joss," he said. " People do funny things when they've got to the stage of making away with themselves. What about injury? If he was murdered he must have been knocked out, or

something of that kind, before he was burnt. Any sign of
that? "

" Impossible to see last night, sir. Dr. Stopp's doing a
P.M. this morning, but I thought perhaps you would
have a word with him, sir, and tell him what to look for."

" Stopp? I don't think I know him."

" Partner of Dr. Faundyce, I understand, sir. He was
at the Surgery when the constable went there last night."

" Know anything about him? "

Joss shook his head.

" Seems all right, sir. In the early thirties, I'd say.
Quick and intelligent, I should say, from the little I saw
last night."

" Well, I'll have a word with him."

" I don't know whether it would be possible to trace if
paraffin was used, sir. Could you ask him to take a section
from the face? Then we could send it along to the County
Analyst and see what he could find."

Kneller nodded.

" That's an idea," he said. " But not the County
Analyst; he's not got any experience of . . . what do
you detectives call it? Medical jurisprudence? This is
a job for the Home Office Analyst; then we shan't have
Mr. Myrtle down on us . . . if there's a link-up with the
Colonel. And that I'm bound to say I doubt."

" I can't say I see it myself, sir; but Mr. Myrtle told me
to look for an outsider, and I suppose it's just possible
there's some connection."

" Well, we'll have to look into the case anyhow,
whether there's a connection or not. If Gannett was
murdered we've got to find the man who killed him.
What do you suggest? "

" I'll find out who his friends are, sir, and what his

background is generally. We might get a line from those glasses."

"Ah, yes, finger-prints. I see Morris is on to that already. I wonder why there are such a lot of them—dirty ones."

"I wondered about that, too, sir. I thought we might have a word with the old woman who looks after him; she lives in that cottage over there."

The two officers found Mrs. Pettitt huddled up on a chair before her kitchen fire, a cup of tea in her shaky hand. By daylight she looked older and more woebegone than she had in the firelight, and her wrinkled face showed evident signs of grief at her late master's fate. She welcomed the police-officers meekly and insisted on their each having a cup of tea, of which there seemed to be an ample supply in the large brown tea-pot on the hob.

Joss explained his point about the unwashed glasses and asked whether it might mean that Mr. Gannett had had a number of visitors on the previous evening. Mrs. Pettitt shook her head.

"It was often like that, sir. Ashamed to see them I was. But he wouldn't let me touch 'em—not Mr. Gannett wouldn't. You know, sir, I think he was ashamed of it really. Of his weakness, I mean, his . . . his drinking. He used to say to me: 'You cook my meals, Jane, and wash 'em up if you'll be so good, and make my bed. But I'll look after that mess myself.' And he did; once a week or the like he'd wash them all up and put them back clean on the dresser. And then start again. Oh, it was a sad pity, gentlemen; a fine man gone wrong, if ever there was one. And all because of the war; he was never the same again after that knock on the head he got in Messypotomy."

" But did he always drink by himself? " asked Kneller.
" Or did he have visitors? "

" Sometimes he did. One or two of the farmers was good friends to him, though they didn't stop him drinking. Nobody couldn't rightly do that, nobbut himself."

"When would that be? These visitors, did they come during the day or in the evening? "

" In the evening mostly, sir. I didn't often see them, though sometimes I'd hear a car drive up. Winter-time, he'd have his supper soon as it fell dark, and wouldn't let me come over after; said I'd got to stay snug and comfy by my own fireside. Wonderful thoughtful he was, Mr. Gannett."

" When did you last see or hear a visitor? "

Mrs. Pettitt thought for a minute.

" Tuesday," she said. " Or it might be Monday. I couldn't say for sure. Days is much alike to me. I heard a car, somewhere about six or fareing to seven, I'd say, but I didn't see no one."

" And yesterday evening? You saw or heard no one? "

Mrs. Pettitt shook her head.

" I was away yesterday evening to my gran'daughter's— I always goes Wednesdays, as I was telling this gentleman last night."

" That's very unlucky," said Superintendent Kneller.

" It might be significant, sir," said Detective-Inspector Joss.

CHAPTER XII

The General's Memory

WHILE the County Constabulary were interesting themselves in the fire at Manor Farm, Chief Inspector Myrtle, C.I.D., was following his own line in London. Before catching the train, however, he had begun his day with a call at Monks Holme at the wicked hour of 8.15 a.m. In reply to his summons Captain Hexman came downstairs in pyjamas and dressing-gown, rather white about the gills and blue about the chin. Myrtle had the grace to apologise.

"Very sorry to disturb you at this early hour, sir," he said. "The fact is I've got to run up to Town for a day or two, and there's something I must ask you about before I go. Something we came upon yesterday."

Myrtle paused, perhaps to see how Hexman would take this rather disquieting remark; certainly it did not have the effect of making him look any happier, but he said nothing.

"We came across some signs that seemed to suggest that this house might have been entered from the outside recently."

George Hexman raised his eyebrows.

"Not an unnatural way of entering, is it?" he asked.

"I mean . . . not by one of the normal entrances, the front or back door."

"The chimney, perhaps? Christmas time, you know, Chief Inspector."

There was a twinkle in George Hexman's eye, and Myrtle realised that this was the first time he had seen him smile. Slightly ruffled, the detective managed to raise one of his own.

"Well, I wasn't thinking of Santa Claus, sir. And just at the moment I would rather not go into any more detail, but the point is that it suggests that some outsider might be connected with your father-in-law's death."

"Then you really think he didn't shoot himself? I still can't quite make out why."

"I've got quite an open mind about it, sir," said Myrtle untruthfully. "There are one or two details that seem to point away from suicide, and of course there's the difficulty that we still can't find any reason why he should have done such a thing."

"And have you found any reason for the other—for murder?" asked Hexman quickly.

Avoiding the obvious answer, Myrtle came to the point of his visit.

"That's the very thing I want to ask you about, sir. With this possibility of an unlawful entry we have to find out who might have done it. Was there anyone had a grudge against your father-in-law, sir? Bad enough to lead him to murder, I mean."

George Hexman lit a cigarette before answering.

"That's a thing that I never thought about," he said.

Myrtle found that very hard to believe. Knowing the police were sceptical of suicide, surely an innocent man would be bound to think over the other possibilities.

"Of course," went on Hexman, "my father-in-law might have upset one or two people. He was a magistrate, you know, and I fancy a pretty hard one. I suppose it's possible that he made enemies in his early life—in India, for instance. Perhaps he stole the green eye of a Goddess—the Moonstone or something—but I'm bound to say I've never seen it. Seriously, I just don't know enough about the old man's murky past to say."

" Perhaps you'll think it over, sir. Talk it over with your good lady. If we could put our hands on some likely outsider it might . . . well, it might save a lot of unpleasantness, sir."

Chief Inspector Myrtle rose to his feet, and Hexman did the same.

" I see," he said, drawing deeply at his cigarette; " it's like that, is it? "

" Oh, and just one other thing I wanted to ask you, sir," said Myrtle. " I think you told Superintendent Kneller that your father-in-law had lost five or six thousand pounds over an investment or speculation in Mexican Oil shares."

Hexman nodded.

" Do you happen to know if that was the total of his recent losses on the Stock Exchange? "

" So far as I know, yes."

" It would be a matter of surprise to you to hear that he lost altogether twenty thousand pounds in that way? "

George Hexman's look of astonishment seemed genuine enough.

" Twenty thousand? I don't believe it! I mean . . . I can't . . ."

" Quite a sum, isn't it, sir? It made me think quite a lot. Well, I must be off now, or I shall miss my train. You'll be staying down here yourself for the time being, sir? "

" Yes, Chief Inspector," said Hexman quietly. " You'll find me if you want me. I shan't run away."

*   *   *   *   *

Myrtle only caught the train by the skin of his teeth,

and then had five and a half weary hours in which to regret that he had ever set foot in it. He reached Liverpool Street in time to find the streets full of City gentlemen returning from their excellent lunches, and took himself straight to the offices of Phayle and Cornish, the firm of stockbrokers for whom George Hexman worked on a half-commission basis. Myrtle sent in his card, and was received at once by Mr. James Eggleman, senior member of the firm.

The detective explained that his business was of a highly confidential nature. Certain doubts had arisen in connection with the sudden death of Captain George Hexman's father-in-law, and though there were absolutely no grounds for supposing that Captain Hexman was guilty of any crime, he, Myrtle, had been instructed to make inquiries into the Captain's financial position, his business affairs, and his life generally. Mr. Eggleman would understand that anything he said would be treated with absolute confidence, unless of course a case had to go to court, in which case he would be advised.

James Eggleman—a man of wide experience—understood all this, and expressed no surprise. He was extremely pleasant to Myrtle—extremely pleasant. He handed him a cigar, lit it for him, and explained that while Captain Hexman certainly had a business connection with the firm, the connection was of a rather spasmodic nature, and not a great deal was known about him. He was, so far as Mr. Eggleman could say, scrupulously honest, and certainly had never done anything of a shady, let alone a criminal nature; he would not have retained his connection with the firm if he had.

Mr. Eggleman's answer to Myrtle's inquiries lasted some ten pleasantly smoke-laden minutes, and at the end of that time the detective realised that he knew no more than before he came; realised, too, that he would know no more, so far as Mr. Eggleman was concerned. A tentative suggestion that perhaps some other member of the firm might have a more intimate acquaintance with Captain Hexman was received with the blandest possible negative. Myrtle removed himself, ruefully regretting a polite defeat. But he enjoyed his cigar for another ten minutes before presenting himself at Dacre's Hotel in Maundy Street, Mayfair.

The manager of the hotel did not look too well pleased when he saw Myrtle's warrant card, which was produced only in his office. But no hotel manager can afford to annoy the police, and Mr. Stipple expressed himself willing to help in any way he could, provided it was consistent with his obligations to his clients. Myrtle did not, in this case, go so far as he had done with Mr. Eggleman. He did not make any mention of Colonel Cherrington nor any reference to crime, but said that in accordance with his instructions he had to make certain confidential inquiries into the financial position of Captain George Hexman; could the manager help him with any information on this point?

Mr. Stipple replied that Dacre's Hotel was most particular as to the soundness and general suitability of visitors, though naturally mistakes of judgment did occur. So far as Captain Hexman was concerned he had always paid his bills, though sometimes, it was true, after a little delay. There had never been any serious trouble in this connection, and he had never heard of any disagreeable incident in the way of pressure for payment by firms or tradesmen. His general impression was that while Captain and Mrs. Hexman were not rich, and probably not so well off as they had been in the early days of their marriage, they were well able to afford the standard of living implied by fairly regular residence at Dacre's Hotel.

This did not help Myrtle much, and he decided to carry his inquiry a stage farther. Did the manager, he asked, know anything about the Hexmans' social background? For instance, were their friends of a quiet type, or did they move in one of the faster sets? But here Mr. Stipple could not help him at all. Dacre's was a residential hotel, and though there was of course, a restaurant, it did not cater for non-residents, and so was not often used by residents for entertaining. Occasionally, of course, residents did have friends or relatives to dine with them, but Mr. Stipple thought that the Hexmans seldom if ever invited their friends here, and he personally, therefore, had no knowledge at all of what set these friends might belong to. On the other hand, the Hexmans frequently dined out, and he believed that the Devonshire and Valtano's were the restaurants they most commonly patronised; their favourite night-club was, he believed, the Sixty-Six.

Myrtle felt that it would be useless to go hunting for 'background' in a popular restaurant or night-club, certainly unless he had something more definite on which to base his inquiries than he had at present. On leaving the hotel, therefore, he went next to Captain Hexman's club, which, he had learned from Mr. Eggleman, was the Boot and Saddle. Myrtle did not look forward to drawing this covert; having served in the Army himself during the war, he knew something about Service clubs, and he doubted whether a detective would receive a very warm welcome.

Major Helder, secretary of the Boot and Saddle, left him in no doubt as to his prospects. He was perfectly polite, but he told Myrtle that the affairs of members were entirely confidential and in no circumstances would the Committee allow him to answer the questions asked; no doubt there were legal means of extracting information —through the Courts, for instance—but apart from that the Chief Inspector's quest was useless. It was not even permitted to divulge a member's address, though a letter would be forwarded.

"Oh, I know his address," said Myrtle drily. "Would you be allowed to tell me what his Regiment was?"

Major Helder thought for a minute.

"Yes, I see no reason why I should not tell you that; you could obtain that information from other sources and it is not confidential. His Regiment was 1st/40th Lancers, but you realise, I suppose, that he left the Regiment some ten years ago. If my memory serves me right, the Regiment is now in India."

That, thought Myrtle, was on a par with his luck for the day, and there seemed every good reason for bringing the wretched day to an end, so far as detection was concerned. Major Helder courteously showed him out—no doubt to ensure that this —— detective did not try to pump any of the staff.

As they crossed the large hall the outer door was pushed vigorously open and a tall, grey-haired man, erect and keen-eyed, entered the club. His glance immediately fell on Myrtle, and he stopped in his stride.

"Myrtle!" he exclaimed, holding out his hand. "My dear fellow, delighted I am to see you. Helder, this is my old Staff Captain; '17 wasn't it, Myrtle? Arras, Third Ypres, before they pushed me out to command a Division in Palestine for the Bull's last show. I didn't realise . . . you not still in the Army, are you? No, no, I remember . . . and what are you up to here? Not running Helder in for keeping immoral premises, I hope?"

The General's spate of words flowed on; he hardly seemed to expect an answer, and Major Helder presently detached himself and returned to his office, not too pleased that the —— detective should have made contact with one of the most loquacious members of the club.

Major-General Hector Jallworth had retired from the Army soon after the war, but had kept his interest alive by membership of two Service clubs and regular attendance at anniversary dinners. He had a good memory for faces, and this, with his genuine friendliness and hospitality, made him popular with men who had served under him, though his contemporaries found him rather a bore.

" I won't ask what you're doing, if it's business," he said, " but you must come and have a sundowner and tell me all about yourself that won't disclose vital secrets, what? "

Myrtle was very ready to enjoy the stiff peg of whisky that he soon found in his hands, and before long he found that the General was skilfully worming out of him the object of his visit to the Boot and Saddle. Realising that the General's hearty voice was attracting attention, he pulled himself up short and said that he must be going. But Jallworth was not to be so easily shaken off.

"What about a spot of dinner? " he asked. " Not here; can't talk with all these fellows whispering and listening. I'm a thought deaf now, and whispering's no good to me. Come along to Teddy's, if you've not got an engagement; in that noise one can shout secrets and no one else will hear them."

Well, here was chance—just a chance that the General, with his obviously wide circle of acquaintances, would be able to fill in some of the background that remained so drearily blank. As soon as they were settled in the crowded restaurant and had sent away the waiter with their orders, Myrtle returned to the subject of his enquiry.

"Hexman? George Hexman? Thirtyish? Yes, by Gad, that'll be Letty's boy. Haven't set eyes on him for years, but I used to know his mother and father. Old Bats Hexman died in Simla in . . . what would it be? '08, '09? Something like that—just before the war. Letty—that's the boy's mother—was a pet; we all lost our hearts to her; but she was a silly woman so far as the boy was concerned—I remember that now. Bats wasn't too well off and didn't leave a lot; Letty had something of her own, but the two together couldn't have amounted to much. Letty was determined that the boy should go into his father's Regiment, the 40th—before the amalgamation, that was—and she put him in without enough money; an expensive Regiment it was, too, in those days. Greatest possible mistake; not fair on the boy, not fair on the Regiment."

Myrtle realised that his luck had changed, and he blessed his old Brigadier's remarkable memory.

"The boy was popular enough, I heard—I never came across him myself after he joined—the men liked him, and so did his brother-officers till the money shortage became a bore. I fancy the senior officers weren't so sure about him and weren't altogether sorry when he left. Married money, you know, and like a damn young fool chucked the Service. Let me see, now who . . .?"

The General snapped his fingers, racking that excellent memory for a name.

"He married a Miss Cherrington, sir," said Myrtle quietly.

"Cherrington; that was it! Bob Cherrington's girl.

And don't you call me 'sir'; I'm not your superior
officer now. Bob Cherrington. God! how that brings
things back to one. Indian Cavalry, he was—Maxwell's
Horse. A tiger if ever there was one. Hard as teak,
body and mind. A damned fine soldier. Might have
gone anywhere, right to the top; nothing to stop him,
you'd have thought. But he was stopped. The old
story, a woman . . . but I'd better let that old tragedy
lie; no point in raking it up now."

General Jallworth shook his handsome head sadly, took
a long drink, and relapsed momentarily into silence. But
Myrtle was not going to let the fountain dry up if he could
help it.

" I heard that his wife ran away from him, sir," he said.
" Can you tell me who with? "

Jallworth stared.

" You heard that? How the devil? Why . . . you
don't mean? I read that the poor fellow had shot himself; you're on that, are you, Myrtle? That's why you're
asking about young Hexman. I'd forgotten the connection. My memory's not what it was. There isn't . . .?
You don't mean there's anything funny about it? Why
did he shoot himself? What's young George got to do
with that? "

" That's just what I'm trying to find out," said Myrtle
quietly.

" God in Heaven! You don't mean . . .? It's not
possible, man. A cavalry officer. I'll never believe it,
never."

Myrtle could see that the old man was deeply shocked.
He hastened to ease his mind.

" I don't say that Hexman had anything to do with it,"
he said. " I don't know. But we're not happy about

the suicide idea. In fact, we're pretty sure that it wasn't suicide. Even if it was, we've got to find out why, and you may be able to help me there, General. And if he was murdered . . . well, I don't suppose you'd like the murderer to get away with it."

"No," muttered the General. "No, I wouldn't want that. But . . . that boy. I can see you've got some good reason for suspecting him, otherwise you wouldn't have come barging into a Services Club with your inquiries. Bit of nerve that, you know, Myrtle, though of course you've got to do your duty. I don't see, though, that that old tragedy of Bob Cherrington's can possibly have any connection with what you suspect. Why, it happened before George Hexman was born. Well, no, not that, perhaps; but he was a mere kid."

Myrtle appreciated the quickness with which the old General had spotted this point. The soldier's keen brain was still active enough.

"No, I don't think that old story can have any connection with George Hexman," he said. "But it may be connected with the Colonel's death, and if it is . . . why, that points away from Hexman, doesn't it?"

"Yes, yes, I see. If it was suicide, it might have some connection; some mental throw-back, perhaps. But you don't think it was suicide. So if it was murder . . . what then?"

"Might someone have borne ill-will for a very long time? You said he was a hard man, and I've heard that, too. That's why I want his background. This may be an outside job, nothing to do with Hexman. It might help him if you can tell me . . ."

"Of course. I'll tell you what I can, but it's difficult to believe . . . What exactly do you want to know?"

"Who did Mrs. Cherrington run away with?"

General Jallworth hesitated.

"I don't like it," he said. "*De mortuis.* Still . . . it was Jack Trellis—quite a youngster—that she went off with, and he was killed three or four years later in Mesopotamia. But it wasn't a case of Norah Cherrington running away with Jack; she was running away from her husband."

It was the detective's turn to stare.

"I told you he was a hard man, but he was more than that; he was a bully, and a jealous bully at that. Norah was a pretty, weak little thing; she wasn't a flirt, but she hadn't the strength of mind to stop men making love to her. There weren't many of them brave enough to do it, because they were afraid of Bob; but Jack Trellis was a light-hearted, mischievous young devil. I don't think he meant anything serious, but Cherrington thought he did, and he gave his wife hell. After a time she couldn't stand it any longer, and she persuaded Jack to take her away. They literally ran away, and if they hadn't I think there would have been an ugly business. Of course that was the end of Jack as a soldier, but he got a commission in another Regiment when the war broke out, and was killed at Kut."

"And Mrs. Cherrington? Did she marry Trellis? Was there a divorce?"

General Jallworth shook his head.

"Cherrington refused to divorce her. He was one of those religious maniacs; pious as a parson and just about as Christian as the devil himself—that's my way of looking at them. What became of her I don't know. But it broke Bob. He was a proud man, and he couldn't stand being talked about. He left the Regiment and got himself seconded to West Africa; got side-tracked for the war and retired soon afterwards as a Colonel, when he might have been a full General if he'd stayed on in the Regiment, with his ability and courage. You can't wonder that he hated women."

CHAPTER XIII

About it and About

GREAT NORNE lay once more wrapt in a damp sea-mist; everything out of doors, and even a good deal indoors, was clammy to the touch, and little could be done without artificial light. For a stranger it would have been difficult to find one's way about in the town; but the inhabitants knew every stone of it by heart, and could have got about blindfold, without any risk of falling into the harbour—which was one of the reasons why people still felt surprise that their Vicar, who, while not a native, had lived in Great Norne for a quarter of a century, should have done that very thing.

Anyhow, nobody thought of staying indoors because of the mist, and Miss Emily Vinton, buttoned up to the throat and muffled round the mouth, strode bravely forth to do her shopping on the Friday after Christmas. She was not happy. She could not get over the death of her dear Vicar; the new man was not the same at all—a stupid, timid creature, who did not seem to know his own mind. What was one to think of a Vicar who genuflected to the altar but not in the Creed?

And then Colonel Cherrington's dreadful death. Nobody had mentioned the word 'murder' to Miss Vinton, not even the faithful and loquacious Minnie, but suicide was shocking enough. Surely it must have been an accident; it was impossible to believe that a true Christian would deliberately take his own life. Miss Vinton had not much liked Colonel Cherrington—had, indeed, been rather afraid of him—but she had respected him, and it was terrible to feel one's respect shaken in this tragic way.

And now another dreadful event; poor Mr. Gannett. Such a good man he had always been before that terrible war, like his father before him. It was fighting the Turks that he got that wound in the head, and they were infidels, so it was really like a Crusade, and one ought not to say hard things about him, especially now he was dead.

It just did not bear thinking about, and she would not think about it; she would go to Bilbow's for the fish, and Mr. Johns had promised her a nice sweetbread this week; and after that there were only one or two things at Perks's, and she would be able to get back home to a nice warm fire and a chat with dear Beatrice. If possible she must pick up a little gossip on the way, because Beatrice liked to know what was going on, so long as it was nothing scandalous. Beatrice seemed to be made of much sterner stuff than herself; she had been shocked—deeply shocked —by the Vicar's death, but about Colonel Cherrington she had not turned a hair. "Never liked the man," she had written on her tablet; "thought himself Moses and St. Paul in one." Then she had lifted the wax sheet and the tablet was blank again, ready for her next comment or command.

It was at the grocer's that Emily Vinton met Mrs. Faundyce. The doctor's wife was a younger counterpart of himself—rosy, cheerful, full of fun and enterprise. It was she who organised the entertainments in Great Norne, ran the Women's Institute, visited her husband's patients and took them little delicacies, books, comforts.

"I have to do something to counteract Jim's horrid medicines," she would say laughingly, "otherwise all our patients would leave us, and then where should we be?"

But everyone knew that Mrs. Faundyce did those things out of the kindness of her heart.

" Emily, how nice to see you! " she exclaimed. " How brave of you to come out on this horrid, clammy day! But, then, you're a brave family, and set us all an example. I hope Miss Beatrice is as cheerful as ever."

Mrs. Faundyce, a woman of fifty-seven, called the younger Miss Vinton by her Christian name, but the elder never anything but ' Miss Beatrice '.

" Oh, Mary, she's wonderful. It's she who keeps the stiff upper lip, as the dear Vicar used to say; I'm afraid I'm a poor-spirited creature, like Chuchundra the musk-rat in ' Rikki-tikki '. I'm so upset by all these dreadful things happening. One after the other; there seems no end to it."

" Well, it is dreadful," agreed Mary Faundyce. " But it doesn't do any good to get upset about it. We've been so fortunate in Great Norne; we've really been spoilt, because we've had so little tragedy, so now when it comes we feel it all the more."

Emily Vinton shook her head.

" I don't know where it's going to stop," she said. " It preys on my mind."

" Oh, you mustn't let it do that," said Mrs. Faundyce briskly. " Now, Emily, collect your parcels—look, Mr. Perks has got them all ready for you—and slip home with me and have a cup of coffee to warm you up and take the fog out of your throat."

" Oh, I couldn't do that, though it's so good of you to ask me. I must get back to Beatrice; she'll be expecting me."

" Now look here, Emily, you left Beatrice with a nice fire? Yes. And a book? Yes. And Minnie in the house to get her anything if she rings? Of course you have. Then what can it matter if you're ten minutes later rather than earlier? You might have been kept waiting ten minutes in one of the shops. If you're afraid Miss Beatrice will scold you, you can just tell that as a nice little fib. It would do you good to have something on your conscience for once in a way. Now come along; it's all on your way. I told Alice to have some coffee ready by the time I got back; I always do on a day like this. Jim laughs at me, but I say it keeps the doctor away."

Chuckling at her own joke, Mrs. Faundyce enticed the nervous little lady into her own comfortable home, sat her down in front of a cheerful fire, and presently was pouring out for her a large cupful of steaming hot coffee.

"What we all want is a good cheering up," said Mrs. Faundyce. " Christmas was spoilt for everybody, and we're all letting ourselves get down in the dumps. I tell you what, now, how would it be if I got up a nice bridge party? we haven't had one for a long time. We'll have it here, not at the Institute, with tea and later on refreshments; it's high time the doctor stumped up for a party. You and Catherine Beynard—I'm afraid the Squire won't come—and the Willisons and Mr. Carnaby and Julia Furze and the Hexmans and Jim and me; that's ten, one always wants one or two extra in case someone is called away."

" Do you think the Hexmans would come? " asked Miss Vinton. " So soon . . ."

She had brightened at the suggestion of a party. Any party was a joy to her, and she loved a game of bridge, though fellow addicts dreaded her as a partner.

" Oh, of course. I always think it's wrong to keep the blinds drawn, so to speak, once the funeral is over—so repressive. Winifred has so little fun down here; it's bad for her to sit moping in that gloomy house. I don't know whether George Hexman will come; I'm afraid he doesn't enjoy playing with women."

Emily Vinton bridled.

"And I don't enjoy playing with a man who smells of whisky," she said tartly.

But planning the party soon drove away her ill humour and depression; she hardly noticed that the ten minutes had stretched into more than half an hour before she tore herself away and padded cheerfully back home through the lifting mist.

. . . . .

It was not only Miss Emily Vinton who had been feeling worried by the series of tragedies that had befallen Great Norne. In many houses, in shops and inns, men and women were talking, arguing, wondering. Their hearts had not been greatly touched; both the Vicar and Colonel Cherrington had been too aloof and austere to attract affection, except from the few, and poor Bert Gannett had been an object of good-humoured contempt for many years, not only among his fellow-farmers, but among the townsfolk and fishermen who so often saw him in his cups. But sudden death was a terrible thing, and fire had a special horror of its own. He must have suffered fearful pain, poor man; it was difficult to understand how such a thing could happen.

By arrangement with Inspector Joss, Sergeant Plett had switched from the 'Silver Herring' to the lounge-bar of the 'Royal George' as the likely ground for picking up useful hints. Plett was beginning to feel uneasy about his own position. There was a limit to the time he could pose as a craftsman in search of an opening for his trade; such people did not kick their heels about for days on end; time was money, and so were hotel bills. He had gone the

length of actually negotiating for some vacant premises,
and was discussing them with Mr. Winch over a pre-
luncheon pint, when the front door swung open and a
good-looking young man in riding breeches and a skirted
coat strode into the lounge.

" 'Lo, Dad," he called cheerfully, throwing his bowler
hat and cane into a chair. " Come to hear the news."

" Morning, Gerry," said the landlord. " I thought
you couldn't have come just to see your father. My boy,
Mr. Plett; doesn't often find his way to Great Norne.
Mr. Plett's thinking of setting up in the electrical business.
What'll you have, Gerry? "

" Pink gin for me, Dad. It'll take you all your time to
electrify this old burg, Mr. Plett. Gas-light where it isn't
paraffin. But what's all this about Gannett? "

Gerry Winch was an enterprising young man, not yet
thirty, who was already making a name for himself as a
breeder of cattle and horseflesh. His business lay on the
far side of the county, but his father maligned him in saying
that he did not often visit the parental roof; probably
twice in a month he attended the market, and during the
summer he was often over for a week-end, playing tennis
and taking part in the modest social functions of the town.
His father, Simon Winch, was one of the warmest men in
the town, and Gerry was regarded as a matrimonial plum,
much sought after in the neighbourhood. There had even
been a time when the attractive but lonely daughter of
Colonel Cherrington was supposed to be interested in him,
but that was before her marriage to a dashing young
cavalry officer. They still met occasionally, but it took
all the vivid imaginings of the ' Silver Herring ' to keep
that old rumour alive.

" Gone, poor old chap," said Simon Winch. " Burnt
himself to death."

Actually, Albert Gannett was some years younger than the landlord of the 'Royal George,' but he had aged out of all proportion to his years.

"So I heard, but it didn't make sense to me," said Gerry. "How does a grown-up man burn himself to death?"

"Knocked the lamp over, I hear. Too sozzled to get out of the light, poor fellow."

The young dealer shook his head.

"Not possible," he said. "The pain would have sobered him. You sure nobody dotted him one?"

There were several other people at the bar now, including the burly Fred Pollitt, Gannett's friend of Yeomanry days. They all stared at the speaker, and Plett began to hope that the conversation was taking a useful turn. He had felt certain that until the word murder was mentioned in connection with Gannett's death—and the police had so far kept their mouths shut about that—he would be merely wasting his time listening to gossip about the fire; now, perhaps, there might be a hint or two to pick up. But Gerry Winch's suggestion was treated with ridicule.

"Dot him? Bert Gannett? Who on earth would want to do that?"

"Well, I don't know," said Gerry. "I hardly knew him, except as a chap with a skinful. Thought someone might have a grudge against him, perhaps."

"Grudge against poor old Bert?" said Pollitt indignantly. "Why, he hadn't an enemy in the world."

"Oh yes he had," said the landlord of the 'Royal George.' His customers turned to him in surprise.

"Who do you mean?"

"Himself. And you can take it as certain sure that he hadn't another."

Dr. Fred Stopp was late back from his evening round. As he hurriedly put his car away in the ramshackle garage behind the surgery he barked a knuckle against the door. Cursing, he examined it by the light of his headlamp; an abrasion was no joke for a doctor, with the constant risk of infection from his patients. This would mean at least another five minutes delay while he dressed and bandaged it, and that probably meant a spoilt supper.

He had been out of temper all day. The special requirements of the police had meant that his autopsy on the farmer Gannett had taken considerably longer than he had intended it to. The fog had added to the day's delay; even though he cut down his visiting list to the minimum, only going to the people he really must look at, there was no chance of getting through it by the proper time. He hated unpunctuality, hated it in other people and no less in himself, even though it was not his own fault; he had sufficient imagination to realise what it meant to a tired woman to have to sit for an hour or more in a draughty passage waiting her turn for the doctor.

Still, Stopp knew that a doctor must never look disgruntled, so there was a smile on his face as he went in at the surgery entrance and apologised to the people who were waiting in that passage which was by courtesy referred to as the hall.

Fortunately there were not many of them. Mrs. Haynes with a carbuncle; young Creech with a badly cut hand—playing with his father's edged tools; a swollen face; an old man with a dirty bandage round his forehead; a young girl with no apparent injury, but looking white and frightened—the usual trouble, probably; and Josiah Chell with his arm in a sling.

Stopp sighed his relief. This lot should not take long,

and then he would be able to have his first drink of the day, which he never took until—so far as he could tell—his work was over.

"Just a minute or two while I put a bandage on this finger," he said cheerfully. "Who's first? You, Mrs. Haynes? Right; I'll call you in a minute."

Stopp's hopes were fulfilled. By half-past seven the last patient—the sexton with a sprained wrist—was shown out of the surgery.

"Awkward for you just when business is so good," said the young doctor with a grin. "You'll have to take a partner; if you try heaving with that wrist you'll have it out of action for a month."

"Ay, the harvest is ripening and the labourer must be found," said Josiah, leaving Stopp in some doubt as to whether it was not a psychiatrist rather than a surgeon that Chell was in need of.

Dr. Stopp lived in the house where he and Dr. Faundyce had their joint surgery. It was an old house, but large and comfortable, so far as the main rooms were concerned. On the first floor he had a bedroom and sitting-room, whilst he took his meals in the dining-room on the ground floor which also served as a waiting-room for the better-class patients, which were usually those of the senior partner.

Stopp washed his hands again and, lighting a cigarette, made his way up to the first floor. Opening the door of his sitting-room, he was just making for the corner cupboard in which he kept bottle and syphon, when he stopped abruptly. George Hexman was sitting in the arm-chair on the far side of the fire.

"Sorry to gate-crash you like this, Fred," said the soldier. "I told your old girl not to bother you while you were at surgery. She seemed to think I was to be trusted.

Though I'm not sure that you do, from the look of you."

"Sorry, George," said Stopp with a laugh. "You startled me, that's all. Very glad to see you. First time for days."

"Lucky to be allowed out," said Hexman gloomily. "If you look out of the window you'll probably see a plain-clothes man leaning against a lamp-post."

"What the hell are you talking about? Doubt if I could, anyway. Fog's getting thick again."

He walked to the cupboard and took out a bottle of whisky, a syphon and two glasses.

"Just in time to join me," he said cheerfully.

"I didn't come to cadge a drink. I came because I had to talk to somebody—somebody who doesn't think I'm a murderer. But perhaps you do."

"I don't know what the hell you're talking about. Say when."

Hexman took no notice of the glass, and his host stopped when there were three generous fingers in it.

"I tell you, Fred, I can't stand this much longer. It's getting on my nerves. I suppose . . . of course, it was a shock to me when the police began talking as if it wasn't suicide, but I could see their point of view; they had to make sure. I didn't take it very seriously at first, but it's damn serious now. Damn serious; I shall be lucky if I don't get the feel of a pair of handcuffs before long."

George Hexman sat rigidly in his chair, staring in front of him. There was an hysterical note in his voice that his friend had never heard before.

"Just get outside that," the doctor said sharply. "No, go on, drink it; it's what the doctor orders."

Hexman shook his head and pushed the glass away.

"I shan't talk to you till you've drunk it," said Stopp

quietly. He took a pipe from the mantelpiece and began slowly to fill it from a large brown jar ornamented with a gaudy crest. With a shrug of the shoulders, Hexman took the glass of whisky and drank it straight down. Instantly his rigidity relaxed and his eyes became more normal.

" That certainly is your best prescription," he said.

" The only one any good, really," said Stopp. " But it's no good telling most of my patients that. Some of them know it already, and the rest would think I was a pretty poor doctor if I didn't give them something nasty to drink. Now, what's biting you? "

" The police think I shot old Cherrington."

" Rot. They've got to look at all the possibilities, and naturally you're suspect number one; on the spot and in the will; or your wife is, any way. Just routine questioning; not the slightest need to worry."

Hexman shook his head.

" I rather thought that myself at first," he said. " But that Scotland Yard man was at me this morning about not going away. He went off to London himself, and a pal has just rung me up and told me that the fellow has been nosing round about me at the office, asking about my financial position and all that. He wouldn't do that if it wasn't serious. Fred, do you know that that virtuous father-in-law of mine has gambled away twenty thousand pounds in the last two years? That's my motive. The police think I wanted to stop him losing any more. I could tell from the way that detective spoke to me that it was damned serious. Besides, I'm pretty nearly sure that I was followed when I came out this evening. Obviously they think I may do a bunk."

" Well, that's a bore for you if it's true, George. But honestly I can't take it so seriously as you do. Granted the premise that they aren't satisfied that the old man shot himself, they *must* look at you pretty close. But if you didn't shoot him—I'm taking that as a premise, too— why should you worry? They can't prove you did something that you didn't. Honestly, George, I quite see how bloody their questioning and snooping must be for you, but it'll fade out in a day or two when they've found there's nothing to hang on you. Is your wife worried, too?"

Hexman shifted uneasily in his chair.

" That's why I came round to see you, really," he said. " I wouldn't have bothered you if I could have talked things over with her, but . . . but I can't. I believe . . . I sometimes think she thinks I did it! That's really what's getting me down, Fred. She doesn't seem to want to talk to me about it. I can't make her out. I haven't been able to make her out for a long time."

The hysterical note was creeping back into Hexman's voice. He drew deeply at his cigarette.

" I ought not to talk about her like this," he said. " But it's a hell of a relief to tell somebody, and I know you'll keep it to yourself. She's been . . . different for some time now; ever since we came down this autumn. I sometimes wonder whether she doesn't care for me any longer; whether there's . . . some other fellow."

Stopp took a pull at his own glass.

" Anyone special? " he asked quietly.

Hexman hesitated.

" No, no one special. Who should there be? "

" Exactly; who should there be? The fact is, George, the girl's bored. As I told you only a day or two ago, I can't make out why you stay in this dead-alive hole; nothing for you to do here, except a round of golf occasionally and a little shooting, and your wife hasn't even got that.

" Obviously, she's bored. And she takes it out on you, as any normal woman would. And you're worrying yourself about these police inquiries, and that makes you see everything through green spectacles. What you both want is a bit of fun. Take her over to Ireland, George, for a hunt, or to Switzerland or Monte or whatever she would enjoy. You'll forget all about this inside of a month."

For the first time George Hexman smiled.

" And that's the doctor's orders, too, eh? Well, I must say, Fred, they sound quite sensible. It is pretty boring down here for Win. The fact is, we've been hard up this last year or two—much harder up than people think. But that ought to be all right now—if only this infernal business clears up. Anyhow, you've done me good, you or your whisky. I mustn't bore you any longer; pretty near supper time, too—God, I'm keeping you from yours, I expect."

Stopp laughed.

" You are, George; you are. I'll put it all down on the bill."

He saw George Hexman downstairs and opened the door for him.

" Bit thick, isn't it? " he said. " Never mind, you'll have company."

Dr. Stopp clapped his friend on the back and watched him disappear into the mist. As he shut the door he smiled.

" Nothing ever happens in Great Norne," he muttered to himself.

CHAPTER XIV

Conference

AFTER his excellent dinner with General Jallworth, Chief Inspector Myrtle went to bed in an optimistic frame of mind, feeling that he had not only enjoyed himself, but had gathered a lot of useful information. The cold, clear light of the morning after, however, soon showed him that, while the General's story had been interesting and picturesque, it really did nothing to throw light on the problem of whether, why and by whom Colonel Cherrington had been murdered. As regards Hexman, all that he had learnt was that the young man had been liked by his contemporaries, not entirely trusted by his seniors, and chronically short of money—until he married Winifred Cherrington. That brought the story back to what Myrtle already knew. The other and more vivid part of the old General's tale now appeared practically irrelevant. It was inconceivable that an elopement of more than a quarter of a century ago could have anything to do with what had occurred at Great Norne the previous week. If the third party to the triangle had been still alive there might be some point in following up the story, but General Jallworth had been positive that ' Jack Trellis ' was dead.

It would be advisable to confirm that fact, and as there were two other small points that needed clearing up, Myrtle rang through to Superintendent Kneller and arranged to come down by the afternoon train which would land him at Snottisham—the County town—about supper time. Kneller undertook to put the C.I.D. man up for the night. As they were speaking on a public line, neither police officer made any reference to the case.

Myrtle's first visit was to Somerset House, where he soon confirmed the fact that Captain John Trellis, then serving in an Indian cavalry regiment, had been killed at Kut-el-Amara on 24th December, 1915. He was unmarried at the time.

Myrtle then turned his attention to Mrs. Robert Cherrington, but the record of her did not go beyond her marriage to Major Cherrington in 1908. She had been born in 1888, which would make her fifty now, if she were still alive. In any case, Somerset House had got no record of her death, so that it was to be assumed that it had not occurred. It was just conceivable that steps would have to be taken to trace her, but not unless some more substantial reasons for doing so emerged.

Of the other two points which Myrtle wanted to clear up while he was in London, the first concerned the scrap of paper which Inspector Joss had extracted from among the ashes in Colonel Cherrington's study—the scrap on which were written the rather melodramatic words: ' Unless you pay up ' . . . ' make public all I ' . . . ' last chance '. Myrtle wanted to discover whether there was the remotest chance of tracing the writer—whom he strongly suspected to be the murderer—through the paper itself or the ink. This was a matter for the Yard, whose experts on the subject were second to none in the world.

Detective-Inspector Bodley had often helped Myrtle in his cases, and the Chief Inspector knew that if anything could be made of the yellowish scrap with charred edges, Bodley would make it, but the latter gave him no grounds at all for hope. A cursory examination showed it to be a cheap paper without water-mark, its colour being the only factor which might act as a guide; the ink would have to be chemically tested, and a report should be ready in three days.

Myrtle's last visit before going to Liverpool Street for his train was to a doctor in Harley Street. He had learned from Mrs. Hexman that her father, though practically never in need of medical attention, did go once a year to see this man, whose address she gave to the detective. Although he had practically eliminated the possibility that this was after all a case of suicide, Myrtle wanted to make quite sure that the dead man had not been suffering from some malady which, unknown to his family, had driven him to take his own life. If that really had been the case it would mean finding some other explanation for the points which had caused Myrtle to reject suicide for murder, but the Chief Inspector was not a man to shut his eyes to facts that did not suit his theories.

However, Dr. Masterly soon settled the point. He was an elderly man, and had known Colonel Cherrington ever since his return from West Africa in 1919; Cherrington had formed the habit of coming to see him once a year just for a check-up. The Colonel was a remarkably healthy man for his age; he was bothered by some of the usual old man's troubles, including hardened arteries and high blood pressure, but there was absolutely no physical or mental cause for self-destruction, and Dr. Masterly had been astonished to read of his violent and apparently self-inflicted death. The possibility of murder had crossed his mind as an alternative, but he knew of no reason why anyone should wish his patient out of the way. He knew little of him except as a patient, and had never met his daughter or son-in-law.

Myrtle felt that this was all he was likely to get from this source. The information was negative, but it was definite, and therefore useful. He thanked Dr. Masterly for sparing him a quarter of an hour of his valuable time, and took his own way to Liverpool Street.

The journey down, long and tedious as it was, did at any rate lack the final misery of the slow local train running from Snottisham to Great Norne. Myrtle found a police-car waiting for him at Snottisham station, and within five minutes was at the Headquarters of the County Constabulary. To his surprise he found Superintendent Kneller still in his office.

Kneller was, in fact, still hoping to save part, at any rate, of his week-end by clearing off routine work before the inevitable conference on the Cherrington case and the developments that must arise from it. However, he was all ready for a break now, and he greeted the C.I.D. man cheerfully.

" Glad to see you back, Myrtle," he said. " You're just in time for supper. We won't talk shop till we've had it—not, that is, unless you've reached the handcuff stage and can't stop to eat."

Myrtle shook his head.

" No such luck," he said gloomily. " Anyhow, I'm all set for some food. A railway sandwich since 8 a.m. leaves a notable void unfilled."

" My dear chap, you must have been hot on the trail. Come along. I warned Mrs. Kneller you might be hungry. I must just ring up the chief and tell him you're back. He wants to come in and see you after supper."

The Scotland Yard detective raised his eyebrows. This was not what he was accustomed to in the provinces.

" Fact is, there's been a development this end. But we'll wait till the Major comes; he'll want to hear your reactions."

Mrs. Kneller had risen nobly to the occasion, and Myrtle was feeling replete and almost somnolent when he and the Superintendent returned to the Headquarters building. Major Statford was already in his own office, and sent for them at once.

" Good evening, Chief Inspector," he said. " I'm sorry to keep you at it so late after your long journey. The trouble is, we've had another death at Great Norne, and I've felt a bit uncertain what line to take over it until I could discuss it with you. But before we go into that, how have you got on yourself? "

" Nothing very helpful, sir, I'm afraid. All it really amounts to is that Captain Hexman was always short of money until his marriage and is probably a bit short now, though not in real difficulties, so far as I've been able to find. I've also heard something about the Colonel's early life in India and the trouble over his wife leaving him; you know something about that already, sir, and all I've got merely fills it out; it doesn't help us in this case, as far as I can see. There's nothing that can't wait, sir."

" All right. We'll switch to this end, then. You'll remember that on Wednesday night there was a fire at the Manor Farm, just outside Great Norne. I understand that you were at the police-station when the news came through."

" That's right, sir. Inspector Heskell and Inspector Joss went off to have a look at it."

The Chief Constable nodded.

" They found the body of the farmer, Gannett, in the ruins."

The Chief Constable handed the story over to Superintendent Kneller, who told it clearly, if rather ponderously. Myrtle, who was more tired than he had realised, found it difficult to concentrate his attention on a story that did not seem to hold much of interest for himself. No doubt a fire and a man burnt to death was quite an incident to these country policemen, but he was investigating a murder, and he didn't see much why he should be bothered with an accident. He pricked up his ears, however, when Kneller came to the point where Inspector Joss began to suspect that this was no accident, but murder.

" You take the same view, sir? " he asked Kneller.

" I do. There seems to me to have been an unnaturally fierce blaze round the body."

" Any sign of his having been struck? "

" None that Joss or I could see—I had a look at him in the mortuary. The flesh of the head is very severely charred; no bruise would be recognisable in that state. There was no fracture; the doctor confirms that."

Myrtle had forgotten his somnolence now; his mind was alert again.

" It might be as well to get Sir Hulbert Lemuel to have a look at him, sir. He can spot things that an ordinary doctor would miss."

Major Statford nodded.

" That's an idea, certainly. Meanwhile we've done the next best thing; we've sent a bit of him to Sir Hulbert."

" You've done that, sir? "

" It was Inspector Joss's idea. He thought that if paraffin or petrol had been used to hot up the fire there might be some trace of it in the flesh or the clothing. We got the doctor to take sections from the cheek and one or two other parts of the body and we sent them and what was left of the clothing up to the Yard this morning; a Sergeant took them up by train this morning; we asked if the Home Office analyst could have a look at them."

Myrtle felt a sudden increase of respect for the ' country policeman '.

" Very good idea, if I may say so, sir. May I ask what other steps are being taken? "

The Chief Constable tapped his pipe out in the grate.

" Nothing very definite. We felt—Superintendent Kneller and I—that this was your case, or at any rate, that it might be, and that we ought to wait until we'd talked it over with you before coming to any tactical decision about a line of action. So far the public think it is an accident; if we start asking questions they'll soon realise that we suspect murder. It's just possible that it might be wiser to let the murderer think we've swallowed the accident. Anyway, that's a tactical decision, and I wanted your opinion about it."

Myrtle nodded.

" That's certainly a point, sir. I'd like to think about it and hear a little more about the man himself and so on before deciding. Then you've made no inquiries so far? "

" Joss is just nosing round a bit," said Kneller. " Your man is helping him, too; not asking questions, but keeping his ears open; naturally there'll be a lot of gossip round Norne for the next few days."

" Has he found anything yet? "

" Hasn't reported. We've got no direct line to the Station there; only the public line. I told him we'd come along to-morrow morning and hear what he had to say."

" That's the trouble," said the Chief Constable. " We've only got direct lines from here to the Divisions. I'd like to have teleprinter lines to them, too, but my Standing Joint Committee is very sticky about expense; they wouldn't look at it."

Myrtle grinned.

" Perhaps this is the ill wind that'll blow you a bit of good, sir. Make out a case that bad communications hindered your hunt for a murderer. This case is going to make a splash, I fancy, as soon as the London papers realise what's in it; so far they only know that an old Colonel has shot himself; the adjourned inquest doesn't seem to have put ideas into their heads."

Major Statford laughed.

" That's quite an idea. I'll work something up about it. Meantime we've got to do our best with the tools we've got."

There was a pause for a minute or more while the three men followed their own thoughts. Chief Inspector Myrtle was the first to break the silence.

" Is there any possible connection between this farmer, Gannett, and Colonel Cherrington? " he asked.

" Must be," said Kneller. " But I don't know what it is. I had a talk to Heskell this morning, and he knows of none. Colonel Cherrington wasn't a man to mix much with people out of his own class; not only that, but he was pretty stiff in his ideas about behaviour; Gannett, as I said, was a drunkard, and I can't see any point where they could make contact. Except possibly the fact that they were both soldiers."

" They were? Not . . . Gannett wasn't with the Colonel at any time? "

" No, no; he was a Yeoman. Wounded in the Middle East somewhere—Palestine or Gallipoli, I think. Colonel Cherrington was in West Africa all through the war and in India before that. They can't ever have met as soldiers."

"They might have some contact as 'old soldiers '," said Myrtle quietly. "Remember that the Colonel was killed after a British Legion dinner."

Superintendent Kneller stared.

"Good Lord! I never thought of that. But surely . . . surely that's a pretty slim thread?"

"Very slim, I should have thought. But we've got to find one."

The Chief Constable had been listening in silence to this discussion, a sceptical look on his face.

"Surely that's a bit far-fetched?" he said. "There seems to me a danger that we shall waste our efforts hunting for a connection that doesn't exist. Surely the simple explanation is the true one; this is just coincidence. Strange coincidence, certainly, that two murders should take place in the same neighbourhood at the same time, but . . . isn't it, perhaps, just the law of averages? In that quiet little town there have been no deaths by violence for perhaps fifty years; now there have been three all together."

Myrtle sat up sharply.

"Three, sir?"

"Oh, well, the first one was only an accident. The Vicar had a fall in the fog and broke his neck. Nothing in that, but it stirred people up in Great Norne simply because violent death was almost unknown to them."

"I've heard nothing about that, sir," said Myrtle, hardly attempting to keep the rasp out of his voice.

"No. Why should you? As I say, it was an accident. Happened a month or two ago. When exactly was it, Kneller?"

The Superintendent, a guilty look on his face, consulted his diary.

" 18th November it happened, sir.   Inquest on 22nd."

He turned to his C.I.D. colleague.

" I'm very sorry, Myrtle," he said.   " I probably ought to have told you about that, but it never occurred to me. I don't see what possible connection there could be . . ."

" Of course there couldn't," said Major Statford curtly. He was not going to stand any criticism of his subordinate from a Scotland Yard man.

But Myrtle stuck to his point, whilst modifying his tone.

" I'd like to hear all about it some time, sir," he said. " I quite understand that there wouldn't appear to be any connection with Colonel Cherrington's death.   But this Gannett business seems to throw a new light on things. If you come to think of it, sir, there have been—as you say—three deaths by violence; the first an accident, the second suicide, the third an accident.   What if they were all three murders? "

It was the Chief Constable's turn to stare.

" Good God! " he said.   " You think . . . you suggest that poor old Torridge was murdered too?   But why on earth?   A harmless old parson!   Who could want to kill him? "

" I don't know, sir.   I know nothing about him.   I know nothing about the accident.   But I should very much like to."

Superintendent Kneller was looking little less astonished than his chief.

" You shall," he said.   " I don't know a great deal about the details of the Reverend Torridge's death; Heskell said it was quite straighforward, and so did the doctor. There was an inquest, of course—verdict of 'accidental death'. He lost his way in a fog and fell over the edge of the quay on to some steps—fractured the base of his skull; I think that was the actual cause of death."

Myrtle gave a short laugh.

"Sounds not unlike our old friend the 'blunt instrument'," he said.

Major Statford was evidently greatly shocked by the Chief Inspector's suggestions. He was nervously rubbing the side of his face.

"Quite incredible," he muttered. "Torridge! What earthly connection can there be?"

"It'll take us all our time to find one, sir," said Kneller, ". . . if it exists."

Myrtle could see that both the County men were highly sceptical. He decided not to press the matter that night, but he was going to find out all about it in the morning. Two violent deaths might conceivably be unconnected, but three . . .? In this dead-alive little corner?

The Chief Constable was still grumbling over his bone.

"What one person could want to kill a retired Colonel of the Indian Army, an elderly clergyman, and a drunken farmer?" he asked.

A buzz sounded on the internal telephone. He took up the receiver, and his companions could hear the metallic crackle of a voice.

"All right, send him along."

He replaced the receiver.

"Morris thinks he's got something off those glasses. He's working late, that young man, Kneller."

There was gratification in his voice. The detective branch was his own child.

"He and Gilbert have been working at them all day, sir, as well as most of yesterday. There were a lot of bottles and glasses, and they were in a pretty good mess—difficult to identify any prints. That's the glasses on Gannett's dresser I was telling you about," he explained to Myrtle.

There was a knock at the door, and the young detective-constable, Morris, came in, a large envelope in his hand. On the Chief Constable's orders he drew a chair up to the table and carefully extracted two photographic prints from the envelope. One of them showed a blur of prints, on which no one finger appeared to be identifiable.

"We'd practically given it up as a bad job, sir," he said. "Put them all away, and then after supper came back and went over them again."

He took two magnifying-glasses from his pocket and a hat-pin from the lapel of his jacket. Handing one glass to the Chief Constable, he looked through the other himself, and then put the point of his pin on a spot on the print.

"That bifurcated ridge just above the whorl, sir; there's a slight break in the ridge on the left-hand side of the bifurcation; it's very slight, and you can only see it through the magnifying glass or, of course, the microscope, but it is identifiable."

"Yes, I follow that," said Major Statford. "But what about it?"

Morris substituted the other print, on which appeared the very clear impression of four fingers against a background of fainter impressions. Again he put the point of his pin on a spot on the print, but said nothing. The Chief Constable studied the print carefully through his his magnifying glass.

"Yes," he said quietly; "that certainly appears to

my amateur eye to be the same break in the same ridge of presumably the same finger. Where did this very clear print come from? Do you know whose finger-prints these are?"

"Yes, sir; they are prints of Captain Hexman's left hand."

CHAPTER XV

Third Murder?

THE three senior police officers were too experienced to display any surprise or undignified excitement in front of their young subordinate.

"How did you get Captain Hexman's prints?" asked the Chief Constable calmly.

"Inspector Joss got them, sir, on the night that Colonel Cherrington was killed. Superintendent Kneller will remember, sir, that Captain Hexman was drinking whisky in the dining-room when he interviewed him there. As soon as everyone had gone Inspector Joss went in and collected that glass and substituted another from the pantry, into which he splashed some whisky and soda so that the maids shouldn't notice anything odd in the morning."

"H'm," said Major Statford, concealing his pleasure. "I don't know that that would be accepted as an identification in a court of law; still, if it comes to that point we shall have had other opportunities of taking official prints. Did he happen to get Mrs. Hexman's, too?"

"Yes, sir, and the two maids, all without their knowledge. Not all that first night, but subsequently."

"First I've heard of it," said Kneller rather stiffly.

"Routine detection work, my dear Kneller," said the Chief Constable, with a sly look at his Superintendent. "No doubt he thought you would not be interested unless he got an important check from them. What about it, Morris? I haven't asked about finger-prints in the study. What have you identified there?"

"The Colonel's, sir—a lot of them. A fair number of the housemaid's. A few of Captain Hexman's. None of

Mrs. Hexman's, nor the cook's. Also one or two of Dr.
Faundyce's; we asked him for his to help us check up. A
few of Inspector Heskell's, Inspector Joss's, and Superintendent Kneller's. And one or two of yours, sir."

"Mine? How the hell do you know they were
mine?"

Detective-Constable Morris allowed himself a slight
smile.

"There happen to be one or two of yours in the office,
sir, for record purposes."

"The devil there do! Seems I've started something;
I shall find you on my tail one of these days. Well, we've
got nothing from them so far as the Colonel's concerned,
but this print of Hexman's in Gannett's house . . . you
feel confident about that, Morris?"

"Pretty confident, sir. Of course, I've very little
experience. I should like to have this checked by the
Yard, sir."

"He's right there," said Chief Inspector Myrtle, who
had been listening with quiet amusement to this rustic
comedy. "Our people will soon confirm that, or otherwise. It looks to me a pretty good bit of work for an
inexperienced man, if I may say so, sir."

"I'm glad you think so. Now we must consider the
implications. Do we need Morris any more? No.
Well, you can fall out now, Morris, you and Gilbert.
You've done a good job. Good night."

When the blushing young detective had gone, the three
elder men started to discuss the significance of this new
development. It would not do of course to jump to the
conclusion that Captain Hexman had killed Gannett just
because a glass with his finger-prints on it had been
found at the farmer's house. There might be a simple
explanation of that, though the association between Colonel

Cherrington's son-in-law and a drunken farmer did not at first leap to the eye.

" If you'll allow me, sir," said Myrtle, " I'll approach the Captain about that. I should like to think over what line we ought to follow now."

" Exactly. Tactics, as I said. And that seems a good moment to close this conference. If you two aren't ready for bed, I am."

. . . . .

Myrtle was too tired that night to think over the implications of the new developments in the case, but he was up early the following morning and, after an excellent breakfast provided by the hospitable Mrs. Kneller, settled down in a chair to use his brains.

He felt extremely sceptical of the Chief Constable's suggestion that Gannett's murder, following so close on that of Colonel Cherrington, was a coincidence. It was not yet definitely established that Gannett's death was homicidal and not accidental; it had not even been *proved* that the Colonel had been murdered, though Myrtle felt little doubt on that score. If it should also transpire that the Vicar's death was not the accident it had appeared, then it seemed almost certain that there must be some connection between the three, though what that connection could be it was difficult to imagine.

The first step, he thought, was to look into the circumstances of the Vicar's death; if that proved to have been accidental beyond all doubt it would remove a complication from the case. That he had only heard about it through a chance remark of the Chief Constable's was typical of the unmethodical thought-processes of the provincial police—or so it appeared to the Scotland Yard man.

The second development—the discovery, or supposed

discovery, of Hexman's finger-prints on a glass in Gannett's house—was, on the other hand, a matter of some credit to the local force; it was a point that might so easily have been missed. He did not propose to jump straight to the conclusion that Hexman had killed Gannett—there might be a straightforward explanation of his presence in the house and it might well have happened on a different day —but it was a decidedly suggestive discovery. Myrtle thought he could foresee an interesting interview with the Captain.

Having decided first to tackle the question of Mr. Torridge's death, Myrtle thought the best order of procedure would be to read the police report, then to interview the Coroner and possibly the doctor who conducted the post-mortem. A copy of the police report was filed at Headquarters, and it was soon in his hands; a straightforward account of an accidental death, with nothing to suggest murder and nothing to preclude it. Myrtle then inquired about the Coroner and, having discovered that he was a Snottisham solicitor, Mr. Oswald Harkins, secured an appointment and was, without unreasonable delay, received by that gentleman in his bleak, old-fashioned office.

Mr. Harkins was, in fact, an old-fashioned man—one of the dwindling race of legal practitioners who regarded the proper, dignified conduct of life and business as more important than the gaining of sharp advantages and quick profits. He was sixty-five years old, lean, clean-shaven, sombrely dressed, but there was a humorous gleam in his eye that came to the surface at slight provocation. The Scotland Yard detective quickly sized him up, and made his approach with appropriate respect.

" I am investigating the death of Colonel Cherrington, sir," he said, " and certain circumstances have made it necessary for me also to learn something about the previous death of the Reverend Theobald Torridge. I understand that you held an inquiry into that."

Mr. Harkins's eyebrows showed a fractional degree of elevation, but he only said :

" That is so, Chief Inspector."

" You found that it was a case of accidental death, sir ? "

" My jury found that, yes. I agreed with them. Have you read the report ? "

" I have, sir. As I understand it, the reverend gentleman fell down the harbour steps and fractured the base of his skull. There was, I suppose, no suspicion of foul play ? "

The solicitor regarded his visitor steadily for a few seconds before answering.

" I wondered whether you were leading up to that," he said. " There was certainly no suspicion of it, nothing to suggest it, and, so far as I know, no reason for it. What makes you suspect it . . . if it is not indiscreet to ask ? "

Chief-Inspector Myrtle had no wish to find himself answering questions, but neither did he want to be brusque with this courteous old man.

" Nothing in the story I have heard and read so far, sir. The suspicion arose from the case I am investigating. You will, perhaps, forgive me if I don't go into that."

" Of course, of course. I should not have asked. What you say is disturbing, Chief Inspector. I do not like the possibilty of a mistaken verdict. I can only say that nothing in the evidence aroused any suspicion in my mind, or, I am sure, in the mind of the jury, that the death was anything but accidental."

" And was there anything to make you sure that it *was*

accidental, sir? Anything, that is, that put the possibility of any other explanation out of court?"

Mr. Harkins frowned, but the frown was one of consideration rather than annoyance.

"Suicide, I think, was clearly impossible. Normally such a slight fall would not cause serious injury. It was the unlucky fact that the back of his head came in contact with the edge of the steps that caused death."

Myrtle leaned forward.

"What proof was there that his head did make contact with the steps?"

Mr. Harkins raised his hand in an involuntary motion of protest, but he did not flinch from the question.

"I take your point," he said. "There was no proof that that was what happened. We assumed it from the general circumstances. I do not think it would have been possible to obtain proof unless someone actually saw what occurred; there was a thick fog at the time; no one came forward to report having seen the occurrence. Really, I think, Chief Inspector . . ."

"I am sure it was a most natural assumption, sir. I only want to make sure that you know of nothing that makes it impossible that this death might—I only say 'might'—have been homicidal."

Mr. Harkins nodded.

"It might have been, certainly. No circumstance suggested that it was, no circumstance proved that it was not."

Myrtle realised that he could expect no more, at any rate until he had more exact knowledge of the incident on which to base his questions. He rose to his feet.

"Thank you, sir, that is very clear," he said. "You will not take it amiss if I make some more detailed inquiries, as discreetly as possible? It is really vital to my other inquiry that this point should be cleared up."

The solicitor had also risen.

" Of course it must be cleared up. And if there was foul play, that must be exposed—at whatever risk to the Coroner's reputation."

He smiled and held out his hand. With an exchange of courtesies the interview ended.

There was nothing here, Myrtle realised, either to strengthen or weaken his suspicion. Before going to the doctor he thought he would have a word with Inspector Heskell, who had made the police investigation on the spot. Heskell was not a very bright specimen, but he appeared to be trustworthy and conscientious.

Borrowing a car to take him to Great Norne, Myrtle soon found himself at the police-station. Superintendent Kneller had decided not to accompany him, realising that the C.I.D. man would probably prefer a free hand. Inspector Heskell was, by telephone arrangement, in his office, and a constable had been sent to rope in Detective-Inspector Joss, who was out on his mission of discreet inquiry.

Heskell showed considerable surprise at the resurrection of the late Vicar as a subject of inquiry. He confirmed the Coroner's statement that there had been nothing to suggest foul play, but he did produce, rather reluctantly, one item of information that had not appeared in either the police report or the report of the inquest. Certain fragments of broken glass had, he said, been found in the Vicar's coat pocket; these, and the pocket itself, had held a slight, a very slight, smell of whisky.

A gleam came into the detective's eye as he heard this scandalous embroidery to the simple tale.

" The suggestion being that the reverend gentleman's loss of direction or balance was due to whisky rather than to fog, eh? " he asked.

Heskell was not prepared to admit this.

" I took it to mean that he was in the habit of carrying whisky when visiting sick persons, sir," he said with dignity.

Myrtle nodded.

" And was he visiting a sick person when he met his death? I understood from your report that he was visiting a Club of some kind."

" That is so, sir. At least, that is what we assumed. But he might have been on his way to visit a sick person."

Myrtle sniffed.

" I should hardly have thought it was that kind of spiritual sustenance that he administered to the sick," he said. " In any case you made no mention of this curious fact in your official report or in your evidence before the Coroner? "

" I did not, sir," said Heskell doggedly. " I could not see that any good would be served by mentioning it, and it might well have given rise to most undesirable talk."

Myrtle looked thoughtfully at the uniformed Inspector.

" I see your point," he said. " You exercised your discretion . . . and it's just possible that you obliterated —or nearly obliterated—a very important clue."

Heskell appeared startled by this suggestion, but he wisely kept his mouth shut. By this time Joss had returned to the station, and he was now called into the Inspector's minute office. He told Myrtle that he had been able to learn little to help him in his search for a possible killer of the farmer, Gannett.

" My hands are tied, sir," he said. " If it's still got to be thought an accident, so far as the public are concerned, how can I ask anyone what enemies the man may have had . . . or any other really useful question? They all tell me the same thing because they're all thinking the same thing—that he was drunk, knocked over the lamp, and was burnt to death. Your Sergeant Plett did hear one man suggest that he might have been knocked on the head, but people just laughed at him."

" And who was that intelligent imaginer? " asked Myrtle.

" Young Winch, sir, son of the landlord of the ' Royal George '."

" I will treat myself to a word with him later. But I agree with you, Joss; we shall do no good working with our hands tied. The Chief Constable put the point to me last night, and I asked leave to think it over. I shall ask him to approve our revealing that we suspect murder; we may hear something then."

Joss grinned.

" We certainly shall, sir; there's gossip enough now, when it's only thought to have been an accident; there'll be a flood when murder's out."

Myrtle nodded.

" And what'll there be if there's a third murder? "

Joss stared.

" A third murder, sir? "

" In the past, not in the future . . . I hope. And only a vague possibility at that. Did you happen to know, Joss, that the Vicar of this parish recently died a violent death? "

Joss opened his eyes still wider.

" I knew he was dead, sir; had an accident and broke his neck, if I remember rightly. I didn't attend the inquest."

" No, he didn't break his neck," said Myrtle quietly. " He died from a fractured base of the skull . . . as the result of a blow. The blow may have been the impact of his head upon the steps of the harbour, where he was found lying, or it may have been the impact upon his head of . . . you know the rest."

" A . . . a blunt instrument, sir? "

" Exactly. The classic weapon. And in this case probably a figment of my unhealthy imagination. But it'll bear looking into, Joss. Ask Heskell, here, to let you see his report upon the . . . accident. And perhaps he will tell you the insignificant fact that does not appear in that report. Or perhaps not."

　　　.　　　.　　　.　　　.　　　.

Myrtle found Dr. Faundyce at his home. As it was Saturday, the doctor had managed to squeeze all his work into the morning, and was spending the afternoon doing a little winter pruning of apple-trees in his small orchard. Reluctantly he closed his knife and led the detective indoors.

" And have you come to any conclusion about poor Colonel Cherrington? " he asked.

" There are still some points to be cleared up, sir," replied Myrtle. " But at the moment it was on another matter that I wanted some information."

" Oh, what can that be? Sit down, Inspector . . . Chief Inspector, I should say. A cigarette . . . or your own pipe? "

" Thank you, sir, I won't smoke just now."

" On duty. Of course, I can't when I'm on duty, but I'm not now, am I? You'll excuse me . . .? "

The little doctor beamed cheerfully and dragged a large leather pouch out of his old tweed jacket.

" Go ahead, Chief Inspector," he said, beginning to cram tobacco into his well-worn briar.

" About the death of the Reverend Mr. Torridge, sir."

The busy forefinger momentarily checked its plugging operations.

" Really.   And how does that interest you? "

" I want to make quite sure what the gentleman died of, sir."

Dr. Faundyce glanced sharply at his visitor.

" I stated that in my evidence at the Coroner's inquest," he said.   " He died of a fractured base of the skull.   I can give it you in more technical terms if you like."

" For the moment that's quite all right, sir.   I don't doubt the medical facts.   The fracture, of course, was due to a blow, and the blow is thought to have been caused by the back of the head striking the stone steps of the harbour. Am I right, sir? "

" Quite right;   that all came out at the inquest."

" Not exactly, sir, I think.   It came out that that was how the injury was *supposed* to have been caused.   But I believe no one saw it happen.   The first thing I want to ask you, sir, is whether the injury *might* have been the result of a blow which was struck by some other person before the deceased fell on to the steps.   Is there any medical reason why that should not have been the case? "

Dr. Faundyce stared at Myrtle in undisguised astonishment.

" God bless my soul;   what makes you think that? " he asked.

" At the moment I don't think it, sir.   I only want to find out whether that possibility can be eliminated."·

" Most extraordinary.   This is a very disturbing idea, Mr. . . . er . . . Myrtle.   Since you ask the question, I can only say that I know of no reason why it should not have happened as you say, but there was certainly nothing to suggest that it did.   The injury was perfectly consistent with a fall on to the steps. The back of the head was actually lying on the steps."

" Was there any secondary injury? "

" None."

" No sign of a struggle. Nothing on the hands—scratches? broken nails? "

Dr. Faundyce frowned.

" I did not notice anything of that kind. I did not particularly look for such injuries. The cause of death was obvious."

Myrtle did not comment on that statement. He paused for a little, to give the doctor time to feel uneasy.

" Were the contents of the stomach analysed, sir? "

" The stomach? What on earth for? The cause of . . ."

" Yes, sir, you said that. But is it not usual to look for alternative possibilities . . . in a case of violent death? "

There was no doubt about the uneasiness now.

" There . . . there was no reason."

" You think not, sir? And yet, this gentleman may have been murdered."

" I can't believe it. I just can't believe it."

" Very well, sir. We will leave that for the moment. Now, can you tell me, was there anything to suggest that—if the deceased fell—the fall was due to his having lost his way in the fog? "

" I don't follow you."

" I'll put it another way, doctor. It has been suggested that Mr. Torridge's fall may have been due to unsteadiness caused by . . . spirits. Can you confirm or disprove that? "

Dr. Faundyce had drawn in his breath sharply when he heard the word ' spirits '. He was silent for an appreciable time before answering. Then he squared his shoulders, as if he had taken a brave decision.

" I see that I must tell you what I hoped need not have been known," he said. " There was a broken flask in the Vicar's pocket, and a smell of whisky both there and in the mouth."

" Ah ! " There was a glint in the detective's eye. " And in the stomach, sir ? You opened the stomach, I suppose ? "

" No, I did not. I told you . . . there was no reason to do so. I did not wish to do anything to distress his poor wife."

" And the fact that there was whisky in the mouth—you suppressed that evidence ? "

Dr. Faundyce flushed hotly. His usually cheerful face showed signs of his distress.

" I don't accept that," he said. " It was not a question of suppressing. It was quite irrelevant and I . . . did not mention it."

" And did you arrange with Inspector Heskell to say nothing about it either ? "

" Certainly not. I said nothing to him about it. I should not have dreamed of interfering in whatever he regarded as his duty. He did not mention it and neither did I."

There was a grim look on the police-officer's face.

" Very curious, sir," he said. " And so we lose what might have been a vital clue. If the body is exhumed now is there any possibility of finding a trace of alcohol in the stomach ? "

Faundyce shifted uneasily in his chair.

" I should say none at all. I am not a pathologist, but I feel sure that alcohol would have evaporated long ago. But what on earth is the significance of this ? "

" The significance is this, doctor. You say that you found a smell of alcohol in the mouth; if you had at once opened the stomach *and found no trace of alcohol there*, then we should have known for certain that this man was murdered."

CHAPTER XVI

Hexmans at Home

GEORGE HEXMAN sank a four-foot putt and picked his ball out of the hole.

"That makes it six and five, I'm afraid," he said. "You've had no luck, old girl. Shall we play the bye, or call it a day?"

"Oh, I'm all for stopping," said his wife grimly. "I can't think why you wanted me to play; I'm no use at the beastly game."

George laughed.

"You could be if you tried; it needs concentration. I agree that it isn't much fun if one's playing badly, but I thought a day out might buck you up."

They cut across towards the Club House, George quietly relieving Winifred of her bag.

"Shall we have tea here?"

"Personally I'd rather get home, but I expect you want to play bridge afterwards."

"Not in the least. Let's get home, by all means; much more comfortable and a better tea."

Winfred Hexman was puzzled by her husband's un-wonted solicitude for her wishes—and rather suspicious of it. To her surprise, he had asked her to have a round of golf with him—a thing he had not done for years. She was a poor player, whereas George was pretty good, playing to a handicap of six. Giving her a stroke a hole and three bisques, he had still not been able to avoid beating her with ridiculous ease, which was, she knew, little fun for him. He had remained pleasant throughout the game, but the poorness of her own game had made

her irritable, and she had not been able to go half-way to
meet his friendly mood.

The drive back to Great Norne was not a cheerful one,
as George's conversational gambits all seemed to come
to an untimely end. But back at Monks Holme, in the
pleasant drawing-room with firelight glinting on the silver
teapot, the atmosphere seemed to improve, and George
thought the moment favourable for his purpose.

"What would you like to do after all this has cleared
up?" he asked.

Winifred looked at him in surprise.

"Do?" she asked.

George handed up the dish of muffins from its place on
the hearth. Taking one himself, he ate a mouthful before
answering.

"What I mean is . . . well, we don't want to stick
down here all the winter, do we? I wondered what you'd
like to do . . . where you'd like to go to."

Curiouser and curiouser, thought Winifred. She could
hardly remember a time when George had not stated his
own plans and left her to fall in with them . . . or not.

"I thought the police wanted us to stay here," she said.

"Oh, that's only for a short time. That embargo ought
to be lifted any time now. Might as well start thinking
what we're going to do when it is."

"I don't think I'd thought of doing anything. More
tea?"

"Thanks. Well, I thought we needed cheering up a
bit. Been depressing, all this police business, apart from
your poor old father's death."

"Why don't you go to Ireland, then, and have a hunt?"

That was one of George Hexman's favourite winter
amusements. It was some years since he had had horses
of his own, and he seldom hunted in England now, but one

of his brother officers had a place in the Meath country, and was always ready to give him a mount. Winifred herself had been there once, but she had always been frightened of horses, and had hated every minute of the three weeks' visit; she had not gone again . . . and George had not asked her to.

"My dear girl, you don't like Ireland. I thought something in the way of winter sports would be the thing; you always said you wanted to go to Switzerland."

Winifred gave a short, bitter laugh.

"I did indeed . . . but did I ever get there? You wanted to hunt and you hunted; I wanted to ski and I came down here while you went to Ireland."

George Hexman lit a cigarette, to give himself time to think. He was not batting on an easy wicket, and did not quite know how to play this bowling.

"Well, why didn't you go to Switzerland?" he asked.

Winifred shrugged her shoulders.

"You know the answer to that," she said.

Yes, he did know it, and had been a fool to ask the question. Their income hadn't run to both Ireland *and* Switzerland . . . and he had gone to Ireland.

He shifted uneasily in his chair.

"Look here, old girl," he said. "Let's drop the past and look at the future. We shall be better off now, and I want you to have some fun. Let's go somewhere where we can both enjoy ourselves—Switzlerand, Monte, wherever you like. I shall enjoy it if you do."

Winifred Hexman looked steadily at her husband.

"Yes, I suppose that's the key to all this solicitude," she said. "'We shall be better off now', or, to put it more accurately, *I* shall be better off. Rather more worth cultivating—even without that twenty thousand pounds."

George Hexman flushed hotly and jerked his cigarette into the fire.

"That was a pretty beastly thing to say," he said. "But perhaps I've earned it. All the same, it's not true. I *do* want you to have a better time, to be happier. If you are, I shall be happier, too."

There was a pause, husband and wife both looking into the fire . . . and thinking.

"I wonder what's suddenly put that idea into your head,' said Winifred.

George Hexman knew that if he did not convince his wife of his sincerity he would fail in his object.

"All right; I'll tell you. I've been feeling pretty wretched lately, what with one thing and another, and the worst part of it was that I felt I couldn't talk to you about it; you seemed . . . almost a stranger. I didn't know what had made you like that. I thought perhaps . . . well, anyway, I had a talk with Fred Stopp . . . oh, I know you don't like him, but he's the only person down here I felt might be able to help me. He told me flat out that it was my own fault, that I had been a selfish cad, that you were bored to tears, and no wonder you were fed up with me. I don't mind admitting it was a bit of a shock to me, because I'd never looked at things in that light. But when I came to think things over I saw that he was right. So I . . . I want to start again . . . if it's not too late, Win."

If he had been looking at his wife he would have seen some of the hardness disappear from her eyes. She did not answer him at once, but sat for some time thinking over what he had said.

"I'm sorry you had to talk to Dr. Stopp about it," she said. "Why didn't you talk to me? I might have been able to tell you the same thing . . . without charge."

" I . . . I didn't go there intending to talk to him . . . not about you, I mean. I wanted to talk to him about the police. I thought I was being followed—trailed, or whatever they call it. It's been getting on my nerves. I couldn't talk to you, because I wasn't even sure . . ."

George Hexman paused, then took his plunge.

" You don't think I shot the old man, do you, Win? "

" Shot him? Father? Of course I don't! Why, I heard you run downstairs, and I came down just afterwards myself. What an idiotic question, George."

George leant across and squeezed his wife's hand.

" It was that fool policeman. He thought I did . . . or thought I might have. He's been asking questions about me at the office. But Fred says it's all a matter of form, and I daresay he's right. After all, I didn't do it, so they can't prove I did, can they? "

" I wish it hadn't taken a tragedy to bring you to your senses, George. How am I to know that when things get normal again you won't be just the same, doing just what you want to do and leaving me to look after myself? "

George Hexman pushed a fire-stool across towards his wife's chair and sat down beside her.

" Win," he said, taking her hand in his two brown ones, " I won't ask you to believe that I mean what I said; I only ask you to give me a chance to prove it. When this is all cleared up—and I'm sure it will be quite soon now—let's get right away from here and start again. We're still young; it's not too late."

Winifred hesitated. She was not at all sure that it was not too late. She had come very near to making a different decision.

The door of the drawing-room opened and Fanny came in.

" There's that London policeman wants to see you, sir," she said.

Hexman frowned, but pulled himself together quickly.

" I'll come down. Where is he? Show him into the dining-room."

The maid went out, shutting the door behind her. Winifred got up from her chair.

" Like me to come with you, George? " she asked quietly.

" Thanks, old girl. I . . . I should rather. Moral support and all that."

He slipped his arm through hers, and together they went down to face whatever fresh battery Scotland Yard might be preparing to open. Chief Inspector Myrtle was standing by the window, looking out onto the wintry lawn.

" I'm sorry to bother you again, sir," he said, as the Hexmans came in. He looked at Mrs. Hexman. " I hadn't intended to disturb your lady, sir."

" I would like my wife to be here, if you don't object, Chief Inspector. I have no secrets from her."

" That's as you wish, sir. Then I'll go ahead. I have to ask you about your movements on other days than that of Colonel Cherrington's death. You may find the questions rather strange, but I'm afraid I'm not at liberty to explain them just at present."

Hexman shrugged his shoulders.

" I've found a good many of your questions rather strange. I've done my best to answer them, and I'll do it again, but I hope there'll be some limit to the time this goes on."

" I hope so, too, sir. I'm anxious to clear this matter up. Now will you tell me, sir, briefly in the first place, what your movements were on Monday, Tuesday and

Wednesday this week, between, say, the hours of 6 and 8 p.m.?"

George Hexman stared.

" *This* week? *After* my father-in-law's death?"

" This week, sir. On the days I mentioned."

" It's certainly difficult to see what you're getting at, Chief Inspector. Between tea and dinner? Nothing on Monday; I was just here in the house. On Tuesday— that was the day you came, wasn't it? You were here up to about tea-time . . . oh, yes, after tea I went over to the Club House at Teale—that's the Golf Club—and played bridge for an hour or two. On Wednesday I went round to see Dr. Stopp . . . no, that was Thursday. What was I doing on Wednesday, Win?"

" You were here, George. We both were; we didn't go out after tea."

" That's right; I remember now. That doesn't sound very exciting, Chief Inspector, does it? Is it any help to you?"

" You're quite sure about Wednesday, sir? You said first that you went to see Dr. Stopp that day. If that was so, no doubt he could confirm it."

" No, I told you, that was Thursday. On Wednesday I was here."

" I think that was Mrs. Hexman's recollection, sir; but I should like to be quite sure that it is yours. Have you any way of fixing that evening?"

" I have," said Winifred Hexman. " It was the even- ing of the fire. You remember, George, we saw it from my window when we went up to dress for dinner."

" Good Lord! yes, so we did. That fixes it, Chief Inspector. You probably heard; a farmhouse was burnt down and the farmer, a man called Gannett, was burnt to death. Anyone can tell you that was Wednesday."

" I heard about it, sir. Did you know Mr. Gannett? '

" Oh, just slightly. Why do you ask? "

Chief Inspector Myrtle paused for a moment. Then he leant forward.

" You're sure you wish Mrs. Hexman to remain, sir? " he asked.

A little of the colour seemed to leave George Hexman's face, but he answered steadily enough.

" I do. Why not? "

" On the morning after the fire your finger-prints were found in the room in which Mr. Gannett was lying dead. How do you account for that, sir? "

Hexman drew in his breath sharply. There was little colour left in his face now.

" What on earth . . .? You're not suggesting I set fire to the farm, are you? I was there the day before."

" Oh, you were, sir? And what time was that? "

" Somewhere between seven and half-past, I should think. I looked in on my way back from Teale."

" You said nothing about that just now, sir."

" You didn't ask me. I mean, I told you I played bridge at Teale that evening. I didn't think about the Manor Farm. I only looked in for ten minutes or so on my way back, to have a drink with the old boy. The farm's on the Teale road, you know."

" I see, sir. Then I'll ask you again: how well did you know Mr. Gannett? "

" I told you, Chief Inspector; I only knew him slightly. I used to see him at the ' George ' on market days. I don't know whether you know, but he was rather a pathetic old chap, gone to pieces, generally rather tight. He asked me to look in on him one evening, and as I was coming back on Wednesday I just stopped and had a drink. That's all."

"Was anyone else there, sir?"

"No, not while I was there. At least, I didn't see anyone. He let me in himself."

"And all this happened on Wednesday, sir?"

"Yes. No, Tuesday; I told you. On Wednesday I was here. I didn't go out."

"Can anyone confirm that, sir?"

"My wife can. You heard what she said."

Myrtle looked thoughtfully at Winifred.

"Yes, sir. And you have no secrets from Mrs. Hexman, I think you said."

Hexman frowned.

"What do you mean by that?" he asked sharply.

"I was just wondering whether anyone else could confirm it, sir. Did anyone come in to see you that evening?"

"Not that I remember, no. One of the maids might remember seeing me. Would you like to ask them?"

"Thank you, sir; I'll do that as I go out. And your knowledge of Mr. Gannett is quite casual?"

"Quite."

"No special interest in him?"

"None at all. What *is* this all about?"

Myrtle did not answer that, but took out his note-book and consulted it.

"Now, sir; I want you to throw your mind back a bit farther. Have you been here all through the winter?"

"On and off, yes. I sometimes go up to London for a week or two, or the inside of a week."

"Have you got a note of the days, sir? Do you keep a diary?"

" I don't write up a daily diary, if that's what you mean. I've got a pocket diary, and if there's any special engagement—business or golf or a day's racing, something like that—I jot it down. Is there any special day you want to know about? "

" Would you have been down here about the middle of November, sir? "

Hexman took out his Badminton Diary and turned over the page.

" I was in London from the 7th to the 11th; that was Armistice Day. I was in the City, outside the Exchange, for the Silence, and came down by the afternoon train. Came up again on the 22nd for three nights."

" And in between those days you were here, sir? "

" Yes. I was shooting at Chatcombe on the 16th—that was a Wednesday. And I played golf on Saturday the 19th. Otherwise I was here all the time, so far as I remember."

" You would have been here, sir, on the night of the 18th? The 18th/19th, to be accurate."

" Yes, so far as I remember. But honestly I'm quite vague about it. One day or one night is much like another down here. Why does that night interest you? Or mustn't I ask? "

" It might help you to recall it, sir, if I said that it was a foggy night—a very foggy night, I understand."

Winifred Hexman sat up sharply in her chair.

" George, that was the night Mr. Torridge was killed," she said sharply.

" Torridge? What about him? "

Myrtle was looking at Mrs. Hexman.

" You have a very good memory, madam, if I may say so," he said.

" Why are you asking about that? "

Myrtle paused for a moment before answering.

" Because I am interested in the deaths—the violent deaths—that have been occurring in Great Norne," he said.

CHAPTER XVII

Friends of Albert Gannett

MYRTLE got very little more information at Monks Holme that evening. George Hexman's knowledge of the late Vicar had been quite impersonal. He went to church occasionally to please his father-in-law, and had sat patiently through the old man's sermons; had met him occasionally at local doings—jumble sales, fetes, charitable bun-worries of various kinds—and still more occasionally at some hospitable occasion to which they were both invited; quite frankly, he had thought the Vicar a bore and rather a prig, but had really thought very little about him. Winifred Hexman, as daughter of the Vicar's Churchwarden, had known Mr. Torridge very much better and, on the whole, had liked him. She could not believe that anyone bore the old man any serious animosity, and it had never crossed her mind that his death had been anything but an accident. She gave the C.I.D detective to understand that she thought he had a bee in his bonnet—or a capital M on his mind.

Albert Gannett she had not known at all, except by sight. She had heard her father speak of him, critically; she thought her father was unnecessarily harsh in his judgment of a man whose failing was unquestionably due to a wound sustained in action. As to George Hexman, he had not budged from his statement that his knowledge of the farmer was slight and casual. He had given Myrtle the names of the men with whom he had played bridge at the Golf Club, though their confirmation would be no proof that it was that evening, Tuesday, that he had been to Manor Farm; still less was it proof that he had *not* been there on Wednesday.

As to that Wednesday evening, there was only his wife's word to confirm his own that he had not been out at all between tea and dinner. Myrtle had questioned the two maids on this point, and found them hopelessly vague. Fanny, the house-parlourmaid, said she remembered going into the drawing-room at about seven o'clock to give a telephone message to Mrs. Hexman, and was sure that the Captain was there then, but on being pressed she could not swear that this had not happened on Tuesday, or possibly even Thursday. As a matter of fact there had been telephone messages on two or three evenings this week, and she could not remember which was which— which message on which day. The one on Thursday, she was pretty sure, had been from Mrs. Faundyce about a bridge party; but, then, Thursday wasn't the day Mr. Myrtle wanted to know about, was it? Dorothy, the cook, merely knew nothing about anything, except that dinner was late on Wednesday, because she and Fanny had gone upstairs to watch the fire from her bedroom window and that had put her back with everything. Fortunately the Captain wasn't one to complain; the Colonel would have raised Cain about it.

So Myrtle had to leave Monks Holme very little wiser than when he went there, except that Captain Hexman had offered a plausible, and quite possibly true, explanation of the presence of his finger-print on the glass at Manor Farm. After all, he did not appear to be a likely killer of the drunken farmer—but, then, who did?

Myrtle had arranged with the Chief Constable and Superintendent Kneller that the fact of murder being suspected in the case of Albert Gannett should be held back until after he had questioned Captain Hexman.

After that he was to be free to use his own judgment in the matter and to instruct Detective-Inspector Joss as he wished. Myrtle thought he would keep the matter in his own hands for a little longer, using the County detective to dig up facts about the dead farmer's past history.

Although it was now late on Saturday evening, Myrtle did not intend to call it a day. It was now nearly three days since Gannett died, and two of them had been practically wasted, so far as the Gannett case was concerned, by his own absence in London. There was, however, one important qualification to that word ' wasted ', and for it Myrtle gave full credit to the County Constabulary. Owing to the intelligence of Inspector Joss and the prompt action of the Chief Constable, a report had already been received from the Home Office Analyst upon the sections of flesh taken from Gannett's face and the scraps of clothing from his charred body; all these specimens had been heavily impregnated with paraffin, far more than could reasonably have been expected from an exploding lamp. There seemed little doubt now that Gannett had been deliberately soaked with oil in order that his body should be charred and all trace of violence removed. Myrtle had asked that the analyst should come down as soon as possible to examine the body itself.

Myrtle learnt from Inspector Heskell that the man who could give him most information about Gannett was another farmer, named Pollitt. In fact, the Inspector thought that Fred Pollitt was the only man who really knew the dead man intimately. Most of Gannett's contemporaries in the farming world were either dead or had moved out of the district; the younger men treated him as a joke, and probably only met him on market days or in one of the bars which he frequented. Of the nonfarmers it was probable that Winch, landlord of the 'Royal George', knew him best, though Richard Barton, the builder, had been fairly intimate with him in his younger days. Heskell himself had only known Gannett since the war, and had no useful suggestion to make as to a possible murderer.

Myrtle was fortunate enough to find Mr. Pollitt at his farm, which lay a mile or two outside the town on the opposite side to Manor Farm. The farmer had finished his substantial supper, and was on the point of running in to the 'George' for a 'follow' and a gossip, but he was quite ready to forego these in favour of a talk with the Scotland Yard detective—as he was now generally known to be. Pollitt led the way into his parlour and insisted on lighting the ready-laid fire, even though there was little chance of any heat coming from it until long after his visitor had left. He also lit the heavy brass lamp on the round inlaid table which graced the centre of the room.

"Oil, you see, Mr. Myrtle. No electricity in these outlandish parts. Poor Albert Gannett'd be alive now if the Town Council had waked up to the fact that we're in the twenty century."

"Would he?" asked Myrtle. "I'm not so sure."

Pollitt shot a quick glance at his visitor.

"Sit down, Mr. Myrtle," he said. "You'll take something; whisky, will it be, or beer? I've got naught else."

Myrtle was on the point of declining, but it occurred to him that the farmer might be offended by a refusal. Besides, he had had a long day, with very little of either food or drink.

"Thanks, Mr. Pollitt; a drop of whisky would be very welcome."

As soon as their mutual wants had been attended to and

two pipes were in full blast, Fred Pollitt returned to the remark of Myrtle's which had startled him.

" You don't think it was the lamp that set Manor Farm alight? " he asked.

" Not entirely, though it obviously contributed to the blaze. I want your help, Mr. Pollitt, and I'm going to tell you one or two things that for the moment I don't want to go any farther."

" They'll be safe with me," said the farmer ponderously.

Myrtle felt doubtful of that, but he did not really mind if the news was broadcast now. He had spoken of confidence because he thought it would flatter his host.

" We've some reason to believe that Gannett was murdered," he said quietly.

Pollitt's massive jaw dropped.

" Go' bless my soul! " he said. " Who'd want to do a thing like that? "

" That's just the question I've come to ask you, Mr. Pollitt. Who *would* want to kill Gannett? I'm told you knew him a lot better than anyone else did; I want to know who his enemies, or enemy, might be. If you can't help me I don't know who can."

" You're sure of this? Seems a daft idea to me."

" I'm as sure as no matter, though perhaps I couldn't prove it yet. Who might want to do it? "

Fred Pollitt banged his heavy fist down on the table, jerking whisky out of the half-empty glasses.

" No one. There isn't a man in this place that had a hard thought for Bert Gannett. He had his weakness, as you likely know, but he was a kind-hearted man and never did no one a wrong—except himself. Someone did say something about it at the ' George '—suggested some fellow might have knocked Bert on the head—but we all laughed at him. ' Bert hadn't an enemy in the world,' they all said. 'Yes he had,' I said, 'he had one.' 'Who was that?' they said. 'Himself,' I said, 'and you can take it from me he hadn't another.' And take it from me you can, Mr. Myrtle."

"And yet someone murdered him," said Myrtle quietly.

"I don't believe it. Pardon, Mr. Myrtle, that sounds rude. But I can't believe it; I just can't."

"From what you tell me of him, I can quite understand your doubt. Now there's a question I want to ask you that you may think very strange, and again I'd be glad if you forget that I asked it. Is there any connection between Gannett and Colonel Cherrington . . . and your late Vicar, Mr. Torridge?"

Pollitt stared in astonishment at his visitor. Then, pulling himself together, he picked up the whisky bottle.

"Here, have another drop. I knocked the last lot out of your glass. I need a stiff one myself; the questions you do ask. The Vicar?"

"Yes, I'll explain. Colonel Cherrington's dead; I believe he was murdered. Mr. Torridge is dead; accident, I know . . . or wasn't it? Now Gannett's dead; accident again, on the face of it, but I'm sure it wasn't. It makes you think, Mr. Pollitt, those three deaths by violence within a couple of months in a quiet place like Great Norne. That's why I ask: 'what's the connection?'"

The farmer drank deeply of the rich yellow liquid in his glass.

"Don't know whether I'm on my head or my heels. The Colonel murdered? Well, I heard talk of that. But the Vicar . . . who'd want to do in that old —— pardon, that old gentleman? And now Bert. Colonel Cherrington hadn't a civil word for Bert—called him a backslider or what not, even though they was both members of the British Legion. Bert was wounded at Gaza, you know, Mr. Myrtle; that's what started him drinking. And the Vicar . . . ah, Bert did have a row with him, along of his drinking, I'd forgotten that. Vicar ticked him off, and Bert wasn't standing for it. Long time ago it was. But Bert bore no malice; never heard him say a word against the Vicar, never heard him speak of him. There's nothing there, Mr. Myrtle."

"It certainly doesn't sound as if the same person had a motive for killing all three. If Colonel Cherrington and Mr. Torridge were harsh with Gannett that might be a reason for his bearing malice against them—if he'd been that sort of man—but it's no reason for anyone else bearing malice against all three. I don't see it, Mr. Pollitt. You've told me a lot, but it hasn't helped me to an answer —other way, if anything. Who else might help me? Inspector Heskell thought Winch, at the 'Royal George,' or Barton—a builder, I understand—might know something."

Pollitt shook his head gloomily.

"Simon Winch won't tell you any different to me, though you can ask him. Barton I don't know. They were friends at one time, before the war. But Dick Barton's a queer chap, mighty queer; never been the same since his wife died."

"When was that?"

"Oh, time ago. Way back in '19 or '20, or that-like. Always was a hard chap, Dick was, but since Ellen's death, grim's the word and no other. Dropped all his friends, goes about his business—and makes a good job at it, never has a lark, never looked at another woman—that I know of."

"Any special row with Gannett?"

"None at all. Bert had nothing to do with it. Of course, Bert was beginning to go wrong then, after the war; Dick Barton might have dropped him anyhow, like other folks did, more shame to them. But there was no row between them, nothing at all."

"Perhaps I'd better have a word with him."

"I should that. Lucky if you get him to talk, though."

.   .   .   .   .

Having taken his leave of Pollitt, Myrtle thought it really was time to ease off. He was tired and hungry; he wanted time to think over what he had heard. But as he drove through the town he saw Dr. Stopp, who had been introduced to him that morning by Superintendent Kneller, getting out of his car to open the gate leading to his garage. Myrtle stopped his own car and got out.

"Just a word with you, doctor? Sit in your car, private as anywhere. Shan't keep you a minute."

"Sure you wouldn't rather come in? Just time for a quick one."

"Thank you, doctor, supper's what I need. But just two questions first. Captain Hexman told me to-day that he'd been round to see you one evening this week. Mind telling me which evening that was?"

Dr. Stopp looked surprised, but did not beat about the bush.

"Thursday evening it was."

"Sure?"

"Dead sure. I was late with everything that day because I'd been doing a P.M. on that chap Gannett for your people; you know all about that. Day after the fire. Thursday was the evening he came."

"Thank you, doctor; that leads me to question number two. What did he come to see you about?"

" You can't ask me that, Chief Inspector. Doctor and patient, you know."

" Sorry, sir. I don't want to tap professional confidence. I'll put it another way. Did he come to ask you—or did he ask you—anything about the P.M. on Gannett? No doctor and patient in that."

" Gannett? No, why should he? "

" I just asked if he did, doctor."

" Not a word; never mentioned him, that I can remember."

" Thank you, doctor, then I'll not keep you any longer."

Myrtle reached for the door, but Dr. Stopp laid a detaining hand on his arm.

" Just a minute, Chief Inspector. One good turn deserves another—whatever that means. You've asked me two questions; may I ask you one? "

" Can't promise to answer, sir, but go ahead."

" I'm speaking now as Captain Hexman's doctor; I'm worried about his health—his mental health. I realise that as long as you're investigating Colonel Cherrington's death he's got to face any amount of questioning, but must you really have him followed about? "

Myrtle stared.

" Followed about? I don't have him followed about."

" He thinks you do. He told me he was followed here on Thursday."

" Not by my orders. Must be his imagination."

" I'm glad to hear that. May I tell him so? "

Myrtle hesitated.

" Better not quote me," he said. " If for any reason I found it necessary, later on, to keep an eye on him, he might think I was going back on my word."

.   .   .   .   .

On the following morning, which was a Sunday and

New Year's Day into the bargain, Myrtle went round at the respectable hour of 10 a.m. to interview Mr. Simon Winch, host of the 'Royal George'. He learnt from him, however, nothing that he had not already heard. His opinion of Albert Gannett coincided with that of Mr. Pollitt; he was no more helpful in the suggestion of potential murderers, and he thought that a lot of undue fuss was being made about a simple act of God—well, not perhaps that, but an accident was an accident, and that was all there was to it. Myrtle did not feel inclined to take the innkeeper into his confidence by giving his reasons for thinking otherwise, but he thought that his time had not been entirely wasted; Winch would undoubtedly talk to his customers about the detective's inquiries—Myrtle had put no embargo on this—and someone might come and tell him something.

His next visit was to the builder, Richard Barton, and as it was now getting on towards eleven o'clock, Myrtle was afraid that he might be hindering a church-going. His first sight of Barton confirmed him in this—the builder, a dark, sturdily built man, not tall, but erect and handsome, was dressed in a dark suit, with a white collar; on his feet, however, were a pair of carpet slippers. Myrtle held out his warrant-card.

"I'd like a word with you some time, Mr. Barton, but if you're going to church . . ."

"I'm not."

Barton turned his back on his visitor and walked back into the house, leaving Myrtle to follow or not as he thought fit. Myrtle followed. The builder was in the kitchen, where a comfortable chair stood on one side of the open range. On a table beside the chair were two books which looked like a Bible and, perhaps, a prayer-book; a pair of spectacles lay on the book which was open. Barton was looking at the fire; he did not invite his visitor to sit or to speak.

" I wanted to ask you about Mr. Albert Gannet," said Myrtle. " I understand that you knew him pretty well at one time."

Barton looked up quickly.

" I've not spoken to Albert Gannett for close on twenty years," he said. He spoke quietly, but there was a harsh note in his voice.

" But you knew him well at one time? " persisted Myrtle.

" I did."

" Any reason for the change? "

" That's my business."

Myrtle felt a growing doubt as to whether he was on the right lines in this interview. It might not be advisable to be too candid with Mr. Barton.

" You don't know much, then, about his recent life? "

" Nothing at all. Nothing beyond what any man with eyes could see for himself."

Barton's lip showed the curl of a sneer. Handsome as he still was—Myrtle put his age at about fifty—he was not an attractive man to look at; his eyes were cold and without even the vestige of a twinkle; throughout their talk, Myrtle realised afterwards, no sign of a smile or even a softening of expression had crossed his face.

" Would you say he had any enemies? "

" He had one obvious one."

" Any others besides himself? "

Barton shrugged his shoulders.

" That's not for me to say."

Myrtle noticed that the builder showed no surprise at these questions and did not ask the reason for them. He also noticed that he was himself not getting one step nearer his objective. He felt disinclined now to carry his inquiries as far as he had done with Mr. Pollitt; if he had learnt anything at all it was that Richard Barton himself seemed to bear some ill-will to Gannett, but if there was a grudge it was evidently twenty years old, and that could hardly account for this sudden outburst of homicidal activity.

Abruptly deciding to drop this line of inquiry, at any rate for the present, Myrtle thanked the builder for his help and turned towards the door. Barton made no attempt to see him out; out of the corner of his eye the detective saw him sink down into the armchair and pick up his book.

CHAPTER XVIII

Mrs. Faundyce's Party

TUESDAY was the day chosen by Mrs. Faundyce for her
'cheering-up' party, and by three o'clock in the afternoon Miss Emily Vinton was already in a state of twittering excitement. Most unfortunately, Tuesday—being
market day, with friends coming into the town—was also
Minnie's afternoon off, so that there would be no one to
look after Beatrice while Emily was at the party. The
younger sister had made a gallant, if half-hearted attempt
to stay away from the party, but this had been instantly
and contemptuously crushed by the strong-willed Beatrice.
Minnie, being of the 'modern generation', had not
offered to forgo her afternoon off, and as Minnies were
practically irreplaceable, neither sister even thought of
ordering her to stay in; the girl had, however, displayed
a glimmering of proper feeling in saying that she would
come back at four o'clock to get Miss Beatrice a cup of
tea.

So now Emily was fussing round the drawing-room of
'The Chestnuts', giving the final touches to her arrange-
ments for Beatrice's comfort. Her elder sister sat in a
wheeled chair on the side of the fire farthest from the
door. Her book was on a swivelled book-rest attached to
the arm of the chair, and her crochet-work lay on her lap.
By an ingenious arrangement of cord and pulley she could
operate the incandescent gas when darkness fell, for Beatrice
Vinton had still some use of her hands, though her legs
were paralysed; this was some slight mitigation of her
dumbness, as it enabled her to write on a wax pad anything which she wished to say. Fortunately her eyes

were excellent, and, as her courage was indomitable, she still extracted from life an interest and enjoyment which seemed incredible to people in full possession of their faculties.

" Now, Beatrice, are you sure you've got everything? Your rug, your book, your work, your pad. Is that the book you want, dear? Shall I get you any other in case you want a change? "

Beatrice's hand moved slowly over the wax pad.

" No. Don't fuss, child. Go," she wrote.

" I don't like going and leaving you. It isn't right that I should go and enjoy myself and leave you here all by yourself, Beatrice darling." Emily kissed her sister tenderly on her withered cheek. " Now, Minnie will bring you your tea at four o'clock, and draw the curtains, and I shall be back at six to get supper."

Again Beatrice's hand moved.

" No. Seven. Be off."

The stiff fingers lifted the wax sheet, and the message disappeared.

" Well, seven at the latest, then. There's only the soup to hot up, and an omelette won't take five minutes. So good of Mrs. Pollitt to let us have those extra eggs; they make everything so easy. Well, now, I suppose I must be going, or Mary may not be able to make up her tables."

Another kiss, a last look round, and Emily Vinton fluttered out of the room and, five minutes later, out of the house, her squirrel jacket buttoned up to the chin and a muffler over her mouth. At the end of the street she passed porter Blake, sitting on his barrow, evidently waiting for a load from the ironmongery at the corner. Crooky touched his battered cap and gave her a grin and an ' Afternoon, Miss '. Emily smiled back, because she was a polite woman; but she did not really like the porter—he had a rough look, and there was sometimes a glitter in his eye that rather frightened her; besides, she knew he was addicted to strong drink, which, in Vinton eyes, was the hall-mark of the devil. However, she soon forgot him as she hurried on, almost trotting in her eagerness for the party.

Two tables were already in operation when she arrived at the Faundyces' house, the doctor himself at one, with Mrs. Willison, Catherine Beynard and the Vicar; at the other were Winifred Hexman, Mr. Carnaby, Mr. Willison and a friend of the Beynards whom Emily Vinton did not know.

" Oh, here you are; Emily dear," said Mrs. Faundyce cheerfully. " I knew you wouldn't mind if I got some fours started. There will only be three tables, I'm afraid. That naughty Captain Hexman hasn't come, and nor has Dr. Stopp."

" My fault, I'm afraid," said Winifred Hexman, who was dummy at her table. " I wouldn't let him. He's only a nuisance at a mixed bridge party; he gets so restless and he will argue. I sent him off to play golf with Dr. Stopp."

" Very sensible, too," chipped in Dr. Faundyce, whose attention was not entirely concentrated on his own game. " Much better for their livers. That young partner of mine is getting fat. But they'll play bridge after dark, and that means whisky and all the good of the exercise wasted."

" Norris is just as bad—about not coming here to-day. I mean," said Catherine Beynard. " And he's not even got the excuse of exercise; he's just poring over some stuffy treatise or other."

" Ah, here's Julia at last," exclaimed Mrs. Faundyce.

" Now we can make up a hen table and play really *serious* bridge."

Serious was perhaps hardly the word, but everybody seemed to enjoy themselves. From time to time a rubber ended, fours broke up, there were intervals of gossip, an interval for tea, and more bridge, less serious, perhaps, but no more silent. At half-past six appeared trays of sherry and lighter drinks, biscuits, almonds, raisins, preserved fruits—all the pleasant ingredients of a Christmas party. Soon afterwards the Willisons left, and five minutes later Winifred Hexman said good-bye and started off for home.

It was dark now, and a cold wind had sprung up; she buttoned her coat up high, but did not quicken her pace. Presently she heard hurrying footsteps behind her and a hand slipped through her arm.

" Thank God that's over," said the voice of Cyril Carnaby. " Win, I've been longing for a word with you; I was terrified that you'd go before that interminable last rubber at our table ended."

Winifred Hexman smiled in the darkness.

" Well, I don't know that I wanted that to happen myself," she said in a low voice.

Cyril Carnaby squeezed her arm.

" Darling, I love you."

" You mustn't call me that. And you mustn't say that."

" I suppose I may think it, mayn't I? "

" An unprofitable pastime, I'm afraid."

" Yes, but is it? I thought . . . I rather hoped . . ."

Winifred was silent. She was glad that the darkness hid the doubt and indecision which her face must show.

" You're not going on with him, are you? I thought you had decided . . ."

" I can't leave him now. He's in trouble."

" You mean . . . about your father? "

" Yes, and . . . other things. I can't understand it. That London detective keeps on at him."

" Oh, but that's nonsense. Of course he didn't shoot your father. You know that yourself; you told me so."

" Yes, I know that. But it's only my word, and I'm his wife. I'm supposed to be prejudiced in his favour." She gave a bitter little laugh. " Besides, it's not only father."

" What do you mean? "

" I suppose I ought not to tell you. But . . . oh well, why should I keep their secrets? They think that man Gannett was murdered, too."

" I heard a rumour of that. But what of it? "

" George's finger-prints were found there."

" Good God. How . . .? Why . . .? "

" The fool went there one evening for a drink. He's always drinking with farmers. Now the police are trying to make out he was there on the night of the fire."

" But surely he can prove he wasn't? Where was he? "

" At home. My word again . . . and his; that's all we've got to prove it. And even that's not all. That man Myrtle thinks Mr. Torridge was murdered, too."

The solicitor stopped in his stride, almost pulling Winifred off her balance.

" Torridge? Murdered? "

" Seems mad, doesn't it? But the whole thing's mad."

" But he can't have got anything against George over that."

" He was here—at Great Norne; that's all."

They walked on in silence for a minute, Carnaby pressing the girl's arm a little more tightly to his side.

" I can't believe there's anything in all this," he said at last. " I just can't believe it. No doubt if Scotland Yard really think there has been a series of murders they've got to look pretty close at everyone connected with the dead man. George is an obvious first choice, so far as your father is concerned. But as he didn't do it—and you know he didn't—they can't pin anything on him. That just doesn't happen, outside a book."

" I know; one keeps on saying that. But . . . well, anyhow, you can see that I can't just walk out on him in the middle of all this."

Again Carnaby was silent for a minute.

" Perhaps you can't," he said at last. " Not just now. But, Win, even if you want to stick to him while he's in trouble, that doesn't mean you love him. It doesn't mean that you must go on tying yourself to a man you don't love."

It was Winifred who was silent now.

" He's been rather . . . different just lately," she said in a low voice. " I . . . of course the shock of all this probably accounts for it, but he really does seem to be trying to think about me instead of only himself."

Carnaby gave an impatient grunt.

" He's got the wind up; that's all. And what difference does it make? You're not in love with him any longer, are you? "

A little pause, then:

" No, I'm afraid I'm not."

" I hoped you were beginning to be a little bit in love with me."

"Oh, what's the good of saying that now? Why didn't you say it ten years ago, before I married George?"

"But, Win, you were only a child then, and I wasn't much more than a boy myself. If my uncle hadn't sent me off to London, everything would have been all right. Goodness knows I was fond enough of you, but I didn't really think much about love in those days, still less about getting married."

"I was in love with you, Cyril. It broke me up when you went away and didn't come back. So I married the first attractive man who came along and made love to me. And now it's too late."

But Cyril Carnaby had heard the tremor in her voice and knew that it would not take much to tip the scale. He stopped again and pulled her roughly to him.

"It's not too late, Win darling. It mustn't be. We love each other, and I'm just not going to give you up now."

He had his arms round her now, and as he pressed his lips against hers he felt their eager response.

"Win, darling, come with me now. There's no one there; no one can see. Come with me now."

"Oh, Cyril, I can't."

"Why not? George won't be back for an hour, and even if he was he would think you were still at the Faundyces'. Come with me now."

She did not answer, but stood trembling in his arms. The man's voice was husky as he pressed her to him.

"My darling. My sweetheart. Come with me now."

.   .   .   .   .

Five minutes after the Willisons and Winifred Hexman had gone Emily Vinton began to twitter.

" Oh, look at the time! Five minutes to seven, and I *promised* Beatrice I'd be back by seven. I never ought to have come, on Minnie's day out, but Beatrice just made me. You know how *firm* she is, and here I am late. Mary, it has been a most lovely party. I shall remember it for months and it has *quite* cheered me up. And now I really must go."

" I'm coming with you, Miss Emily," said Dr. Faundyce cheerfully. " I'm going round to the surgery to make sure that Stopp got back in time. These young fellows; you can't rely on them nowadays."

This was a libel on Frederick Stopp, who was most punctilious about his professional duties, whatever his private failings may have been. But Mrs. Faundyce had warned her husband for this escort duty. Emily Vinton had been in a highly nervous condition last Thursday, and was not fit to go walking home in the dark alone. Emily herself was by no means sorry to have an escort. Three months ago she had told the Vicar that she had no qualms about going home in the dark, nobody would hurt her; but the Vicar's death had been a great shock, and then the Colonel's and Mr. Gannett's coming so quickly on top of it—all accidents, of course, or practically accidents—but they had upset her. She did not really like being out alone, and the streets on her quiet side of the town were lonely at night. Nevertheless she made her gallant protest.

" Oh, but it's not on your way, doctor. It's *miles* out of your way."

Dr. Faundyce laughed.

" Half a mile at the outside. I shall enjoy stretching my legs after all this sitting and eating."

So, after reiterated and affectionate thanks, Emily

Vinton set off, with the little, tubby doctor pattering at her side. They were well matched for size, though not for weight, and they found plenty to talk about on their way—cheerful, unmalicious gossip, that was very manna to their souls. Emily thought nothing of the darkness, the almost deserted streets, the cold, piercing wind; almost before she realised it they had reached the gate of the little drive leading up to ' The Chestnuts '. She pressed Dr. Faundyce to come in and have just one little word with Beatrice while she prepared supper, but he declined—he must get on to the surgery and see that all was right there before going back to his own evening meal. So he watched her safely into the house and then turned away.

There was a Yale lock to the front door, so that Emily Vinton could let herself in. As soon as the door was shut she called out cheerfully to let Beatrice know she was back, then went into the kitchen to make sure that all preparations for supper were ready for her. A minute later she was walking upstairs, eager to tell Beatrice all about her lovely evening. The hall and staircase were brightly lit; Minnie would have turned up the gas after getting Beatrice her tea and before going out again herself.

Emily opened the door of the drawing-room and stopped in surprise. The room was in darkness. Beatrice must have decided to have a little nap and have turned out the gas. Tip-toeing into the room, so as not to wake her sister, Emily realised that it was not really in darkness; the fire was burning brightly, its light reflected on the bright fender, the furniture, the silver teapot, on her sister's face . . .

Emily drew in her breath with a gasp of horror.

Beatrice's eyes were open, staring, protruding from a

face blotched with dark colour. Her mouth was open. Round her neck was something dark, something that pressed into the flesh.

A scream rose in Emily's throat, but it was never heard. Hands fastened round her neck, hands of steel that squeezed and stifled sound, crushed out life.

CHAPTER XIX

Connecting Link

" THAT'S as grim a business as any I've seen in my time,"
said Chief Inspector Myrtle.

He was standing in the drawing-room of ' The Chestnuts ', looking at the dead bodies of two old ladies,
brutally strangled, their faces distorted, their wide-open
eyes still reflecting the horror of their violent end. Inspector Joss stood beside him; Joss, who imagined himself
tough enough for anything, was feeling physically sick.
Dr. Faundyce had just finished his examination; white
and shaken, he stood looking at the stiffening bodies of his
old friends.

" Must they be photographed? " he asked, in a voice
that was little more than a whisper. " May I close their
eyes? "

" Afraid we must wait, doctor. It won't take long once
the camera-man is here, and then they can be taken away.
There'll have to be a P.M., of course."

Dr. Faundyce nodded.

" I'll do it if you wish. But perhaps it would be better
for Stopp or one of the Snottisham men to do it. I'm . . .
perhaps I'm getting too old for this sort of thing, and I
don't want to make the same mistake again . . . that you
say I did with the Vicar."

" I'll have a word with Superintendent Kneller when he
comes, sir. But can you just give me a line about the
time? "

" Only very roughly. I think Miss Beatrice—the elder
sister—certainly an hour or two before Miss Emily. Emily

was alive at seven o'clock, but it must have been soon after that."

" You know that, sir?—the seven o'clock limit? "

Dr. Faundyce's voice faltered as he answered.

" I brought her back here myself—to her death. She asked me to come in and talk to her sister for a few minutes. I wanted to get back to my supper, and I refused. If I had come in she would be alive now . . . and perhaps this foul brute would have been caught. My God, that poor little woman owes her death to my selfish gluttony."

" Oh, come, doctor; that's over-stating it. Very likely you'd be dead, too, yourself if you had come in. This man's a killer, whoever he is. Well, it's a help to have that limit, and you think it can't have been long after that? And the elder lady an hour or two earlier; you can't be more exact? "

" I'm afraid not; it needs much experience to fix the time of death exactly. Rigor varies so much with the conditions; that fire was probably hot when she was killed, and that would delay the onset. But I think not later than five-thirty or six, perhaps a little earlier."

" Thank you, doctor. You'll want to be getting home, I know. The Chief Constable may come to-night, but I can't say when he'll get here, and I'm sure he won't want to disturb you again."

Muttering his thanks, the old doctor went away.

" Poor old buster! A hell of a shock for him," said Myrtle. " Good job he suggested someone else doing the autopsy; I shouldn't have been too happy leaving it to him. Not that there's likely to be much more to learn about how they died. But I wish we'd got that maid here."

It was Minnie who had found the bodies. Coming in

soon after ten o'clock, she had found the lights still on in the hall and on the landing, though her mistresses usually retired on the stroke of ten, Emily putting out the lights before she did so. Minnie had gone upstairs to the drawing-room, to see if they were still there; the room was in darkness, but, thinking that she would just have a look round, she had pulled the chain of the incandescent gas-lamp, and had instantly been faced by the horror that had later shaken two policemen and a doctor off their balance. The girl had run screaming out of the house, and was only able to gasp out her tale incoherently to the first person who met her, before collapsing and being taken to the Cottage Hospital.

On their arrival with Inspector Heskell, Myrtle and Joss, who were both now living in the town, had made a hurried search of the house to make sure that the murderer was not still in it. Then, when the doctor arrived, Myrtle had stayed with him while Joss made a more detailed examination of the premises. Heskell had gone back to the Police Station to telephone to Headquarters, there being no such new-fangled contraption at 'The Chestnuts'.

"I want to know where she was while all this was happening."

Myrtle, of course, had no means of knowing about Minnie's evening out. Neither had Joss, though probably all the inhabitants of Great Norne knew each other's fixed habits.

"Did you find anything? How he got in or out?"

"Bathroom window, sir. It was open; he hadn't even bothered to shut it after him, and there are marks of a knife on the hasp. Might be some finger-prints."

"We'll get your fellow to look for them, but we shan't find any. This man knows his job."

" You don't still think it's Captain Hexman, sir? "
Myrtle hesitated.

" This seems to rule him out, doesn't it? he can't possibly
have got anything against these poor old things. There's
just the possibility, of course, that this and the Gannett
murder were done simply and solely as a cover, to draw
one's attention away from him."

" My God! that's pretty cold-blooded."

" This man's a cold-blooded murderer, whoever he is.
Remember that Gannett wasn't killed until after it was
known that we didn't accept suicide as the explanation of
Colonel Cherrington's death—in fact, not until Hexman
knew we were looking at him."

" But the Vicar was killed before the Colonel, sir."

" True; that's a point. But his death may really have
been accidental, though there's one thing about it that
makes me doubt that. Hexman might have wanted them
both out of the way and then, when we got suspicious
about the Colonel, killed these others to confuse us."

Joss looked shocked.

" Very difficult to believe, sir—a man like him."

" Very difficult, I agree. And probably it's not him,
but I don't rule him out altogether."

" One thing, sir; it's not a sex crime; they're all too
old."

Myrtle looked thoughtfully at his companion.

" They were young once," he said.

The young detective seemed to find it difficult to believe
this, but he did not argue the point.

" What do you make of it all now, sir? Seems mad to
me."

" It may be mad. I think there are two alternatives:
either all these murders are the work of a homicidal
lunatic, or else there's something very deep behind them—

very deep, and probably very far away, in point of time. We must bear the lunatic in mind, and I shall probably ask your Super to let me put you onto that, Joss; but what I've got to look for is the connecting link between these five people who have been killed; if we can find that we shall find the murderer. You probably wonder why I stand here talking instead of hunting round for clues. This is a case, in my opinion, where ideas are more important than clues, and ideas come from talking things over with someone else—provided that one thinks at the same time as talking, which isn't always the case."

The Chief Inspector grinned at his subordinate, and at the same time a car could be heard drawing up outside. Two minutes later the Chief Constable and Superintendent Kneller came into the room, whilst Joss could see the eager faces of his two young detective-constables on the landing outside.

" This is a ghastly business, Myrtle," said Major Statford. " Must be a madman. My God, can't you cover them up? "

" I just wanted to get photographs taken, sir, and then they can go to the mortuary."

" Well, let's go into another room while you tell me about it. I can't bear looking at the poor old things."

Myrtle led them to a room on the ground floor and lit the gas fire, Joss remaining above to direct the taking of photographs and the search for finger-prints. The Chief Constable looked round the room, which had the appearance of a dining-room which was never used.

" I suppose they don't keep whisky here," he said. " I could do with something after that."

" Brandy in the ambulance, sir, if you'd like some."

" No, no; of course I don't need it. Mustn't be soft. Now, Myrtle, what about it? "

The C.I.D. man told what facts he knew and repeated some of the theories which he had discussed with Joss.

"But what earthly connecting link can there be?" asked Major Statford. "A parson, a retired Colonel, a drunken farmer and two old women."

"They're all people of some standing, sir," said Superintendent Kneller.

"Standing? Gannett?"

"A leading farmer, sir, and before this breakdown he was playing some part in local life. If I remember rightly, he was on the Bench, or was being considered for it. And he certainly was on the District Council. I remember he was the man who made such a to-do about that old timber bridge over the river here. He might have been one of the biggest men in these parts if he hadn't taken to drink."

"Well, but what about these old ladies? They were never on the Bench, surely. Nor, of course, was the Vicar. If they had been, one might have seen some light —a crime of revenge, or whatever you call it. Do you see any link, Myrtle?"

"There is just one point, sir. It's very puzzling in itself, but I'm not sure it doesn't throw some light on one or two of the other puzzles."

He drew from his pocket a flat, thin package, wrapped in a handkerchief. Removing the handkerchief he disclosed a paper-covered book, which he held by one corner with a bit of the handkerchief between his fingers and the paper.

"May be prints on it, sir, though I don't expect to find the murderer's. I found this on the paralysed lady's lap under the rug, when the doctor began to examine her. I don't think anyone else has seen it, which is perhaps as well."

Laying the book on the table, he turned over a page or two with a pair of tweezers which he had taken from his pocket. He stopped when he came to a page on which appeared a crude line-drawing.

The Chief Constable and Kneller leaned down to examine it.

" My God."

" French, sir," said Kneller ponderously, after studying a line or two of the letterpress.

" French, yes; but not Paris French, I fancy. This is a grade lower even than the muck sold by touts to the guileless visitor to Montmartre. Marseilles, I should say, was its spiritual home, or possibly Port Said."

Borrowing the tweezers, he turned back to the title-page.

" *Les Rêves de Fifinette* ; the usual tripe. No publisher's imprint, of course. This is incredible, Myrtle; that old lady . . .?

Myrtle smiled.

" I'm sure she never saw it, sir. This is highly suggestive, sir; it works in with similar things in all the cases. One now begins to see the significance of the Vicar's whisky."

Major Statford raised his eyebrows.

" It suggests deni . . . deni . . . I can't quite get the word."

" Denial? "

" No, sir; a word meaning the blackening of character."

" Denigration? "

" That's it, sir. Look at each case : The Vicar, accidental death, due to intoxication—shocking in a Vicar."

" But nothing was said about intoxication."

" No, sir, because Dr. Faundyce sat on the evidence. He didn't tell anyone that there was a smell of whisky in the Vicar's mouth and a broken flask in his pocket. And he didn't open his stomach, so we shall never know now whether he had drunk whisky or had it poured over him after he was dead."

"My God! that's a bad report."

"He never suspected murder, sir, and not unnaturally he didn't want to blacken the Vicar's character—as I believe the murderer intended it to be blackened."

"Well, go on."

"Colonel Cherrington, suicide due to a blackmailing letter. Left to the imagination what he was being blackmailed about."

"H'm. Trust the public to imagine the worst, eh?"

"Exactly, sir. Gannett—well, there was no need to blacken him; he'd blackened himself. But accident again, and due to drink."

"And old Miss Vinton this filthy book?"

"Yes, sir. It seems to click, doesn't it?"

The Chief Constable absent-mindedly drew a pipe from his pocket and began to stuff it with tobacco, then remembered himself and put pipe and pouch away with a shame-faced air.

"There's certainly the suggestion of a connecting link there, but why these five chosen for denigration?"

Superintendent Kneller evidently thought it was time for him to re-assert himself.

"I'd like to suggest, sir, that the Church might have something to do with that. The Vicar, of course; and I happen to know that Colonel Cherrington was his Churchwarden. I don't know about these ladies, but they seem the sort that might be very religious-minded; there's a holy picture in the hall."

"Gustave Doré at his worst," murmured Major Statford. " And Farmer Gannett went to church regularly to confess his sins, I suppose."

" I haven't heard tell of that. We shall want a little more local information, I expect, before we link him up."

" We certainly shall. Well, Myrtle, what's your plan? "

" I haven't really had time to think it out, sir; but following up Superintendent Kneller's idea I'll look up the other Churchwarden to-morrow. No good seeing the new Vicar; he's not likely to know anything. I've got it in my mind, sir, that if we can establish a link definitely connecting these five people we shall be able to hook it on to the man we're looking for. But we shall have to be quick, because of course there may be more than five."

The Chief Constable nodded gravely.

" I was thinking the same thing. It is obvious now that we can wash out ' coincidence ', and we must probably accept murder in the case of Gannett, if not in that of Torridge; but I hope we aren't excluding other possible explanations."

" The only other possible one seems to be a homicidal lunatic."

" Religious maniac," murmured Kneller. " There you've got them all on the same chain."

" It might be. I thought perhaps you might allow Inspector Joss to work that line, sir—the homicidal lunatic—while I work on the link. Heskell might know of some local ruffian with a screw loose, and Joss would do that better than I should."

So it was arranged, and as the photographic and finger-print experts had now finished the first part of their work, the Headquarters party departed. The bodies of the two Miss Vintons had already been removed in the ambulance, and Inspector Heskell had posted a constable in the house for the night.

Before leaving, Myrtle had a last look round the drawing-room with Joss. He had already noted that the strangling had been done with green blind-cord, and that two cords had been cut from the blinds in the room.

" He must have done that when no one was in here, sir."

Myrtle shook his head.

" I suspect he did it under the old lady's eyes. She was dumb, remember."

Joss frowned.

" That's a nasty thought, sir. You said he was cold-blooded. But what about the bell? There's one fastened to the chair."

Myrtle walked quickly across to the wheeled-chair.

" So there is. I missed that. A bad slip."

He pressed the button, and a faint whirr sounded in the lower regions.

" That maid must have been out."

" And he must have known she was out, sir. And the sister, too."

" Yes, probably everybody knows everybody else's business in Great Norne, but it's a local job all right."

" If only we could find a finger-print, sir. There doesn't seem to be a clue of any kind."

The C.I.D. man chuckled.

" I expect I've gone too far in the other direction," he said. " We mustn't altogether shut our eyes to clues. And that reminds me, Joss; if we rule out Captain Hexman—and we may have to—we come back to the premise that Colonel Cherrington was killed by an outsider—an outside, not an inside job. You remember we weren't sure that he might not have faked that window entry; in fact, I strongly suspected that he had. But there was another point that struck us. That cupboard under the stairs, where a man—an outsider—might have hidden. You remember I asked you to have a look inside it sometime, in case I'd missed anything. Did you ever find time to do that? "

Joss nodded.

" I did, sir."

" Find anything? "

" Nothing significant, sir. Unless, perhaps . . . well, the only thing that struck me was that the cupboard was put in after the stairs were built; in fact, after the hall was last painted and papered."

" Eh? How did you make that out? "

" Inside the cupboard, sir, the wall was papered like the rest of the hall and the wainscot painted dark brown, like the wainscot in the hall. But the rest of the cupboard was just painted white. The under-side of the stairs were painted, too, which you would hardly have found if the cupboard was put in at the same time. So I asked the cook, and she said it had only been put in a couple of years ago—mostly for the Captain's golf-clubs and things, that used to annoy the Colonel."

" That's interesting, Joss. Everything in these cases points to local knowledge, and not only local, but inside knowledge. Who put the cupboard in, did she say? "

" Yes, I asked her that, sir. She said Barton put it in; he's the big builder round here. Barton didn't do the work himself, of course; she told me all about the old carpenter who did the work—a regular card, according to her, never spoke all the time. An old man called Ebenezer Creech."

CHAPTER XX

Joss's Line

DETECTIVE-INSPECTOR JOSS was delighted to have a line of his own to follow, after the rather indefinite and manacled gropings of the last few days. He particularly liked the line allotted to him because he thought it was the right one. Theorising about 'denigration' and threads linking with the distant past might be all right for Scotland Yard, but he was a practical man, and thought that the killer would prove to be a lunatic, or possibly an apparently sane man with a kink, a grudge against society, or some form of religious mania. Certainly the man was cunning—the clever way he covered his tracks proved that —and it was equally certain that he was a local man, who knew the comings and goings of his victims and their households, and he also seemed to know his way about their houses.

Before getting down to his trail, however, there was some routine police work to be done in connection with this latest crime. Whatever Chief Inspector Myrtle might say about ideas being more valuable than clues, it would be idiotic not to set in motion the normal machinery for catching criminals. In this case the obvious thing to do was to find out who was seen in the neighbourhood of 'The Chestnuts' between the hours of, say, 4 p.m. and 8 p.m. the previous day. It was even possible that somebody might have been seen entering or leaving the house or its grounds, though the murderer would naturally have taken great pains to avoid being seen.

So, with the help of Police Constables Bridger and Batt, he spent Wednesday morning visiting every house and shop in the neighbourhood, collecting a large netful of well-known and apparently harmless people who had been seen in the locality on the previous evening. No stranger was among the list, nobody had been seen actually entering 'The Chestnuts', and nobody had been seen behaving in a suspicious manner—unless in the latter category you included the report of two film-trained urchins who claimed to have seen Crooky Blake 'lurking' outside the house at some time after six—after their tea, anyway, which they had at that hour. Questioned as to what they meant by 'lurking', they admitted that he had been just walking down the road, but declared that he had been 'squinting about him' in a suspicious manner.

It might, of course, prove necessary to question all the citizens whose names appeared on the list, but Joss thought he would first of all try to narrow the field a bit by other inquiries. His first step in this direction was to have a talk with Inspector Heskell, whom he found helpful enough if treated with tact. Joss explained the theory of the homicidal lunatic, the man with a grudge against society or, alternatively, the religious maniac. Heskell didn't know about a religious maniac, but if Joss wanted a queer customer mixed up with religion, he might do worse than have a look at the sexton of St. Martha's; he himself had no use for Josiah Chell, and wouldn't trust him any farther than he could see him. As for a grudge against society, there wasn't much society in Great Norne; a few gentry, of course, like the Squire and Colonel Cherrington, and he didn't think that any natives of Great Norne harboured a grudge. There was that foreigner, Blake, who called himself an outside porter, which Heskell had always thought might be a cover for less honest activities—a drunken fellow with a temper; he was a type who would bear watching.

Coinciding as this did with the report of the man's presence near the scene of the crime, Joss thought that Blake must certainly be interviewed, and inquired of his whereabouts and those of Chell. The latter, Heskell told him, was usually to be found at the church; he had a whole-time job there, looking after the churchyard as well as doing his duties as a sexton. Blake was a bird of passage, but his home was near the harbour, and he might be expected to be found there at meal-times. Both men were frequenters of a public-house known as the ' Silver Herring ', but that was probably not the best place at which to discuss a murder.

Having fortified himself with a late lunch, Joss went off to St. Martha's, and had no difficulty in discovering the sexton. He was actively supervising the work of a hefty labourer who was already two feet deep in the soil. Chell himself had his arm in a sling, which presumably accounted for his inactive rôle.

" Who's that for? " asked the detective.

" Old Vintons this be for," replied Josiah; " them as croaked last night."

" You're starting very early, aren't you? Who's given the order? "

" Nobody's give the order," replied the sexton resent-fully. " But I knowed what was wanted directly I heard they'd been took. Pegged out their claim, they did, a good time back, and I reckoned it wouldn't be long now. I said to the Vicar—the late Vicar, that is—no longer ago than October last: ' Worthy the lamb to be slain ', I said, speaking of the old one, and he rebuked me sharp, he did. But slain she's been, and not one lamb, but two. Not so much lamb neither, but mutton, and scraggy at that."

The sexton chuckled ghoulishly.

" Worms won't find 'em so tasty as that little bit," he

said, nodding towards a nearby cross on which the name
ELLEN BARTON was engraved. Probably that would be
the wife of Richard Barton, the builder, Joss thought; he
vaguely knew that she had died some years ago in tragic
circumstances.

The detective pointed to two neighbouring mounds, on
one of which the turf was barely set.

" Would those be Mr. Torridge and Colonel Cherrington? " he asked.   " Or is one of them Mr. Gannett? "

" Nay, he's in new part," said Josiah, jerking his head
towards the churchyard's extension.   " This corner's
reserved for the quality.   And the fold's filling up; filling
up quick."

He made to rub his hands together, then winced as if
the arm in the sling hurt him.

" What have you done to that? " asked Joss.

" Strained a ligiman, I have; so doctor says.   Powerful
unfortunate.   I has to get Jim here to do my burials, and
that's lost money to me—good money is burials.   Jim's the
only one bar me that can dig a pretty grave, and that's
why I've began to-day, because Jim's starting on road-
work Friday.   Powerful unfortunate my arm be."

" Show me where Mr. Gannett lies," said Joss.

Chell looked doubtful, but an authoritative jerk of the
head persuaded him.   As soon as they were out of earshot
of Jim the detective halted.

" Tell me about those two," he said—" your late Vicar
and Colonel Cherrington.   Were they men you liked? "

" They were gentry.   It wasn't for me to like them or
not like them."

" Oh, come, we aren't living in the Middle Ages.   I
heard the Colonel was a martinet."

" Don't know nothing about that.   He was tight-fisted
enough.   Never a present came my way, nor yet a picking

—nothing but what was my right. Couldn't please him either—laid his tongue about when things wasn't as he liked. Chastised us with scorpions, like old Rehoboam. Not much milk of 'uman kindness about the Colonel."

" And the Vicar? "

Chell shrugged his shoulders.

" Meant well, did Vicar. Swelled up in his own conceit, though he did like to say that him that humbleth himself shall be exalted. Reckon he got over the humbleth part young and had got on to the exalting."

" You didn't like either of them much, then? "

Josiah looked shrewdly at his questioner.

" What's this all about? " he asked. " Mighty curious you be."

Joss laughed.

" Oh, I just like to know about people. I thought no one could tell me better about the Vicar and his church-warden than the sexton. And the old ladies; they were church-folk, too, were they? "

" Ay, they were the flock indeed—and fold's filling up."

" And Gannett? "

Chell laughed.

" Never seed him inside here these twenty years. 'Twas John Barleycorn he worshipped . . . and I don't blame him."

Joss had not expected to get any definite information from his first conversation with the sexton; he had too little to go on for that. A general picture was all he had hoped for; a basis on which to build the man's character. He did not much like what he had seen and heard, but, apart from a morbid sense of humour, there did not seem to be anything unbalanced or malicious about the man.

His search for Blake was less immediately successful,

and it was not until dusk had fallen that he found him in a house on the edge of the saltings, about four hundred yards beyond the harbour. He had been told that the porter lived in the last of three old wooden houses on the very edge of the mud flats, and in fact they proved to be little more than cabins, such as Uncle Tom might have dwelt in, and certainly nothing half so luxurious as the up-turned boat of the Peggotty family.

It was not, however, in the last house that the detective found Blake. He knocked at the door and, receiving no answer, knocked again more loudly. A moment or two later he heard a man's voice calling from the neighbouring cabin:

" Wanting me? "

Walking back, he saw a sturdy figure silhouetted against the light from an open door.

" Is that Mr. Blake? "

" Crooky Blake I am. Don't know about the ' mister '."

" I'd like a word with you, Blake."

" Come inside, then."

The man moved back into the room behind him, and Joss followed. He found the room larger than he expected, but from the look of the furniture he guessed that it was the only one in the ' house '. There was a bed, a deal table, a mangle, a dresser, a sink, and a small range with an open fire. It was only when he had completed this rapid inventory that he realised that there was an old woman sitting beside the fire—a very old woman with a generous growth of grey hairs on her withered chin, but an alert pair of eyes watching him. He turned towards the porter, whom he had noticed about the town but had not closely examined. He saw a man of no great height, but sturdily built, his appearance marred by a deformed shoulder that gave him almost the look of a hunchback.

Blake's face was rugged, and he showed a mouthful of broken and discoloured teeth when he grinned, but his eyes, too, were alert, and had often a mischievious twinkle in them.

" I wanted a word with you alone, Blake."

" No secrets from mother," replied the porter. " You're Inspector Joss, ain't you? "

" I am, yes, but . . ."

" You'll take a cup o' tea with me and mother. You'll find it warm you."

It was a statement rather than an invitation. A large, thick cup was filled with dark fluid from a big brown tea-pot and a dash of milk added.

" Sugar's in it."

The tea was welcome, and Joss took a deep gulp of it. Instantly he recognised one of the more pleasant of the aromas that filled the cabin; the tea was richly laced with gin.

" Very good that," he said. " Your health, marm."

The old woman looked at him, but did not respond or smile. He wondered if she were deaf or wanting in her faculties. That would simplify the problem of questioning Blake in front of her.

Joss had a definite line of inquiry to follow up here, so he decided to waste no time on a ' general picture ', which would in any case probably emerge during the course of his questioning.

" I'm a police-officer, as you know, and I have to ask you some questions about your movements yesterday."

The twinkle came into the porter's eyes.

" Charging me? " he asked.

" I should caution you if I was going to do that. You'll likely know that two old ladies were murdered yesterday, name of Vinton, and you were one of the people seen near their house at about the time it happened. I have to ask what you were doing there."

" And what time did it happen? "

" I'm here to ask questions, Blake, not to answer them."

" Well, how am I to know what you want? I was past there two or three times in the day. I'm a porter, I am—outside porter, carrier, or whatever you like to call it. I get all over the town in the course of the day. Yesterday . . . now let me see."

Blake scratched a tousled head.

" Morning I was past there, turned eleven, carrying a case from the station to Mr. Perks. Afternoon I was at the end of the road, collecting a delivery from Coote, the ironmonger—I do a round for him; I didn't go past the house then, but I was in the road."

" What time was that? "

The porter, who had been stuffing shag into a dilapidated pipe, picked up a glowing coal in the tongs.

" I don't sport no wrist-watch, nor yet a gold-and-albert, but I reckon not to be far out. I was there at a quarter three, but they weren't ready with their stuff, and I had to wait a half-hour or more. Call to mind I see one of the old things go past there while I was waiting."

" You did, did you? Was she alone? Did you see anyone about there while you were waiting? "

" Alone she was. No followers—a bit past that. There was one or two people up and down all the time. I couldn't call to mind their names."

This was earlier than the first time limit, so Joss did not press the point.

" Any other time that day? "

Blake shook his head, and the detective's interest quickened.

" Ah, but wait a minute. Yes, I come back after dark

to tell Mr. Coote a parcel he'd been expecting by rail for some days hadn't turned up yet. The old boy was fussing about it, so I went to the station after the afternoon train to inquire—and then I went and forgot to tell him till . . . what was it? . . . nigh on seven, I should think."

That, of course, was a statement that would have to be checked—and could be checked. The time was suggestive.

" Did you see anyone that time? "

Blake shook his head.

" Not that I call to mind. But, then, I see so many people, going about the town, I wouldn't reckon to remember."

" It's important, Blake. Think it over, and if you do recall seeing anyone let me know."

" I'll do that."

" Now another evening I want to know about, last Wednesday—the night of the fire at Gannett's. Where were you then? "

" Oh, ah, I remember that. We was at the ' Silver Herring ', talking about the inquest on the old Colonel. A lot of cackle there was and dry throats, and we mostly took a good load aboard. What time would you want to know about? "

" Say seven o'clock to eight."

" It wouldn't have been much before eight that I left the ' Herring '. I was going along to the ' George ' to ask about a job Mr. Winch wanted me to do next day, but I found when I got in the air I wasn't too steady on me props, so I had a doss in me barrow. I could see the fire though from down there by the harbour; remember wondering what it was before I popped off."

There was some confirmation of this in what Sergeant Plett had said. He had spoken of seeing the fire as soon as he left the 'Silver Herring'. He would perhaps be able to confirm the time at which Blake had left the inn, though Joss had not had much conversation with him on the subject. Anyway, he was back in London at the moment, as Chief Inspector Myrtle had thought that his assumed rôle in Great Norne was wearing rather thin.

"Well, that's all very clear, Blake," he said; "now, do you remember the night the old Vicar died—Mr. Torridge? Way back in November that was—the 18th, to be exact."

Joss thought he caught a look of disquiet, or at any rate of surprise, on the porter's face; his colour seemed to heighten, but the twinkle quickly returned to his eye.

"You're all on the deaths, aren't you?" he said. "There was old Mrs. Codling died Michaelmas Day. Where was I then, would you like to know?"

Joss smiled politely at this witticism.

"No, Blake, I'm not interested in Mrs. Codling. I am interested in the Vicar. Where were you that night?"

"And what time would that be?"

That, of course, was a facer. He did not know the time at which the Vicar had died, and he realised that he had made a blunder in not finding out. On a vague period such as 'the hours of darkness' he could not hope to pin Blake to any definite reply. Neither was he any more successful in the case of Colonel Cherrington; he knew the time then—between 11 and 11.30 p.m.—but the porter merely replied that so far as he could remember he was in bed and asleep. And who was there to check that?

Having questioned the man so closely about his movements on those critical nights, it was no use asking him about his relations with the deceased. He would be on his guard, and would have no difficulty in giving evasive answers—if, that is to say, he was guilty and had something to hide. It would be better to think out a plan for trapping him into some admission at a later date. Joss was not a very experienced detective and had not got the skill to plan very far ahead. So he thanked Blake for his information, said good night to the old woman—who throughout the interview had alternately sucked at her laced tea and a pipe but had paid no attention to what was going on—and walked out into the night.

When he had gone a few steps he realised that Blake had followed him.

" You've been asking me some ugly questions, Inspector," the man said. " I've a right to know what you've got on me."

There was a rasp in the thick voice that Joss did not altogether like. This was, he realised, a very lonely place.

" I've got nothing on you, Blake," he said heartily. " We're going to question a lot of people before we find out what's at the bottom of these killings. I hope I didn't upset your mother."

" My m . . . oh, you mean old Ma Hirdle. Jansy Hirdle her name is. She's not my mother, only a neighbour. But a good neighbour. And a good friend to Crooky Blake."

CHAPTER XXI

Winds of Fear

NEWS of the dreadful killing of the Vinton sisters spread through Great Norne like wildfire. Some even heard of it on the same night; these were people who had heard the screaming maid running through the streets and had made contact with those who had come in contact with her. But for the majority of the inhabitants it was Wednesday morning when the news reached them; men going to work met others who had passed ' The Chestnuts ' and seen the police on guard outside; those who were not already too far from home slipped back to tell their wives, and the wives spread the report from door to door as quickly as any ' bush telegraph '.

The first excitement was quickly followed by horror, and then by fear, as realisation of the meaning of this latest tragedy dawned upon those who heard of it. The ten-weeks-old accidental death of the Vicar had done little more than startle, or even amuse, the majority. Colonel Cherrington's suicide, as it was at first supposed to be, had shocked them; then, as rumours spread that murder was suspected, there spread with them a feeling of excitement. But what happened to a man in Colonel Cherrington's position did not touch the lives of the people; they were intrigued but not personally affected; on the whole they had got enjoyment from that death, too. The burning of Manor Farm, with poor Albert Gannett in it, had saddened them; he had been more nearly one of them-selves—a fine fellow once, and even now without an enemy; but then a disquieting report began to spread that the police thought that he had been murdered, too, and people began to feel uneasy, to ask themselves questions, to wonder whether there could be anything behind all these sudden deaths.

But now the stark reality of a horror menacing them all had sprung into being in a single night. The other deaths might have been accidental or suicidal; here was murder—brutal, senseless massacre. There could be no reason, no motive for such a killing. Two harmless old women, one of them paralysed for twelve years, not rich, not malicious, not spiteful or unkind, could have no sane enemy, any more than could poor drink-sodden Albert Gannett. There could be only one possible explanation— a madman, a killer must be loose in the town, too cunning to be caught or even suspected, too brutal to have mercy on the weakest or poorest, too strong to be resisted by normal woman or man . . . Who was safe? Who dared move or live alone? Who dared even sleep while the menace hung over all? Who would be the next victim?

The cool, trained reasoning of the Scotland Yard detective, which had so quickly realised a connecting link between the crimes, was not for the common people of Great Norne. They could see no sense in any of these murders—if murders they all were—except possibly in the case of Colonel Cherrington, where inheritance or resentment might have been possible motives. They could only see that death was loose among them, striking with meaningless but brutal certainty, and apparently with impunity. What were all the police doing, Scotland Yard and all, if they could not protect innocent, harmless men and women in this quiet, peaceful town?

Little work was done in Great Norne that morning. Women stood in their doorways, talking to their neighbours, glad to have a friendly face in sight—though what face could with certainty be called friendly now? Some

went into each other's houses, determined not to be alone
for a minute; cooked or shared their meals with a neighbour, went shopping in pairs, formed escorts to take their
children to school and fetch them back in the evening.
The men were little better. Their lives, except those of
the fishermen and the ex-servicemen, had been so uneventful that danger was almost unknown to them, and they
had not the spirit of adventure with which to greet it. They,
too, when evening came, went home from their work in
pairs, where that was possible, or waited for someone to
come along who was going even part of the way in their
direction. Not many of them would leave their homes that
night, even for the comfort of a bright saloon bar and the
courage-giving glow of spirits or beer.

The weather, too, seemed bent upon heightening the
general sense of depression and even alarm. Rain had
been falling steadily for the last two days, and now an ugly
wind was rising, blowing in sudden, violent gusts through
the streets, banging doors and fluttering window-curtains.
A loose tile crashing to the street was unpleasant at any
time; now, with people's nerves taut with fear, it was
enough to cause a burst of unreasoning terror. West of
the town a great elm toppled across the road with a roar
that, magnified by the wind, startled those who heard it
as if it had been the explosion of a bomb. Men coming
from that side of the town reported, too, that the Gaggle
was in flood and was rushing under the old Timber Bridge
with a force that made it lurch and tremble; they had not
liked the crossing of it, and if they had to go back, having
heard the shocking news and been infected with the spirit
of fear, they would like the return journey even less.

And it was not only among the humbler folk that fear
and uneasiness were felt. The usually high-spirited Mrs.
Faundyce had been shocked from her normal balance by

the tragedy that had befallen two of her oldest friends, one of whom had left her house, under the escort of her husband, to go straight to her death. Mary Faundyce was an intelligent woman, but she no more than her simpler neighbours could see any sense in these killings; a homicidal lunatic seemed the only possible explanation. She got no help or comfort from her husband; his usual cheerfulness and optimism had abandoned him, and he was silent, and snubbed his wife when she questioned him. She understood some of his feelings about the night's tragedy, but she could not know that he had for days been blaming himself for his concealment of evidence in connection with Theobald Torridge's death. He realised that Chief Inspector Myrtle had let him down lightly about that, and he suspected that if he had then told what he had found, and had had the intelligence to search as he should have done, he might have saved the lives of these men and women who had since died.

So James Faundyce gave no comfort to his wife, and when he had to go out on his rounds she found herself in a state of unaccustomed nervousness; she had maids in the house, but they were more nervous than she was, and added to her malaise; so she went round to see Mrs. Willison, and lunched with her, and the two elderly ladies arranged to stay together till their husbands, doctor and banker, should return from the day's work.

At Monks Holme, too, the gloom of the last ten days, which had seemed on the point of lifting, had settled down again. Here it was not only the new and most shocking tragedy that caused depression; there were other and more personal reasons for distress. Winifred Hexman was in a state of remorse and uncertainty that were in no way lessened by the shameful exhilaration that she felt. She did not know what her future was to be now; she did not know what she wanted it to be. She had been swept off her feet by a sudden passion that she had long kept under rigid control; the very strictness of her upbringing had added to the force of the cataclysm when it fell upon her, and she had not the experience and knowledge of the world which would have enabled her to re-establish her ideas with reasonable calmness. With her husband she felt both shamed and resentful; her conscience urged her to tell him what had happened, her innate prudishness prevented her. The result was that she was by turns considerate, morose, affectionate, short-tempered, so that the wretched man did not know where he was, whether he had offended her, or she him; could not tell how to take her or how re-establish the better understanding that had seemed to be growing up between them.

It was a bitter disappointment to George Hexman. After the misfire of their game of golf on Saturday the conversation he had had with Winifred over the tea-table had seemed, after an uneasy start, to be holding out great promise of renewed understanding and even affection between them. Winifred had appeared to be touched by his belated recognition of her loneliness and his own selfish behaviour. The sudden irruption of Chief Inspector Myrtle, with his startling revelations and hostile cross-questioning, had seemed likely to throw their relations back into the state of uneasy suspicion in which they had been since the old man's death; but Winifred had reacted very finely, standing by him while Myrtle pressed his offensive and giving him sympathy and comfort when the bloody man had gone.

So now George could not understand what had upset his wife again, whether it was this ghastly business of the old Vintons—who, after all, meant very little to either of them —or whether it was his own shortcomings that were 'coming

back ', like the evil fumes of a ' night before ', and causing
her to go sour on him. He would like to go out and have
a drink with some men, people whom he could understand
and whose moods didn't have to be humoured, but he
was afraid to put himself in the wrong again with Win,
so he gloomed and read the paper and made spasmodic
efforts to get a cheerful conversation going, and spent his
day and his evening in the aimless depression that is the
special privilege of a man who has no work to do.

There were, of course, men and women in Great Norne
who did not allow the even tenor of their life to be disturbed by mysterious killings and alarmist rumours. Old
Ebenezer Creech finished his day's work—a full day's
work, without a minute wasted in talk—and took his
solitary way home at his usual leisured pace. He had
heard the tales buzzing round the work-shops of Barton's
yard, but had spent no time in discussing them; men had
joined him in his walk, but his slow pace had got on their
nerves, and they had left him for other companions as
agitated as themselves.

When he got home Ebeneezer washed his hands and
settled down to the solid meal that his faithful wife,
murder or no murder, had prepared for him. Then he
sat silently listening while her pent-up nervousness poured
out in a spate of words, stories, theories, questions—not
expecting an answer, knowing Eb—plans and prophecies.
As soon as his meal was digested and his first pipe finished
Eb rose from his chair and, walking slowly to the door,
took down muffler and overcoat from their hook.

" Ebenezer Creech! You're not going out to-night
and leave me and the girls to be murdered where we sit? "

Again the torrent of words, begot of fears for him as
much as for herself, eddied round and over the old man.
Slowly he wound the muffler round his neck, slowly

shrugged himself into the overcoat, pulled his old cloth cap over his scanty hair. Opening the door, he turned for a moment towards his wife.

" Back at eight," he said, and walked out into the night. With two strapping girls just back from their work, and with stout-hearted neighbours on either side to come to a quick rescue, he had no fear for the old woman. As for himself, on his lonely walk to and from the ' Silver Herring '—well, it would take more than a looney killer to keep Eb Creech from the nightly pint that had been his, man and boy, for the fifty years of his working life in Great Norne.

Of the same mould was Jansy Hirdle. Through a rosy mist of gin-laced tea and tobacco smoke she had listened to the talk going on between her friendly neighbour and the man who was some sort of a copper. She was feeling too mellow to follow it very closely, but she had realised that there was hostility, and perhaps even danger, in the policeman's questions. If Nat Blake—Nat to Jansy, though no one else in Great Norne called him by that name—wanted her help she was ready to give it him at any moment and to any extent, even to the use of the sharply pointed scissors that lay on the workbox beside her. But Nat seemed quite happy and able to look after himself, and presently followed the fellow out into the night, no doubt to see him off and then perhaps slip up to the ' Herring ' and come back later with another bottle of comfort and happy dreams for an old woman.

Nat Blake had told her the rumours that were going round the town, told her about the two old hens who had had their necks wrung the night before. But Mother Hirdle was too old to worry much about death. It wasn't likely that anyone was going to bother about killing an old woman like her, a poor old woman with nothing

. . . well, only that stockingful under the flagstone that no one knew about. And if they did—well, what did a year or two more or less matter when you were past eighty. And there was always Nat, a good neighbour, a kind good boy to look after her, to comfort her with what she fancied, and sworn to see her properly laid out and buried like a lady.

So Jansy Hirdle smoked and dozed and dreamed of her young days, when she had been a wild girl and the young fellows had been daft about her and she had lived her life to the full and not regretted it, even though it had meant ending her days in a lonely wooden shack by the saltings. Not so lonely either, because hadn't she got a kind neighbour, Nat Blake? . . .

Nat Blake—Crooky Blake—meanwhile was buffeting his way through wind and rain not fifty yards behind the dimly seen figure of Inspector Joss. He wanted to be quite sure that the detective was really going away and was not intending to slip back and poke his nose in where he wasn't wanted. Nobody likes a policeman asking questions, nobody likes him poking his nose and prying, least of all Crooky Blake, whose activities were not confined to outside-portering, and who was particularly anxious that his wooden castle by the saltings should not suffer invasion and search by hostile officialdom; he was prepared to go to quite considerable lengths to prevent that.

But Joss walked steadily on into the town, and when he was satisfied that this was true intent, and not subterfuge, Crooky left his trail and swung away towards his second home—the public bar of the 'Silver Herring'. He found it strangely empty. Jasper Blossom was there behind the bar, large and hearty as ever, though perhaps less rosy about the gills. Rose was there, too, her colour no wit diminished—but, then, it came from the same pot as usual.

Eb Creech was just settling himself in his accustomed seat behind his accustomed pint, silent and self-possessed as ever. Besides him Charlie Trott, the postman, and a handful of fishermen made up the company.

"Where's it going to end? that's what I want to know," Trott was asking as Blake came in.

"End among the worrrms, as Josh would say," chipped in Crooky with a grin. "Where is the mouldy, anyway?"

"Wind in his funnel, seemingly," commented Ben Hard.

"Ah, it's vertical in many chimneys to-night," said Blossom, helping himself to a tot of courage.

"Staying home with their wives, most of them," said Rose, "and quite right too."

"Well, what about that engineering fellow, Plett? he's only a visitor; he can't have got a wife here."

"Engineer?" queried Blake, with a cock of his shaggy eyebrow.

"Well, he is, isn't he?"

Crooky sniffed loudly.

"Dick, I reckon," he replied, taking a deep pull at his tankard.

The company stared.

"What? That chap?" asked the landlord. "What makes you say that?"

The porter grinned.

"Oh, I don't know. I don't know nothing. I just sits on my barrow and thinks. But when an engineering fellow spends two hours of his own time in the police-station, without going there under escort, I puts two and two together and makes it Dick."

"Well, I'm blowed. And you brought him here your-self, didn't you, Crooky?"

There was a general laugh at this sally.

"Did he feel in your pockets, Crooky?" "Find any rabbits?" "Have you got him at home now?"

The outer door opened with a crash, and a rush of wind and rain burst into the room, bearing with it a white-faced man with his arm in a sling. It was the sexton, Josiah Chell.

"Holy Martha! give me a tot of brandy, quick," he gasped. "A great chimney-pot smashed into the road not five yards from me!"

And so the wind of God and the wind of words and fear swept round the roofs and ceilings of Great Norne, while women huddled together in terror, and men, little less afraid, comforted them with brave words and long-forgotten caresses. And somewhere in the darkness death lay in wait, choosing a fresh victim, perfecting a final plan.

CHAPTER XXII

Stinkin' Fish

THE more he thought over it the stronger became Myrtle's
conviction that the key to this problem lay in the death of
the Reverend Theobald Torridge. Although he might
not be able to prove it, after the lapse of so much time, he
felt certain that the Vicar had been murdered. It
infuriated him that the well-intentioned but incompetent
Dr. Faundyce should have missed the vital clue; if,
after realising the presence of whisky in the mouth, he had
carried out an immediate autopsy and found none in the
stomach, it would have proved beyond reasonable doubt
that Torridge's ' accidental ' death had been staged.

It was no use looking for that evidence now; the alcohol
would have evaporated in less than twenty-four hours.
Nor, after all this time, would it be very profitable to
reopen the inquiry into the Vicar's death; people's
memories were short, and it was unlikely that anyone
would have a clear recollection of what happened one
foggy night ten weeks ago—anyone, that is, except the
murderer, who would be likely to keep his memories to
himself. But Myrtle did not think it would be necessary
to prove to a jury that Torrridge had been murdered;
if this was a multiple-murder crime it would be sufficient
for his purpose to establish guilt on only one of them.
What he wanted to do was to satisfy himself about this
point, so that he could feel sure that he was basing his
theories on a correct premise.

The likeliest way to do this was to have a talk with someone who knew the late Vicar intimately, and it did not take
Myrtle long to discover a suitable person. Mrs. Torridge

had moved away from the neighbourhood, but, as she had gone to live with relatives, she had not taken her staff with her; her late parlourmaid, in fact, was living in the town, having settled down to live with a widowed sister. Myrtle knew that the morning was not a propitious time for calling on any lady, but he was too anxious to establish his point to allow a little matter of etiquette to delay him. So at eleven o'clock on the morning after the murder of the Miss Vintons he presented himself at Rose Cottage, a pleasant little brick-and-flint house on the eastern outskirts of the town. The door was opened by a middle-aged woman with greying hair, neat of figure, and wearing a short apron over her blue-stuff dress. Myrtle raised his hat.

" I have called to see Miss Jane Hollyer," he said.

" I am Miss Hollyer."

Myrtle held out his warrant card.

" If you could spare me a few minutes on an important matter? " he asked.

Jane Hollyer seemed rather taken aback by the sight of the official card.

" Oh," she said. " I . . . I don't know, I'm sure."

But she backed into the house, and Myrtle quickly followed.

" My sister's out shopping; it's her house really."

" I'm sorry to miss your sister, but in a way it's an advantage, because this is a very confidential matter."

Miss Hollyer hesitated.

" Then you'd better come into the parlour. Maggie'll be back any time."

She opened a door and led the way into a small room, grievously overcrowded with furniture of a genteel description. Portraits of a clergyman and his wife were prominently displayed upon a basis of knitted mats on the centre table.

" I'm sure I'd have lit a fire if I'd known you were coming," said the agitated ex-parlourmaid, fussing round the room before coming to rest upon the edge of a gilt chair. " Do take a seat, won't you, Mr. . . . er . . . ? "

" Myrtle. Now you'll understand that what I am going to ask you should not go any farther, Miss Hollyer, and I can assure you that I shall treat as entirely confidential anything you tell me. It is about your late employer, the Reverend Mr. Torridge."

" Oh ! "

Agitation increased upon Miss Hollyer's prim face.

" I'm afraid this may be a little bit of a shock to you, but we are not entirely satisfied that Mr. Torridge's death was accidental, as was supposed at the time. You will know, Miss Hollyer, that there have been a number of rather mysterious deaths in the town recently, and we are bound to satisfy ourselves about them all, even at the cost of causing some distress."

This speech was not entirely calculated to calm troubled nerves, so Myrtle hurried on :

" What I have to ask you is whether the late Vicar was in the habit of taking whisky."

" Whisky ? The Vicar ! "

Here, evidently, was a suggestion even more shocking than murder.

" Yes. I have a reason for asking. Did he take it himself, either at meals or as a pick-me-up ? "

" Never ! "

Miss Hollyer bridled with indignation.

" Never in all the twenty years I was with him did I see him touch the nasty stuff. He was teetotal, and so was madam."

" He wouldn't even have taken it if he was feeling poorly ? A cold coming on, perhaps."

" No, indeed; that he wouldn't."

" Very well, then. Now, did he ever carry whisky—in a flask or a bottle—when he visited the sick? "

" Never! He didn't hold with spirits—not even for an ill person, not even if it was ever so."

" Well, that's very definite. Now, Miss Hollyer, I am bound to ask you this, and I want you to believe that I only ask it because a matter of life or death may be involved in your answer. You will realise that we are all of us sometimes mistaken in our opinions of people; sometimes a man or a woman proves to have some weakness that we never suspected—even the best, the most unlikely person. Now, are you quite sure that you might not be mistaken in this? I must tell you that when the Vicar died he was found to have in his pocket the broken fragments of a bottle or a flask that had contained whisky, and there was trace of whisky, too, in his mouth. Now, if you are right, how is that to be explained? "

The look of horrified incredulity on Jane Hollyer's face was extremely convincing.

" Oh! I just don't believe it. I don't believe it. Why, I've known him twenty years and never . . . Where would the whisky come from? There was none in the house, that I'll swear. If he'd had a weakness . . . like you say . . . I'd have been bound to know it. You can't look after a gentleman twenty years without knowing all about him."

" No man is a hero to his own valet," murmured the detective.

" Oh, he didn't have a valet. I did all his clothes, not only valeting, but mending and seeing to the washing. And I looked after the wine. Not that there was much— only a bottle or two of claret and port that he had from the grocers from time to time in case anyone took it that came to dinner. Only we didn't entertain much; dull it was in a way, as Cook always said. But there wasn't never any whisky; that was spirits, and the Vicar didn't hold with them.''

Myrtle felt that, to his own satisfaction at any rate, the parlourmaid's story might be taken as proving that the whisky found on the person of Mr. Torridge had been planted there by some other person for his own, probably sinister, purpose—the purpose which Myrtle had classified as 'denigration'. He was prepared now definitely to link up the Vicar's death with those of Colonel Cherrington, Albert Gannett, and the Miss Vintons, and his next step must be to find the connecting link between these rather variegated victims. Superintendent Kneller had suggested that the crimes might have a religious basis, and certainly the idea was worth looking into. For the moment he was not inclined to attribute them to a religious maniac; there appeared to be too much cool, calculating method for any madman. But there might still be a religious basis, or one concerned with persons connected with the church. Gannett did not appear to fit in to this, but the old ladies might well do so, and the Vicar and Colonel Cherrington, his churchwarden, certainly did.

So Myrtle, following his own suggestion of the night before, decided to look up the People's Churchwarden, who, he had discovered from Inspector Heskell, was that much-respected townsman and pillar of local trade, Mr. Samuel Coote, ironmonger. Mr. Coote—a rotund figure of immeasurable dignity—evidently knew Myrtle by sight, because, without waiting to be asked, he at once led him into his own house, which connected with the shop. He was not, however, at all helpful. It was perfectly evident to Myrtle that Coote, like nearly everybody else in Great Norne, was now in a highly nervous condition. He probably thought that the very fact of his being questioned by the police might expose him to danger of attack by the maniac who, in the common belief, was now ranging the town. No doubt this accounted for the alacrity with which the ironmonger had led his dangerous visitor out of the public eye.

Having listened, with growing consternation, to the detective's theory of a connecting link between these various murders and his suggestion that that link might be the church, Mr. Coote hurriedly assured Myrtle that he himself knew of no grounds which might be said to support such a horrible idea. He had, as a matter of fact, only been in the town fifteen years, and modestly suggested that it was only lack of enthusiasm on the part of better-qualified Churchmen that had permitted his own selection for an office of such responsibility as he now held. He had heard that there had been some trouble three or four years before his arrival, but, though he had heard the story, he could not vouch for it of his own knowledge, and there-fore declined to say anything.

"Where it's a case of ' stinkin' fish ', Chief Inspector, I'm not the man to cry it unless I know the facts for myself. But I'll tell you the man who could probably give you the truth from an unbiassed point of view, and that's the Squire. I've heard that he knew all about it, and he's one that you could trust."

Myrtle had only heard vague references to ' the Squire ' before, and had not met Mr. Beynard. From what Coote told him he was surprised that the Chief Constable or Superintendent Kneller had not suggested reference to him earlier. He thanked the ironmonger, and noticed with amusement the relief and speed with which the little man ushered him off the premises.

The Manor House was a mile or two outside the town,

and beyond the gutted Manor Farm. Myrtle borrowed Inspector Heskell's car, and arrived there before noon. It was a large, rambling house, some of it dating back to Tudor times, but the haphazard additions of succeeding Beynards had not entirely destroyed its charm. The inside was as haphazard as the exterior; no artistic ' decorator ' had ever been permitted to lay his or her efficient but devastating hand upon the jumble of furniture, curtains, coverings, carpets or wall-colourings of all periods which gave the house its air of untidy homeliness.

Without being asked to explain himself or his visit, Myrtle was at once shown by a dilapidated butler into the Squire's study. Norris Beynard was seated at a large table which was smothered in a chaotic assortment of books, papers, envelopes, and writing paraphernalia, from which it would appear impossible that order or meaning could ever be obtained. When his host rose Myrtle saw that he was a tall, thin man, of between fifty-five and sixty years of age. His face might have been handsome had he not spoilt it by a straggling moustache which hid his mouth; his figure might have been good if it had not been bent by much poring over books; his normal expression was abstracted and rather gloomy, but when he did smile his eyes lit up with a twinkle that had great charm and even youthfulness.

" Come in, Chief Inspector," he said, holding out his hand. " I know you by sight, though I have not had the pleasure of meeting you before. But I am afraid ' pleasure ' is hardly the just word to apply to your visit to Great Norne. Terrible things have been happening in our old town—last night's tragedy above all—but I am too much of a recluse to understand the meaning of it. Sit down; that chair . . . tumble those books on to the floor. I am always in trouble over the state of my room; I won't let anyone else tidy it, and I always forget to do it myself."

Myrtle thought a little licence in rambling on might put the old gentleman—though he perhaps was hardly that—into a forthcoming mood.

" I am sure you have not come about any little peccadilloes of my own," continued the Squire, " though my knowledge of the modern law is so flimsy that I might easily stray into a breach of it. My sister does all that is practical in this house, not only as regards domestic matters, but all the miserable business of income-tax returns and bill-paying. I am a useless dreamer and scribbler, and I am afraid my conversation is loose and probably maudlin. You must tell me just how I can help you."

Wasting no further time, Myrtle explained his theory of the murders in words which he thought would have been comprehensible to a child, fearing that any subtlety would be wasted upon one so vague as Mr. Beynard seemed to be. To his surprise the Squire accepted both theory and suggestion without question.

" That appears the logical conclusion, Chief Inspector," he said, " once you have established the fact that poor Torridge's death was no accident. I confess that that possibility had not crossed my mind, and the news of Beatrice and Emily Vinton's death only reached me an hour or so ago. I felt quite dazed by it, and had not tried to put my thoughts in order. They are, you will have realised, no doubt, devoted Churchwomen, so that there appears only too sound a basis for your suspicion."

" Mr. Gannett's the trouble, sir; I don't see how he fits into my Church theory."

" Oh, but surely that is quite simple. Gannett was a man of standing before the war; it was only that unfor-

tunate wound that upset his balance and caused his
unhappy propensity for drink.   But before the war, and
even after, until things got too bad, he was a member of
the Church Council."

" Ah ! "

Myrtle's eyes sparkled.

" That does seem to lock the picture, sir.   But what's
the meaning of it?   What can it all be about? "

Beynard passed his hand across his eyes.   Myrtle saw
that his face had taken on an expression of haggard
anxiety.

" You must let me collect my thoughts.   There is, I am
afraid, a deep tragedy behind all this, and I blame myself
for not realising it before.   If I were not so immersed in
my own bookish affairs I might even have foreseen—perhaps prevented—what happened last night."

He paused again, and Myrtle waited impatiently.

" Chief Inspector, has anyone told you of the tragedy
of Emily Barton? "

" Only vaguely, sir.   I've met Mr. Barton, and I know
he lost his wife in tragic circumstances many years ago.
But what they were exactly, I don't know."

" I hoped it had all been forgotten, for poor Barton's
sake.   I dread what this may mean.   But I see that I
must tell you the story."

So it was coming at last.   Myrtle could not doubt that
he was very near the solution of his problem.   He would
have liked to take shorthand notes of what he was going
to hear, but was afraid of upsetting the narrator, who
might well be temperamental.

" Richard Barton inherited his father's business as a
builder when he was only a little over twenty, in about
1910.   He was always an ambitious young fellow, and he
worked hard and made a success of it.   He had plenty

of friends then, but when the war came in 1914 Richard made no attempt to join up, and he lost a lot of his popularity, which was only natural. Whether he got exemption as a builder, or whether he had some physical disability I'm not quite sure—I'm afraid that's where my vagueness comes in—but the fact remains that he never went out at all, or even got into uniform. He was a proud chap, and the cold-shouldering he got didn't do his temper any good. Early in the war—I think I heard he was about twenty-seven at the time—he married a girl called Ellen Vaughan, a very pretty girl, the daughter of a widow who had settled in Great Norne not long before and about whom—the mother, I mean—there was a good deal of talk and mystery. As a matter of fact she died soon after her daughter's marriage, and, if she hadn't, the tragedy might never have happened."

Norris Beynard reached absent-mindedly for a cigarette from a big box half buried under his papers. Myrtle noticed that his fingers, as well as his straggling moustache, were stained with nicotine.

"I believe the marriage was happy enough for a year or so, and then Richard began to show signs of being jealous. Young fellows home on leave used to throw their eyes at any pretty girl, and Ellen certainly was that. She was only seventeen or so when she married, so she hadn't got a great deal of balance, and the admiration she got rather went to her head, I suppose. I don't think she meant any harm, but she probably inherited from her mother a . . . what shall I say? . . . lightness of head and heart that you wouldn't find in our native girls. Barton took it very badly. It wasn't long before he was bullying her, and though she stood up to him for a bit, her nerve began to go after a time. For a year or so she kept away from any kind of social life, and though that cooled down Richard's suspicions, it didn't make her own life any happier. Then, not long after the war ended—somewhere about 1919 or early 1920—a young sailor came to Great Norne on leave—not a fisherman, a naval rating. He met Ellen and fell in love with her and she with him."

Myrtle wondered at the precision of this story from a philosophical recluse who accused himself of woolly-mindedness.

" I needn't go into all that; it's a common enough story, but fortunately it doesn't always turn out so tragically. Richard had been very strictly brought up. His father was an almost fanatical churchman, and the boy tended in the same direction. He attended Church regularly—Communion once a month and all that. When the war came, and it was difficult to find any young or even middle-aged men to run things, the Vicar suggested putting Richard Barton on the Parochial Church Council; he was elected, and took it very seriously. I was a member myself at the time, and that was how I first came to know him. Then came this unfortunate infatuation of Ellen's for the young sailor, and there was terrible trouble. How far things went, and whether he actually caught them *flagrante delicto*, I don't know; but Richard Barton brought the matter up before the Church Council—most unwisely, and even wrongly in my opinion."

" If I may interrupt a minute, sir," said Myrtle. " What was this sailor's name? "

Norris Beynard frowned, tapping his fingers on the writing-pad in front of him.

" I don't know that I can tell you that," he said. " It's a long time ago, and he was only a bird of passage, staying with an aunt or something. Bentham? Benbow? Some name like that, I think. As so often happens, he had his fun and sailed away, leaving the girl to face the music. And such music! The full blast of the church organ. I confess that it sickened me; the whole thing struck me as utterly un-Christian, in the most precise meaning of the word."

The Squire was silent for a minute, picking nervously at the blotting-paper.

"What happened, sir?" prompted Myrtle quietly.

"As I told you, Barton brought the matter before the Council, asked whether his wife, as an adulteress, should continue to receive the Sacrament. My dear chap, it was appalling; the most embarrassing thing I've ever sat through in my life. I would have walked out, only I thought I might be able to smooth things over. But I couldn't; Torridge—the Vicar—leapt at it, and Cherrington egged him on. Beatrice Vinton was nearly as bad, and one or two of the townspeople, seeing which way the big guns were pointing, backed them up. I think I probably left my own protest too late; I'm a diffident speaker, and a poor one at that. Anyway, I was a voice crying in the wilderness, and it ended in Torridge formally advising Barton that his wife should not attend Communion until she had fully satisfied him of her repentance. As I say, it fairly sickened me, and I resigned from the Council then and there."

"Barton was present throughout the discussion, sir?"

"No. He was asked to retire while the thing was discussed, and was then brought back to hear the verdict—if that was the appropriate word."

"Then he probably did not know who had spoken one way and who another?"

" No, not at the time, but he may have heard afterwards. Of course the whole thing was over the town within twenty-four hours; that's the worst of those mixed committees. You can imagine the talk, the scandal. Poor Ellen could not put her face outside her house, and I'm afraid she got no mercy from Richard inside it. Within a week she hanged herself in her husband's workshop."

Myrtle drew in his breath sharply.

" And then, sir? What happened then? "

" Everyone felt very ashamed of themselves, when it was too late—poor Barton, I think, most of all, though he did not admit it to a soul. His reaction was curious. Having brought the matter before the Church himself, he appeared to blame the Church for what happened. In any case he never came to a service again, still less to a Council meeting. He dropped all his friends and buried himself in his work. He never showed a sign of remorse at his own behaviour; he just shut himself out of the lives of his fellow-men, except in his professional capacity, and at that—his job as a builder—he was supremely good. At first people were inclined to cold-shoulder him, and his business dropped away, but he was so clearly and outstandingly the best builder in Great Norne, that that did not last very long. To-day he has seventy-five per cent of the work in the place—and still not a friend."

" Not one, sir? "

The Squire looked faintly uncomfortable.

"Well, perhaps I might be allowed to call myself a friend," he admitted. " He does come up to have a talk with me sometimes, or a game of chess. I really think it's the only time he becomes human."

" No doubt that is because you didn't condemn his wife," suggested the detective.

" I don't know. I don't know, I'm sure. We've never

talked about it. I was disgusted with him at the time for parading his trouble—and his wife's trouble—before the Church Council. I saw nothing of him for a long time. Then I realised that he was leading a very solitary life, and I thought I might help him to become more normal. I happened to discover that he was reading some philosophical books of varying merit, and I offered to guide him a bit. He shied away from me at first, but one night he came up here, and he has been coming, at odd times, ever since. That must be for the last ten or twelve years."

Both men remained silent for a time, Myrtle thinking over what he had heard.

" That's a very significant story, sir," he said at last. " I must take a little time to think it over. But one thing I'd like to know now. Who were the other members of the Church Council? "

Beynard nodded.

" Yes, I expected you would ask that," he said. " A number have either died or moved away from the district. Torridge was Vicar, as you know; Cherrington his warden; Coote People's . . . no, it was before Coote's time; Pybus was People's warden—he died a few years afterwards. Then there was Gannett and Miss Beatrice Vinton and . . . let me see . . . that's about the lot."

" And Gannett was against Mrs. Barton too, sir? "

" No, no. I'm sure he wouldn't have taken a line like that. But he wasn't there. He had already begun to fall from grace, as Torridge called it, and he didn't often come to a meeting. Torridge spoke sharply to him not long afterwards about his drinking and non-attendance, and poor Gannett resigned."

Myrtle nodded.

" But, of course, he was a member of the Council at the time. And Miss Emily Vinton, sir? "

"No, she never was. She didn't like Committee meetings, she said—small blame to her."

"Then the only other member was yourself, sir?"

The Squire smiled.

"Yes," he said. "I am the sole survivor."

CHAPTER XXIII

Closing In

AS he drove away from the Manor House, Chief Inspector Myrtle's thoughts were so deeply engaged in the story he had just heard that he hardly noticed the scudding sheets of rain that swept across the bleak winter countryside. His way lay across the swollen Gaggle Brook, and he was momentarily conscious that the car slowed down as it approached the river.

" The old bridge'll be in the sea before long," said his chauffeur as he drove cautiously across the ricketty structure. A glimpse of swirling brown waters barely distracted the detective's thoughts from the problem that he had to solve.

Myrtle did not doubt now that the story told by Norris Beynard, the eighteen-year-old tragedy of Richard Barton's wife, provided the key to the mysterious murders of the last few weeks. But that did not mean that any open book lay before him. Why should this ancient trouble suddenly have flared into active, violent life now? Was Barton himself the murderer—the conclusion to which the mind naturally jumped? Of if not he, who else had cause to avenge himself on those harsh judges who might be thought to have condemned Ellen Barton to her self-inflicted death? Was it the sailor who had kissed and sailed away? Was it some relative of Ellen's? The Squire had said little about her, except that she was the daughter of a widowed mother who herself had some mystery attached to her past. It would be necessary to probe these alternatives before deciding that the sullen builder was himself the brutal killer.

Above all, it was necessary, not only to *prove* what he
suspected, but to prevent any further development of the
tragedy.   It was quite obvious that Norris Beynard himself
must be regarded as being in danger.   Although he had
befriended the injured husband, ostracised by his fellows,
and although Barton was on friendly terms with him,
discussing philosophy and playing chess, this might all be
a cover to intended attack.   It must be remembered that
Barton had at first rejected Beynard's advances, and then
one day had suddenly turned up of his own accord at the
Manor House and got on to terms of intimacy with its
owner.   It was, of course, the case that Beynard had not
been one of the harsh judges; he had stood up for Ellen
Barton when the Church Council was discussing the case;
Barton might have discovered this, and so removed the
Squire from his list of intended victims—if he was indeed
the murderer.   But it was not safe to count on that
possibility;   Beynard   must   be   regarded   as   on   the
danger list, and danger might become death at any
time.

Myrtle's thoughts had reached this stage when he
arrived at Great Norne police-station.   He had at first
intended to ask Superintendent Kneller to come over for
a conference, but he now decided that it would be wiser,
even though it caused initial delay, to go to Headquarters
and discuss the matter there, not only with Kneller, but
with the Chief Constable.   It would be easier to make a
comprehensive plan there, rather than in the constricted
space of this small station, where it was not even certain
that a discussion would not be overheard by constables
and casual visitors.   So Myrtle put through a call to
Snottisham and asked for a conference there.   He also
rang the Yard and arranged for the return of Sergeant
Plett, together with a detective-constable; he thought

that the County detective force could handle the rest of the work that would have to be done.

He would have liked to have had a word with Inspector Joss before going to his conference, to find out if there was any development in the line he had been instructed to follow; but Joss was still out trying to make contact with the porter, Blake—as Inspector Heskell told him—and Myrtle could not wait for his return.

The Chief Constable was astonished to hear the story which Myrtle had been told by Norris Beynard. He had only come to the County in 1925, and so had not heard it before. Kneller, on the other hand, had spent all his service in the County, but before coming to Headquarters had been in the Southern Division, and so had only heard vaguely of the suicide of a builder's wife. The whole story of the ' inquisition ' by a Parochial Church Council seemed fantastic to Major Statford, but he knew enough to realise that fantastic and even cruel things did happen in religious communities, though in the easy-going Church of England less often than in others.

It was obvious that there must be a deeper digging of past history, but the immediate point that concerned the Chief Constable was the safety of the Squire of Great Norne, who, though a quiet, retiring man, was still the representative of one of the oldest families in the County. He therefore arranged with Superintendent Kneller and Myrtle that the County Constabulary would maintain a watch round the Manor House, particularly at night, whilst the Scotland Yard detectives should keep an eye on Barton himself. In the meantime, the other possibilities must be carefully examined; it would not do to concentrate all attention on Barton if he was not in fact the killer.

Dusk was just falling as Myrtle got back to Great Norne. It would be some hours yet before Plett and the other

C.I.D. detective arrived, so Myrtle arranged that Inspector Heskell and one of his constables should keep an eye on the builder's house. Joss was still out, but Heskell suggested that it would be worth while having a talk with Police-Constable Flaish, who had been in Great Norne or the near neighbourhood all his service, and was bound to know a good deal about the story of Ellen Barton.

The ponderous and hearty Flaish—inevitably nicknamed Flesh in reference to his figure or Flash in criticism of his speed—was delighted to have a chance of airing his local knowledge. He recalled the story well; a pretty piece Ellen Vaughan had been, and why she had cottoned to that surly fellow Barton—surly even in those days, though not to compare with what he became afterwards—passed the imagination; but there, girls, you never could tell with them. Her mother had been a good looker in her time, too, but she hadn't any use for men—not after she came to Great Norne, at any rate. No, he did not call to mind any particular man being interested in that direction; he certainly knew of no one, either relative or friend of Ellen Vaughan or her mother, who would be likely to bottle up revengeful sentiments for eighteen years and then suddenly start wringing necks and bashing heads.

The young sailor, cause of all the trouble, had been a lively young spark, what Flaish could remember of him, though he had only been in the town a matter of weeks. Staying with old Miss Dufflin—an aunt, he thought. She had been a character, too; a sharp-tongued old lady with a bit of money, and not afraid to hold her own opinion and let others know it, too. She had died about three years after the trouble, and very upset she'd been, because her nephew had never come to see her again. So far as Flaish knew, that was the only time the lad had come to the town.

Benbow had been the young fellow's name, but the Christian name had slipped his memory, if ever he had heard it. Lively? Yes, that he was, because in three or four weeks he had cast his eyes at Ellen Barton and turned her head over heels . . . well, he wouldn't go into details, but it was common talk that Dick Barton hadn't been so very far wrong when he called her a rude word before the Church Council. A rum do that had been; how a man could go and lay his own wife's shame before a lot of clergymen and old maids passed common understanding. Got what he deserved, Barton had, so folks said, though it was rough that a young girl like his wife should have had to lay violent hands on herself.

Flaish did not know whether the young sailor had realised what Barton was doing. Certainly he had left before the trouble became public; recalled to his ship by telegram, Miss Dufflin had said, before his leave was up. Whether he knew about it after, or even that Ellen was dead, Flaish couldn't say; certainly he had never come back. But there, sailors were like that; no doubt Ellen Barton was just one girl in one port to him, and he'd likely forgotten her as soon as his leave was up.

Myrtle decided that he would ask the Yard to get in touch with the Admiralty. Even without a number or a Christian name it should not be difficult to trace a comparatively rare name like Benbow. But it certainly did not seem likely that a young man who had shown no interest at the time of the tragedy would suddenly come to light eighteen years afterwards with a series of bloody murders of people whom he had probably never met. Besides, there was ample evidence that the killer was a local man, with intimate knowledge of the ways, houses and households of his victims.

As there was still an hour and a half before Plett's train

was due, Myrtle went down to the neighbourhood of Barton's house and yard to satisfy himself that the watch was being intelligently and efficiently kept. The uniformed Inspector and his constable, Bridger, had disguised themselves for the nonce in plain clothes, and at first Myrtle had some difficulty in finding them, but when he did he realised that the apparently slow-witted Inspector knew his job well enough. Promising to bring a relief as soon as his C.I.D. colleagues had arrived and had a meal, Myrtle returned to the police-station.

He found that Joss had at last returned, and at once asked for a full account of his activities—for Myrtle was not a man who believed that his own thoughts and his own investigations were the only ones worth hearing about. Joss told him of his inquiry for suspicious characters—or indeed any characters—seen in the neighbourhood of ' The Chestnuts ' during the vital hours of the previous evening; he told how this inquiry had led to the discovery of no stranger and how the only ' suspicious character ' had been the outside-porter Blake, the suspicion in his case having been supplied by two small boys who had described him as ' lurking ' and ' squinting about him '. Joss would hardly have considered this worth following up if the porter's name had not been one of those given him by Inspector Heskell in reply to his inquiry for local men who might be candidates for the rôle of ' homicidal lunatic '. Why Heskell had picked on Chell and Blake for this category had not been very clear to Joss; neither, when interviewed, had struck him as being either weak in the head or violent in character, though Chell's humour had a churchyard turn and Blake certainly looked a tough nut.

There being nothing definite to take hold of in the case of Chell, Joss had, he explained, concentrated on the porter, who would have to explain his presence in the neighbourhood of ' The Chestnuts ' and also describe his movements on the occasions of the other murders. Joss gave Myrtle the man's answers, and explained the two points that he thought could and should be checked; he had, in fact, checked them after leaving Blake at the hut on the saltings. Blake had said that he had passed the Vintons' house ' after dark '—later he had given the time as ' nigh on seven '—on his way to tell the ironmonger, Coote, that an expected package had not yet arrived at the station—a fact which he had ascertained earlier in the day, but forgotten to mention. He, Joss, had just called at the ironmonger's and discovered that it was indeed the case that the porter had called there some time about seven o'clock; Mr. Coote had not been there himself, but a maid—a very young girl—had taken the message; she had not been very certain about the time, but put it at ' about seven ' because she had begun to lay for supper, which the Coote family took at eight o'clock.

Joss had then gone on to the station, and there again found confirmation of Blake's story. The parcels clerk remembered his calling in the previous afternoon to inquire about a parcel for Mr. Coote; he put the time at about half-past three.

" That's before the first murder could have happened, sir," said Joss, " but it goes to prove Blake's tale for what it's worth."

" How do you know the murder must have happened after three-thirty? " asked Myrtle sharply. " Simply because it got dark later? "

Joss shook his head.

" No, sir. You haven't seen that maid of the Vintons to-day? I called in at the Cottage Hospital to inquire on my way back just now. She's all right; they're keeping her quiet for a day or two to get over the shock, but they let me see her for five minutes. She told me she went back in the afternoon to give the paralysed lady her tea and draw the curtains and make up the fire. She left again at about four-thirty, and the old lady was all right then."

"A useful time limit, though I didn't expect it earlier. Ask her anything else?"

Joss hesitated.

"Yes, sir, I did, though I don't know that I ought to have. There's one thing that's been puzzling me about that murder, and that's the blind-cord they were strangled with. You remember telling me last night that he probably cut it down in front of the poor old lady's very eyes, because she was dumb. That worried me, sir. I wondered whether being dumb was the same as not being able to make a noise. So I asked Minnie—that's the maid —and she told me that old Miss Vinton—Miss Beatrice she called her—*could* make a noise all right. She spilt some hot water on her once, and the old lady let out a squeal that brought her sister running up to see what was the matter."

Myrtle looked thoughtfully at the younger detective.

"That's very interesting, Joss," he said. "I wonder just what it implies."

.　　.　　.　　.　　.

Detective-Sergeant Plett and his companion, Detective-Constable Gwylliam, had been posted soon after 10 p.m., and were relieved by Myrtle just before daybreak, which was about 7 a.m. They had not seen anything of Barton, who had been described to them, nor any activity of any kind near his house.

"That's all right," said Myrtle. "I'll be seeing the gentleman myself later in the day. I've got one or two

questions to ask him. No need to keep a watch here
during daytime; the County people are keeping an eye
on the Squire."

As they walked back towards the police-station, Myrtle
asked Plett what he had seen of the outside-porter, Blake,
during his visits to the ' Silver Herring ', and particularly
on the night of the Gannett fire. Joss had told him Blake's
account of his movements that night, how he and his
friends had been discussing the inquest on the Colonel
and had got ' a load aboard ', how he had been going to
see Winch, the landlord of the ' Royal George ', about a job
but, finding his legs unsteady, had had a nap in his barrow
instead. Blake had declared that he had seen the flames of
the fire before he ' popped off '.

Plett laughed.

" I can confirm that," he said. " Whatever else Blake
may have done—and I should think he's not above a bit
of dirty work if there's money in it—he didn't set alight to
Gannett. He was too soused for that. They all got a bit
tight that evening; Blake was staggering when he went
out, and he filled a flask with gin before he left. I
followed not long after him . . . you'll remember, sir,
that I had to report to you at 8 p.m. . . . and I saw
the flames from the harbour, too, though they weren't
much more than a flicker then. I hadn't gone far before I
stumbled across Blake asleep in his barrow, stinking of
gin and tight as an owl. No, I'm his alibi for that job,
sir."

Myrtle shrugged his shoulders.

" Anyway, there doesn't seem anything to connect him
with these murders, though he certainly was outside ' The
Chestnuts ' at a very tricky time last night. I don't think
myself that we need look much farther than Barton, but
how we're going to prove anything against him is a very

different story. Whoever did these jobs is a cunning devil."

"Have you anything to connect him, sir? Apart from the old story?" asked Plett, who had only heard the barest outline of late developments while he ate his supper the previous night.

Myrtle shook his head.

"Not much. But there are some significant pointers. It was he who put the cupboard into Colonel Cherrington's house that the murderer must have hidden in . . . well, his carpenter put it in, actually, but Barton must have known about it, and that's the point that matters. And who knows better than a builder how to get in and out of a window, or force a lock, for the matter of that? May have had a spare key, even; Barton does three-quarters of the building work in Great Norne, they tell me."

Breakfast and the writing-up of his notes occupied Myrtle till ten o'clock. Then, having detailed Joss to make further local inquiries about the sailor, Benbow, and, if possible, about Ellen Barton's relations, he walked back to the builder's yard. In the office he was told that Mr. Barton was out.

"Be back soon?" he asked casually.

"Couldn't say. He went off soon after lunch—dinner the men call it—yesterday. Hasn't come back yet."

Myrtle felt a stirring of interest.

"D'you know where he went?"

The young man shook his head.

"No idea. Don't confide in me. Not at forty bob a week."

Myrtle wondered whether it would be profitable, or wise, to ask questions of Barton's staff. While he thought, his eyes automatically wandered round the office. It was a large room, partly fitted up as a store-room for the tidier articles of the builder's trade. One wall was covered with racks and pigeon-holes. On one of these pigeon-holes the detective's eye came to rest. He strolled across and had a closer look. As he had thought, the pigeon-hole contained a large roll of blind-cord—green blind-cord.

" D'you sell this stuff? " he asked. " Retail, I mean."

The clerk shook his head.

" No, we don't retail. That's all stuff we use ourselves. You can get it, or something like it, at an ironmonger's. Coote's or Pillford's would stock it, I expect."

" Thanks. Look here, I wonder if you'd be so good as to slip out and ask your chaps if they know when your boss is likely to be back. Some of them might know."

The youth hesitated.

" I oughtn't to leave the office," he said.

Myrtle laughed.

" Oh well, if you can't trust a policeman, who can you trust? "

That bait was swallowed, and a moment later Myrtle was alone in the office. Taking a penknife from his pocket, he cut off a length of the green blind-cord. It was, he felt sure, identical with the cord that had strangled Beatrice and Emily Vinton.

CHAPTER XXIV

Breaking Covert

BARTON returned to his yard at midday. Myrtle had
not thought it worth while to keep the yard or the builder's
house which adjoined it under observation during the daytime, but he had arranged with the young clerk to give
him a ring as soon as his boss got back. In the meantime
Myrtle had reconsidered his course of action, and realised
that when he went down to see Barton that morning he
had not really thought out what line his interrogation
should follow. From his previous interview it was clear
that the man would volunteer no information and, saying
nothing—wisely from his own point of view—would give
nothing away. The interrogation would have to follow
one of two courses. The first alternative was a series of
tricky questions, designed to trap him into lies or admis-
sions which could later be used against him; the second
was a straightforward, blunt inquiry about his movements
on the occasions when the various murders were committed.

In one respect Myrtle was well placed for the first
alternative. As he was not yet certain that Barton was
the guilty man, and was not therefore in a position to
charge him—could not even say that he expected to charge
him—he need not caution him, and he could employ any
tricks he liked without running the risk of infringing the
Judges' Rules on evidence. Against that, he had so far
very little material evidence of any kind against Barton,
and therefore had very little upon which to base his tricky
questions. He would have much preferred to defer this
interrogation until he had more to work on, but the very

real danger of yet another murder being committed forced him to take what might prove to be premature action.

On the whole he thought that the second alternative was preferable—blunt questioning about movements. He could not force the man to answer, but if he did answer it would be very difficult for him, if he were guilty, to avoid inculpating himself. A clever man might well fake an alibi to cover a murder, but the faking of *four* alibis—alibis which would have to be supported by the evidence of other people—was surely impossible.

Myrtle did not propose to waste time upon the murder of Theobald Torridge. Apart from the lapse of time, the circumstances of the murder—a blow struck at some uncertain time on a foggy night—made it practically impossible to pin it on to any individual; or, if not impossible, at least it would be a slow and uncertain business. None the less, Myrtle still regarded that murder as the key to the mystery, because it was only after he had established, or at any rate satisfied himself, that it *was* murder that he had realised the nature of the connecting link.

On the other three murders, the dates of which were very recent, he proposed to question Barton very closely, and he flattered himself that it would take a very clever man to hoodwink him.

There was, however, one other respect in which he accused himself of carelessness on his earlier visit that morning. If Barton was a murderer, on the grand and brutal scale which these killings demanded, he could be little removed from the insane, and he might be extremely dangerous if he found himself in peril. Although to attack a police-officer would be a fatal mistake for him to make, that would be no consolation to the police-officer after he was dead!

So when Myrtle started off for his second call, which he did at a little before two, he took with him an escort in the form of Inspector Joss, who would remain outside, but within close call. He also carried an automatic in his overcoat pocket and a small whistle in the palm of his hand.

Myrtle had calculated that Barton would spend an hour or so in his office, giving a first glance through letters, et cetera, which had accumulated during his twenty-four-hour absence, and would then go into his house for a meal. That was where he hoped to find him, because there would be more privacy than in the office, and if the builder was mellowed by luncheon that would be all to the good.

The door was opened to him by a woman, whom he knew to be Barton's housekeeper.

" Mr. Barton in? "

" Yes, but I don't know that . . ."

" That's all right, marm; Mr. Barton's expecting me," lied Myrtle, and walked through into the kitchen.

The builder was sitting at the table, with the remains of a meal in front of him; he was reading a newspaper, but looked up quickly as the detective entered.

" Sorry to trouble you again, Mr. Barton," said Myrtle blandly, " but there are . . ."

" How did you get here? " interrupted Barton sharply.

" Oh, your housekeeper let me in, but I didn't want to bother her to introduce me."

He was conscious that the woman was hovering uncertainly behind him. He had feared that Barton would refuse to see him if he had sent in his name, though he knew that this brusque intrusion was risky.

The builder hesitated.

" All right, Mrs. Jackson," he said curtly.

As soon as the door was shut Myrtle settled himself, uninvited, on a kitchen chair.

" You've been away, Mr. Barton? "

" I have.   Does that matter to you? "

" It interests me.   Nobody seemed to know you were going or where you'd gone to."

Barton stared at him.   There was a flush of colour on his cheek and a jaw-muscle tightened.

" I went to see my sister who was taken ill suddenly. Snottisham, she lives.   Your fellows at Headquarters can check that."

" Thank you," said Myrtle calmly; " I'll ask them to. Now, you'll remember I was asking you some questions about Albert Gannett.   As a matter of routine—we're asking all his old acquaintances—would you mind telling me where you were on the night of the fire, the night he died?   Wednesday of last week that was, you'll remember."

Barton shrugged his shoulders.

" I don't know what the devil you're getting at," he said, " but I was here.   I'm here every evening—I suppose you mean the time of the fire? "

Myrtle nodded.

" I don't live a social life," continued Barton.   " Sometimes I work late in the office, but I'm always either there or here."

" Always?   Never go out in the evenings at all? "

" Very seldom."

" And is there anyone who can support that?   Your housekeeper, perhaps? "

" She goes home after I've had my supper.   I don't want any women living in my house."

There was a harsh note in Barton's voice as he answered.

" Well, that doesn't get us very far, then, does it? " said Myrtle.   " Now, there's another night I want to know about—Christmas Eve; easy to remember.   I believe there was some kind of a do on that evening—a dinner or something."

" If you mean the British Legion dinner, I wasn't there. I am not a member of the British Legion."

" Oh, I beg your pardon. Perhaps you were out at some other party? A lot of festivities around Christmas time."

Myrtle's tone was hearty, as if the Christmas spirit was still in him.

" I don't go in for festivities. I was here."

" Ah, I see, and . . . nobody with you? "

" Nobody."

This blunt negative, though it proved nothing, gave nothing away, Myrtle realised.

" Well, that's very unlucky. I must try again. Now, only a night or two ago—Tuesday night, to be exact. Where were you then, Mr. Barton, any time between four-thirty and ten p.m.? "

Myrtle saw the builder's hands tighten on the arms of his chair. His face was heavily flushed.

" What are you asking me these questions for? " he asked harshly. " That's the night the old ladies were killed. And Christmas Eve, that was when the Colonel shot himself. And Gannett's fire. What's it all about? "

Now was the time for shock tactics, Myrtle knew. Now was the moment for the tanks and cavalry to go in. He had tapped along the line, probing for a weak spot. He hadn't found it . . . but the tanks must go in. Haig or Allenby would have waited until the weak spot was found, but he, Myrtle, was under ' political ' pressure to strike at once; he must try to force Barton's hand.

Changing the tone of his voice to a sterner note he answered the builder's question.

" In the last ten weeks five people have died violent

deaths. Four at least of them were people against whom
you, Mr. Barton, are thought to have a grudge. They
were members of the Church Council before whom
you laid the story of your wife being unfaithful, and
they . . ."

Barton sprang to his feet, sending his chair crashing over
behind him. His face was livid now.

" Get out of my house ! "

Myrtle, too, had risen.

" You haven't answered my question," he said quietly.
" Where were you . . ."

" Get out, I say."

Barton took three strides across the room, and Myrtle
slipped his hand into his pocket. Then he saw the builder
check, the colour draining from his face; with a sound that
was almost a groan he slipped down into an armchair
and buried his face in his hands. At the same moment
the door opened and the scared face of the housekeeper
appeared.

" Your master's not well," said Myrtle, and walked out
of the house.

The fat was in the fire now. No finesse here. He had
blundered—with mixed metaphor—into this show-up
bald-headed, with all four feet splashing. Myrtle disliked his own performance and its outcome; it was not his
usual style. But it was what the Chief Constable of the
Country wanted and, technically at any rate, he was
working under the Chief Constable's orders. " Force
the fellow out into the open," were the last words he had
said to Myrtle, and, guilty or not, Barton was no longer in
the dark; if he wanted to kill Beynard he would be forced
to do it quick, without finesse of his own, and he would be
trapped.

So Myrtle, with a jerk of the head to Joss to follow him,

walked back to the police-station, silently chewing the cud of his self-criticism.

Arrived at the station, he quickly wrote out a report of what had happened, and asked Inspector Heskell to send it over to Headquarters by motor-cycle. Then he sat down to think out his future action. He was still uncertain in his mind about Barton's guilt. The background showed up the builder prominently; the whole tragic story pointed to him. He had the motive, the opportunity—those evenings alone, with no witness to mark his coming and going; the means—the cupboard in Colonel Cherrington's house so conveniently at his disposal, the means of entry into houses all of which he must, as a builder, know intimately, even the green blind-cord—though the murderer *apparently* had used cord cut in the house of his victims. But where was the proof?

There was none at all, and the detective was perfectly well aware of that inconvenient fact. In normal circumstances he would have set about quietly, methodically collecting evidence, and—if the man were guilty—within a few weeks, a few months perhaps, he would have proved him so. But a few weeks were not at his disposal. It was impossible, over a prolonged period of time, to keep a man under such close watch that he could not slip out of it and commit that other murder which was so strong a possibility. There was no time for finesse. He would try his utmost to find proof with all speed, but he must be prepared for instant action.

The first thing he must do was to secure a sample of Barton's finger-prints; there should be no great difficulty about that. Then he would have the cupboard in Colonel Cherrington's house hunted over again, both for prints and for any other tell-tale evidence; Myrtle felt sure that the murderer had worked in gloves, but there was always the possibility of a moment's carelessness. Then he would try to trace the purchase or possession of the yellow paper, on which the Colonel's 'threatening letter' had been written, to the builder. Bodley had not been able to help much about that, as it was a common type of paper. Still, if it had been bought locally, the colour might help somebody to remember selling it.

The possibility of Barton having been seen in the neighbourhood of the Vintons' house, Gannett's farm, Monks Holme, even down at the harbour on the night the Vicar died, must be examined; so familiar a figure as the builder might have been seen without being noticed, like the postman in the Father Brown story. Was Barton a whisky-drinker? If not, had whisky been bought by him about the time of the Torridge murder? Could he have known where Colonel Cherrington kept his revolver? Were *his* finger-prints, too, discernible on one of Gannett's glasses? If he had drunk with Gannett he could hardly have worn gloves. As regards Gannett, too, another piece of evidence was now available. The Home Office Analyst, Sir Hulbert Lemuel, had found indications that the man had received a severe blow on the left temple with some heavy but soft weapon—perhaps a sandbag— before being burnt. The *left* temple was interesting; either the striker, if he struck from behind, was left-handed, or, if right-handed, must have struck from in front, which suggested his being well known to Gannett. All these were lines which must and would be followed up, if only he had time.

Meanwhile there was the immediate plan to be considered. As soon as darkness fell the watch on Barton's house and business premises—had he not said that he often worked late in the office?—must be re-established.

Fortunately they adjoined one another. Plett and Gwylliam could do that job, reinforced by one of Heskell's constables to act as a messenger; Plett and the constable in front of the house, watching both doors, Gwylliam behind it; a thin wire joining the two watchers would give rough and ready means of passing signals.

He would have liked to be there himself, but he knew that this vigil might go on night after night, and he must be fresh to work by daylight; for the same reason he did not wish to employ Joss, of whose ability he had formed a favourable opinion, on routine observation. All the same, he did not propose that either of them should take off their clothes until the situation was a little clearer; both of them would sleep at the police-station, on camp beds next to the telephone, merely removing their boots for reasonable comfort.

At tea-time Police-Constable Bridger returned from Snottisham on his motor-bicycle, bearing a note from Superintendent Kneller. No comment was made on the interrogation of Barton, but the Superintendent said that all was ready at the Manor House end. He also reported that Barton's sister, Mrs. Hyles, was in fact ill, and that he had visited her on the previous day; he had not stayed the night at her house, and there had not so far been time to establish whether he had spent it anywhere else in Snottisham.

Indications of reconnaissance, thought Myrtle, with renewed confidence.

To give his brain a rest and to while away the time till supper—to be provided for him and Joss by Mrs. Heskell—was ready, Myrtle challenged the County detective to a game of draughts. In this they presently became so deeply absorbed that the trill of the telephone bell sounded twice before Myrtle became conscious of it.

Flaish, the constable on duty, answered the call, and at once put his hand over the mouthpiece.

"Your call, sir," he said. "Batt."

A moment later Myrtle was listening to the eager voice of the young constable.

"Barton's off, sir. Slipped out the back way. Gwylliam passed us a signal, and we went round behind, but he'd disappeared; no sign of either of them. We found an open door at the back of the yard leading into a lane that runs behind it. No doubt Gwylliam couldn't wait for us to come up with him; there's not much light."

"Any idea which way he went?"

"Not for certain, sir. Sergeant Plett used his torch, and thought he could make out some fresh footprints turned west. If they went that way they may be heading for the road that goes over Timber Bridge and passes the Manor."

"What if he turned east?"

"The lane turns north after a couple of hundred yards and joins the coast road running east out of the town."

"Where are you speaking from?"

"Mr. Lucy's house, a hundred yards from Barton's."

"Right. Go back and watch Barton's; he may double back."

Myrtle replaced the receiver. Glancing at the clock, he saw that it was six-thirty-five.

"Come on, Joss, we must gamble on it—cast right ahead and try to come up with them. Car, I think; if we spot them and drive straight past, Barton won't know who we are. Then we can park the car out of the way and join in behind when he re-passes us. The hunt's up; we've forced him to break covert, anyway."

Huddling on raincoats and pulling their hats well down on their heads, the two detectives hurried out into the night. It was, of course, by now quite dark; a full moon was rising early, but there was so much cloud that little light could come through. Visibility could not be much more than twenty yards, even for eyes accustomed to the darkness. The wind and rain, which had slackened somewhat during the afternoon, were now again sweeping in violent gusts across the landscape; this had one great advantage for a trailer; he could keep close to his quarry without being heard.

The police car was standing outside the station, and Bridger was already in the driver's seat. Myrtle wanted freedom of action for himself and Joss.

" He's bound to go over Timber Bridge, sir," said Joss, " if he's making for the Manor. In these floods there's no other way of getting over the Gaggle. If he's walking it'll take him half an hour to get there, I should think."

" Right. We'll get there before him, debus the other side and send the car on. It could wait at the Manor Farm, couldn't it? That's on the way, if I remember rightly."

The car was now running through the almost empty streets. At each crossing the wind, seeming to rush out of a funnel, shook and nearly overturned it. Lashing rain forced its way in through the smallest aperture, and the driver had the greatest difficulty in seeing where he was going. A chimney-pot and several slates were flung into the roadway, and they were glad to get clear of the town; but in the open country things were little better, as branches were flying about, and the risk of falling trees made the drive anything but pleasant.

About a mile short of the bridge the headlights picked up a figure battling forward against the storm.

" Here he is! One of them," exclaimed Myrtle.

In accordance with his orders, Bridger did not slacken

speed, but drove straight on. Myrtle saw that the storm-
buffeted figure was Sergeant Plett, but the headlights
picked up no other trailer and no quarry in front of him,
and when they had gone on a hundred yards Myrtle
stopped the car and waited for Plett to come up.

" Get inside, man," shouted Myrtle, slightly opening
the window.

Plett flung himself into the back seat beside Joss. He
appeared almost exhausted, and lay back panting.
Myrtle waited impatiently for him to recover himself.

" I've lost him, sir," gasped Plett at last. " I came
across Gwylliam just outside the town; Barton had
slipped him. I sent him off up a path that seemed an
alternative to this road. I thought I should catch up
with him."

" You're sure he's ahead of you? "

" Must be, sir, if he came this way; the road took an
awkward turn, and I seemed to go out of my way, but it
turned back again. If he cut across the fields or by a
path he must be ten minutes ahead of me. I tried to
catch up, sir."

" Of course, man; you've done your best," said Myrtle,
reaching back over the seat to pat the dejected Plett's
knee. " Push on now, Bridger; we'll catch him if he's
on the road between here and the Manor. May have
crossed the bridge by now, though."

But there was no ' pushing on ' for the car. A hundred
yards farther on an elm lay across the road; there was
nothing for it but to get out and follow on foot. As they
emerged from the car the detectives were almost flung off
their balance by the wind. The roar and scream of it
through the trees was almost deafening, and the sound was
intensified by the crash of falling branches. They had
not gone far before a deeper roar fell on their ear. Myrtle

was puzzled by it at first, and then realised that it must be the river in torrent. The thought of crossing that rickety wooden bridge, which had shaken under the car as he crossed it earlier in the day, was not a pleasant one. He remembered the driver's words the previous day: " The old bridge'll be in the sea before long." If that was near the mark yesterday, how much nearer to-day.

As if to give point to his thoughts, the sound of a sharp crack penetrated through the roar of wind and waters. It was followed by another, prolonged and deeper, and then the crash of a heavy structure collapsing. Above it all rose suddenly the piercing cry of a human voice, a cry of terror or pain, and then . . . silence. Only the rush of waters, the howl of the wind through the trees.

" My God, he was on it! "

The three men rushed forward, and then pulled up abruptly as they found that the roadway had disappeared in front of them. Myrtle's powerful torch showed a raging torrent crossing their path only a few feet below the level of the road, that and the remains of wooden balustrades dipping into the waters.

" Look, sir, look! "

Joss's hand in the beam of light pointed to the wooden framework on the left side of what was left of the bridge. Clinging to it was a man, his legs and part of his body in the water. The torch-beam, swung directly on to him, showed a white, terror-stricken face staring up at them.

" It's Barton! "

" He'll never get himself out of that. He won't hold long; we must help him."

Myrtle struggled to get out of his macintosh, but the stalwart Plett pushed him gently back.

" My job, sir," he said quietly. " Hang on to my legs, Joss."

Getting down on to his stomach, he wriggled forward and downward until he could get a grip of the drowning man's wrists, first with one hand, then with the other. Joss, also, prostrate, clung on to his legs, wriggling forward with him; Myrtle, knowing the drill, clung on to Joss's; he wished he had Bridger holding his.

As soon as he felt that his grip was secure, Plett shouted at Barton to leave go of the wooden framework, but the man was either too bewildered or too frightened to loosen his hold. Plett gathered up all his strength, and with a tremendous effort heaved himself backward, tearing loose Barton's grip. Then the dead weight of the body on his arms pulled him forward and down; for a moment Myrtle thought that all four of them were going into the river. But union is strength, and the well-trained policemen held their grip and, gradually wriggling and heaving back, drew Barton slowly up from the water and on to the roadway. He lay there on his face, and for a minute or more his rescuers lay beside him, utterly exhausted. Then one by one they rose slowly to their feet.

Myrtle laid his hand on Plett's shoulder.

"Well done, my lad," he said. "That won't be forgotten."

To cover his embarrassment, Plett knelt down beside Barton and turned him over on his back. His eyes were open, and he was breathing in heavy gasps, but he seemed to be unconscious of the men beside him.

"Don't think he's swallowed water, has he? But better be on the safe side."

They went through the well-known drill, but no water came out of Barton, and presently he began to breathe more easily.

"Shock," muttered Myrtle. "We must get him to the car. I don't like the look of him."

Barton's appearance was certainly changing for the worse. There was a sickly green tinge about his face, and his eyes were dull and lifeless. He hardly seemed to be breathing at all.

" Anyone got brandy? " asked Myrtle shortly.

His companions shook their heads.

" Come on, then. We must be quick."

Plett and Joss bent down to take shoulders and legs, but even as they did so Barton made a sudden effort, as if to rise or to speak. He gasped, but no words came through his lips. Then, as suddenly, his head rolled over on his shoulder and his whole body seemed to collapse.

Hurriedly Myrtle tore open waistcoat and shirt, thrusting his hand over Barton's heart. There was a pause, then slowly he withdrew his hand.

" My God," he muttered. " The man's dead."

CHAPTER XXV

Tidying Up

"AN unsatisfactory end, I'm afraid, sir, but it is the end."

Chief Inspector Myrtle, his clothes dry now, but still crumpled and soiled, sat in the Chief Constable's office at Snottisham at noon on the day following the death of Richard Barton. Superintendent Kneller sat near his chief, and Inspector Joss beside the Scotland Yard detective.

"Thank God for it," said Major Statford soberly. "You think Barton was on his way to kill the Squire?"

"One can't doubt it, sir. He must have realised we were closing in on him and that the storm gave him his best chance. He did slip us for a time. If the bridge had held he might have got to the Manor without our seeing him. Of course, he couldn't know that you had a guard posted over Mr. Beynard."

The Chief Constable frowned.

"It will be a shock to Beynard," he said. "I don't think we had convinced him that Barton was a murderer and meant to kill him, too."

"This ought to convince him, sir."

"Yes, I suppose so. And yet . . . we haven't really got much evidence against him, have we, Myrtle?"

The Scotland Yard man shifted uneasily in his chair. He wanted to get back to London, and this was exactly what he had feared; the Chief Constable would want him to tie up every loose end before he went.

"That's only too true, sir," he said. "In a way it's lucky the man's dead. We hadn't got enough evidence to arrest him; it might have taken weeks to get it, and in the meantime there was always a risk of another murder."

" Beynard; yes, I suppose so. Always supposing that the crimes really did hinge on that old tragedy. Not just the work of a madman. I should like to be sure."

Myrtle sighed inwardly. Still, one could see the point.

" I don't think you need feel any doubts, sir," he said. " Now we know the story, the list of victims is too clear to allow of doubt."

" I suppose so. And Barton the killer; Ellen Barton's husband. What about her lover? "

" The sailor, sir; Benbow? I've had a report about him from the Yard this morning. They've managed to get something out of the Admiralty. Naval Intelligence must have been pretty hot so soon after the war, and they got close tabs on the young fellow. He deserted his ship."

" Did he, indeed? "

Myrtle pulled a large envelope from his pocket and extracted a foolscap document. Turning over the pages slowly, he ran his thick forefinger down the lines.

" Here it is, sir. Deserted Hong Kong, October 1920."

" When did it happen? The girl's death: Mrs. Barton."

" July '20, I think, sir."

" Time enough for a letter to reach him."

Myrtle rubbed his chin.

" You think that's why he deserted, sir? "

" It might be. If someone told him what had happened —that aunt he was staying with, perhaps—it would be a pretty good shock. Still . . . he never came back to Great Norne, did he, Kneller? "

Major Statford turned to his Superintendent.

" Not so far as we've been able to trace, sir."

" And if he had, he'd hardly have waited eighteen years before doing something about it. And he could not have lain doggo all that time. Do they know what happened to him after he deserted? "

" Just a bit, sir. but they never caught him; they were always just too late. They got word of him at Cape Town, where he was thrown out as a stowaway early in '21. He was drinking then, and evidently well on the way downhill. But they couldn't find him. They think he had shipped to South America, because he was heard of at Montevideo in '25. At least, they think it was him, but the man who saw him couldn't be sure; said if it was Benbow he'd gone all to pieces, looked twice his age and sodden with drink. That's the last they heard of him. It doesn't help much, but it seems hardly likely that he showed up in Great Norne again, or would be capable of engineering a series of ingenious murders if he had."

" No, I suppose not. If that really was Benbow, and not just someone like him. Do the Admiralty give any description of him? "

Again Myrtle ran his finger down the typewritten pages.

" Here it is, sir. Born 1896. Joined September 1914. Age on joining . . . parents . . . height five foot eight, weight 163 pounds, chest . . . we don't want that. Brown hair, grey eyes, complexion clear, good carriage. Distinguishing marks: apendectomy scar, butterfly tattoo on left breast."

" That description applies to the time of joining, I suppose? "

" I suppose so, sir."

" And that was twenty-four years ago. Not much help

to us now.   One doesn't keep one's schoolboy complexion
at the age of . . . what would it be, forty-two? "

The police officers smiled.   None of them could pose as
advertisements for a beauty soap.

Major Statford leant back in his chair, scowling at the
blotting-pad in front of him.   For five minutes there was
silence in the room, each officer engaged with his own
thoughts.

At last the Chief Constable sat up and spoke crisply.

" We must make quite certain," he said.   " I don't
doubt you're right, Chief Inspector, but we must have
some definite proof that Barton killed these five people.
Now that we know so much it should not be hard to get
the evidence.   Will you stay and help us, Chief Inspector,
or do you want to get back to London? "

It was Myrtle's turn to sit up.   This was a challenge.

" Certainly I'll stay, if you'll allow me, sir.   There's
quite a bit of tidying up to do, and it's my job to do it."

·   ·   ·   ·   ·

Myrtle and Joss drove over to Snottisham for the most
part in silence.   Myrtle was silent because he was not
pleased with life.   The case had reached an anti-climax,
dead but not buried.   The interest had gone out of it;
the interest of the puzzle, the hunt.   There remained the
dull, routine job of tidying up the loose ends, finding
evidence to prove what he felt sure was true.   And it
might well be a long job, whatever the Chief Constable
might say.   To prove his case he would have to connect
Barton definitely with at least one of the murders, and that
meant proving his physical presence at the scene and at
the time of the crime.   With a solitary man, who lived

alone and did not mix with other people, it might be extremely difficult to trace his movements on any one day. Especially when, as with these murders, it was night rather than day with which he was concerned.

So Myrtle sat in frowning silence, pondering over the work ahead of him.

Detective-Inspector Joss was silent primarily from tact—or discretion. He realised pretty well what was in the mind of the big noise from Scotland Yard, and he did not want to attract any of the irritation to himself. Moreover, he also was thinking about the case. He had had his own line to follow—the ' homicidal maniac ' line—and he was not yet entirely convinced that the injured husband, nursing an age-old revenge, was the correct answer to the conundrum. Certainly he could not see that any real proof that this was the case had been found. An attractive theory, yes, but his Hendon training had discouraged theorising and emphasised the vital importance of hard facts.

As the car approached Great Norne—by a roundabout route, to avoid the broken bridge over the Gaggle—Chief Inspector Myrtle at last broke the silence.

" We'll concentrate on the Vinton case," he said. " That's the latest in point of date, so that people's memories will be freshest; and earliest in point of hour, so that there is more chance of his movements having been seen. I believe you did look into that, didn't you—people seen near the house? "

" I did, sir, and I got nothing—except that fellow Blake."

" Ah, yes, one of your homicidal maniac candidates," said Myrtle with a grin. " You didn't get far along that line, I fancy."

" Not far, sir, but I can't say I've worked it right out yet," said Joss doggedly.

"Well, I don't know that I can spare you for non-essentials now. We've got to concentrate on Barton. I expect you'll have to re-work the neighbourhood of the 'Chestnuts'; you may have missed somebody, and that somebody may have been just the one who saw Barton—and thought nothing of him because he was a familiar figure. But we'll go first to his house, get a line from there, and then probably separate."

It was to Barton's place of business, actually, that the detectives went first, because the time of Miss Beatrice Vinton's death had been fixed at between 5 and 6 p.m. The workmen would probably have knocked off by then, but the clerk might still have been there.   In any case, if the killing was at the earliest limit, 5 p.m., Barton must have left his place between 4.30 and 4.45 p.m. to get to the 'Chestnuts' by then, let alone the time taken in breaking into the house. Myrtle thought 5 p.m. was really too early because, though the sun had set at 4 p.m., it was not quite dark an hour later.

The young clerk, Hopper, greeted Myrtle with ghoulish eagerness. He had evidently been sharp enough to realise that the detective's previous visit had been ' hostile ', and to guess that his late employer might have been something more than the sixth victim.

Myrtle wasted no time on finesse.

" I want to know about Mr. Barton's movements on Tuesday afternoon and evening," he said.   " Say between 4 p.m. and 6 p.m."

" Tuesday this week, sir? " asked Hopper eagerly.   He knew well enough what had happened that evening.

Myrtle nodded.

" I can't cover all that time, sir, because I was out for

an hour or so. Mr. Barton was in the office up to ten
minutes to five, when I went out. I got back a little
before six, and I thought he'd gone to his house, but when I
went round to see that all was locked up—that's my job at
6 p.m.—I found him in the carpenter's shop."

"With somebody?"

"No, sir, alone."

"What was he doing?"

"I couldn't see. He was at one of the benches, but he
turned when I looked in and told me to go home; said
he'd lock up."

"You didn't see him again?"

"No, sir."

"And how did you happen to be out from 4.50 to 6
p.m.?"

"Mr. Barton sent me down to the station to find out
about some timber that hadn't come."

"It really hadn't come?"

"Really not, sir. It was a genuine job," said the acute
Mr. Hopper.

"And likely to keep you away for an hour or
so?"

"Well, it wouldn't have taken so long if we hadn't had
to telephone from the station to Snottisham."

It was not entirely convincing. But at least Barton
could have been sure of being alone for from half to three-
quarters of an hour; probably long enough for the killing
of Beatrice Vinton. Nobody else had remained in the
builder's yard, and there was no reason why Barton should
not have come back to establish a six o'clock alibi and
then returned for the killing of Emily at seven. How,
though, could he know that she would not return till
seven?

Feeling slightly uneasy, Myrtle walked with Joss the

few yards to Barton's house, to which they were admitted by a woebegone Mrs. Jackson.

At Myrtle's first question the housekeeper burst into tears.

" Oh, sir," she said, " I told him not to go.   I told him it wasn't safe."

" What wasn't safe? "

" The storm, sir, and that old bridge; not safe it's been these twenty years.   Mr. Beynard shouldn't 've asked him."

The detective stared at her in bewildered amazement.

" You knew he was going to the Manor? "

" Oh, yes; he told me.   Grumbling he was.   Natural enough he wouldn't want to go out on a night like that, and I tried to stop him.   But he would go.   Mr. Beynard had been his only friend for years.   Telephoned, Mr. Barton said he did; wanted to see him urgent."

Myrtle shook himself, as if to throw off his bewilderment.

" Joss, slip round to the office and find out what they know about this call."

While Joss was away, Myrtle continued to question Mrs. Jackson about the previous evening.   Barton, it appeared, had made no attempt to conceal from his housekeeper his intention of going to the Manor House.   He had even told her that he was going out by the back-yard because he believed the police were watching him and he didn't see why they should follow him wherever he went.   Strange behaviour for an intending murderer, thought Myrtle, with a growing feeling of uncomfortable doubt.

Joss was back within five minutes, to say that there had certainly been a telephone call for Barton just before four o'clock the previous afternoon.   Hopper had been having a cup of tea, so had noticed the time.   He had not paid much attention to the conversation, but thought it had ended with his employer saying: "Tell him I'll come."

And Mr. Beynard? For what earthly reason could he have sent for Barton, the very next day after being warned that he might be the murderer's next victim? Surely it was inconceivable that he had done so. Could this be some blind of Barton's? Some attempt to throw them off the real scent, to create an alibi to cover the murder of some other, unsuspected victim?

"Here, Joss, let's get down to the station," said Myrtle abruptly.

The detectives left the tearful Mrs. Jackson without ceremony and without even formal condolences; their surprise had driven away their manners. At the police-station Myrtle put a call through to the Manor House, intending to get at least preliminary confirmation or denial of the housekeeper's story.

After a slight pause the operator's nasal voice came through:

"Sorry. Line's out of order."

"Out of order? What do you mean?"

"The line's down. Been down since yesterday morning."

Myrtle's eyes glittered with excitement.

"Get me Supervisor," he snapped. And ten seconds later: "Supervisor, this is Chief Inspector Myrtle. I want to trace a call that was supposed to have been put through from the Manor House to Mr. Barton's office yesterday afternoon just before 4 p.m. The line was down at that time. I want to know if a call really was put through to Mr. Barton at that time, and if so where from."

"I'm sorry. We don't keep a note of calls."

The bored, would-be-refined voice of the Supervisor pricked Myrtle to irritation.

"Young woman, I am investigating five murders," he snapped; "possibly six. I expect you to help me. I shall be round at the Exchange in ten minutes, and I want that information."

He got it. The possibility of appearing by name in the papers, perhaps even a photo in the 'Sundays', stirred Miss Jook and her staff to unwonted energy, and even intelligence. Within half an hour Myrtle was in possession of the fact that a call had been put through to the builder at 3.55 p.m. on the previous day from the kiosk outside the railway station.

Myrtle and Joss hurried there, and soon had the station staff buzzing with a fever of inquiries. But no one knew anything about a telephone-call from the kiosk at four o'clock the previous afternoon. It was a quiet time, no train due in or out; the staff would be mostly engaged on their afternoon cup of tea.

"Crooky might 'a seen summat," suggested an elderly porter.

"Crooky?"

"He means Blake," explained the Stationmaster. "Calls himself 'Outside porter'. Nothing to do with the Company. Quite unauthorised really, on the Company's premises; but he makes himself useful, and we allow him. It's true he's the most likely person to see anyone using that outside kiosk."

"Where is he?"

No one, as it happened, had seen Crooky Blake that day, though no one had, up till now, particularly noticed his absence.

"Come on, Joss, we must find him. We've got to trace this call. Where's he likely to be?"

" He was down at his hut near the harbour when I
looked for him before, sir. Or rather, in the one next to
it, belonging to an old woman called Hirdle. Friend of
his, I gathered."

" Let's go. We may get news of him on the way."

But no one of whom they inquired had seen the outside
porter that day. One man—a fisherman down at the
harbour—reported that he had not been at the ' Silver
Herring ' the previous evening.

Leaving the harbour, the two detectives took the muddy,
cindered track that led to the small group of ramshackle
cabins on the edge of the saltings. Although it was not yet
sundown, a haze of thin fog had darkened the afternoon,
and it was not possible to see more than a hundred yards
or so. Presently a spark of light showed from one of the
cabins, the one next from last; the light came, they saw,
from a crack under the door.

" That's Mother Hirdle's," said Joss. " Blake's is the
end one."

Suddenly the sound of a man's voice caught their ears.
It sounded almost like a cry, a shout, but there was a
wavering quality in it—no strength, weakness rather. It
came from the old woman's hut.

" That's where he was before," said Joss. " I wonder
. . . it didn't sound like him."

" Sounded to me like someone in pain," said Myrtle.
" Let's look."

They walked up to the door and tapped. There was
no answer, but the man's voice could be more distinctly
heard, though no words could be distinguished. Myrtle
lifted the latch and opened the door.

The room was lit by an oil-lamp on the table in its centre.
In one corner stood a bed, partly hidden by the body of
an old woman—Mrs. Hirdle—who stood bending over it.

Her head was turned over her shoulder now, and she glared at her visitors.

" Is that Mr. Blake? " asked Myrtle quietly.

For a moment Ma Hirdle continued to glare, then her withered face crumpled and she began to whimper.

" He's bad. I don't know what to do for him."

" What's happened? "

" He was in the water last night. Dragged himself here, he did, all soaking and shivering. I got him into bed—I don't know how. He's been going on terrible. Shaking, too, and all hot."

" Fever," said Myrtle shortly. " Been going on, has he? What's he been saying? "

Suspicion flashed into the old woman's eyes. She shook her head, muttering.

The two detectives had moved to the foot of the bed and stood looking down at the sick man. Blake was clearly in a bad way—his face was flushed, his eyes bright and staring. Unshaven chin and tousled hair added to the wildness of his appearance.

Suddenly a torrent of words burst from him, at first unintelligible, then distinguishable, though thick and slurred :

" Why don't he come? . . . Him and me. . . . At last . . . last of them . . . Him or me, him or me . . . there he is ! . . ."

Then, rising to a sudden scream:

" CHRIST; IT's GOING ! "

The scream, a cry of mingled terror and rage, sent a shiver through the listening men. Old Mrs. Hirdle whimpered and twisted her gnarled fingers together.

Myrtle pushed her gently from the side of the bed and leant over the sick man.

" Bring the lamp here, Joss," he said quietly.

As the light fell on Blake, Myrtle gently opened the front of the coarse flannel nightgown in which the old woman had somehow managed to dress him. There was a thick mat of hair on the chest, and streaks of grime, but clearly the light showed, just above the left nipple, the crude outline of a tattooed butterfly.

CHAPTER XXVI

A Good Job

DR. STOPP frowned as he read the thermometer.

" Can't very well move him yet," he said. " We must get that temperature down a bit if we can. I shall have to get a nurse from the Cottage Hospital."

He glanced at Mrs. Hirdle.

" Better shift her if we can," he muttered to Chief Inspector Myrtle.

But the old woman heard him. Clutching her shrivelled arms in front of her, she glowered at the doctor.

" I'll not go," she said. " 'Tis my house. I can nurse him, better'n any chit from the hospital."

Dr. Stopp looked doubtfully at Myrtle.

" I'd like a word with you outside, sir," said the detective.

Out of earshot of the hut the two men stopped.

" Is he bad? " asked Myrtle.

" About as bad as can be. Double pneumonia. I doubt if he's got the constitution to pull through. Hopeless place to nurse him, that hovel, but I must get his temperature down if I can."

" Any chance of his talking? "

" You want him to talk? "

" Like hell I do. Look here, doctor, that man's got the key to all these murders—I want it. I can't question him, not as things stand now, but if he *did* happen to talk it'd save a lot of time and trouble. Is there any chance of his being able to? "

Dr. Stopp did not answer for a moment.

" Possible," he said. " If it's as you say, I'll use pretty

drastic methods, but keep that to yourself. I can't shift that old woman, I suppose?"

"Not very well, sir. It's her house."

"The Englishwoman's castle," said Stopp with a short laugh. "Well, I'll try to get Matron to let me have Sister Newling; she's the last word in discretion."

After making Blake as comfortable as possible, Dr. Stopp went off to plan his battle. Myrtle, leaving Joss on guard, made his way to the police-station and sent a discreet message to Headquarters. He also had to make his plan.

It was clear enough now that this man Blake was the sailor Benbow, cause of all the trouble that had led to Ellen Barton's suicide. It was pretty clear, too, that he and not Barton had been methodically wiping out the people who, in his eyes at any rate, had driven his lover to her death. Last night was to have been the final act in the tragedy; he had lured Barton out by a faked telephone message and waylaid him at the Timber Bridge, where the flooded Gaggle had played the hand for him in a way he had not intended.

How Benbow, only forty-two years old, had transformed himself into the crook-backed, elderly Blake was a mystery that probably only Benbow himself could explain. Would he? He could not now be questioned, because it was the clear duty of the police to charge him with the murders. Only a voluntary statement would be accepted in court, and it hardly seemed likely that that would be forthcoming.

Dr. Stopp and Sister Newling flatly refused to have a policeman permanently in the cramped cabin which was now a sick-bay. There was really no necessity for it, as by no possibility could a man in Benbow's condition escape. So Myrtle arranged that either he or Joss should be in Blake's cabin next door, and fixed up a bell by which

Sister Newling could call them if necessary. Dr. Stopp said that it would be at least twenty-four hours before the sick man was able to talk coherently, if at all.

From time to time during the following day Myrtle looked in to see how Benbow was getting on. Towards evening there were definite signs of improvement, and Myrtle once caught a gleam of intelligence in the man's eye. But it was ten o'clock at night before Sister Newling summoned him by a ring on the electric bell.

Benbow was lying rather higher on his pillows than before. The flush on his face had subsided and the glitter disappeared from his eye, but he looked tired and worn.

Myrtle walked up to the side of the bed and looked down.

" Evening, Benbow," he said quietly.

Crooky's shaggy eyebrows contracted in a quick frown.

" You know that, eh? " he muttered.

He closed his eyes and lay back as if intending to take no more notice of the detective, but after five minutes he opened them again.

" If you've got that far there's no gain in holding on," he said. " Sit down. I'll talk."

Myrtle sat down, wishing that he had a shorthand writer with him. But he had not wanted to choke the man off by too much formality—at first.

" I must warn you, Benbow," he said, " that I shall probably charge you with the murder of one or more persons. There's no need for you to say anything, and I'm not allowed to question you. Anything you say may be used as evidence."

" I know all that. But I've done a good job, and I'm proud of it. I don't want any of the fine points missed."

Crooky grinned. Myrtle had noticed that the man's voice and manner of speaking were much less coarse than his appearance. No doubt young Benbow of the Royal Navy had been a well-educated man; later coarseness of appearance and speech might have been, to some extent at any rate, deliberately assumed.

" To cut it short, how much do you know? "

" I know you are Nathaniel Edward Benbow, and that eighteen years ago you had an affair with a Mrs. Barton who subsequently committed suicide. I know that her suicide was thought to be due to some action taken by her husband and the Church Council, that you subsequently deserted your ship, and that now her husband and all the surviving members of the Council, except one, have met violent deaths within the course of a few weeks. That's all I'm prepared to tell you about my knowledge."

Benbow nodded.

" You've got the old story. You know the ' why ', you'd like to know the ' how ', eh? "

" I would—but you needn't say anything."

" I won't talk about her—or I may want to kill someone else. We fell for each other, and if I could have got her away from Barton I would have. He was a dirty swine even then, and I hated him. But she wouldn't leave him and . . . and I was recalled off leave, and no time even to talk to her alone. We sailed directly I got back—Mediterranean first, then China. It wasn't till we called in at Hong Kong two months later that I got a mail. And then it wasn't from Ellen; it was from my old aunt I'd been staying with when I was up here.

" My God, shall I ever forget that letter! She told me Ellen was dead—hanged herself. Said Barton had found out, or thought he'd found out, about Ellen and me, and gone to his Church Council and . . . Christ, the swine! "

Myrtle saw Benbow's eyes begin to glitter again. He feared a return of the fever.

"Better leave that, Benbow," he said. "I know what Barton did, and the Council. You deserted your ship. Tried for leave, I suppose, and not granted?"

"That was it. The Old Man was good to me, but he couldn't grant me a compassionate—no relation; I couldn't even tell him the truth. So I took it, but from the start my luck was out. I was doped by some Chinks and all my money taken, got a ship to Colombo and broke my wrist. Like a fool, instead of waiting for it to mend, I stowed away in a Dutchman that was making for the Cape and up the West Coast; of course I was spotted, and the skipper threw me overboard at Cape Town. By that time I'd lost heart, and I let myself go. Lost all my wish to get home; didn't care what became of me."

"So you kicked about the world a bit . . . and someone saw you in Montevideo."

Benbow stared.

"Don't you know something, then! You're right. 'Knocked about' is the word. Smashed up by shifting cargo in an Argentine tramp. No doctor aboard, and the the skipper was a drunken brute who knew nothing of setting a broken shoulder. I got to hospital—what a hospital!—and look at me now! Who'd recognise the smart young matlow that turned the head of the prettiest girl in . . . oh well, what's the good?"

"Lucky to get over it, I should think," said Myrtle quietly.

"Lucky? Better dead, I thought then. But it was in hospital that I started thinking, and it gradually came on me that perhaps there was something to live for, after all— Barton. It was only him I thought about then. Aunt Annie, in her letter, had given me the names of some of the people on the Church Council, the Vicar of course, and Colonel Cherrington, Gannett—an easy name for a sailor-

man to remember; Pybus was another name and Vinton,
They all stuck in the memory, but there were one or two I
forgot. But just at first I was only thinking of Barton.

" As I lay on my back it came to me what a fine thing it
would be to go back to Great Norne and punish Barton for
what he'd done to Ellen. I planned to let him know who I
was and why he was going to die. I enjoyed that planning; it was the first thing I had enjoyed since I said
good-bye to Ellen all those years ago. I made out it
should be a good job, an artistic job, so that I shouldn't
swing for it; that meant preparation, long preparation.
It wouldn't do to go blundering into Great Norne, a
stranger, and a week or two later a man dead. It wouldn't
do either to turn up as a seaman; that might start people
thinking, directly things happened. No, I must have a
trade, and gradually fit into the background of the place."

Sister Newling walked up to the bed with a cool drink.
Her fingers quietly felt the man's wrist, but she said
nothing. The drink refreshed Benbow, and he went on.

" I landed in Liverpool in June 1929, and got a job as a
docker. Then I gradually worked south, picking up what
I wanted—a background. I fetched up in Great Norne
at the end of 1930, and when I found my old Auntie was
dead I knew no one would recognise the crook-backed,
broken-toothed wreck I now was; I looked nearer fifty
even then than the thirty-four I was.

" I got a job with the local Council, as a roadman;
not much skill needed for that. I soon began to pick up
the names, and I had a good look at them—Torridge,
Cherrington. I began to hate them, too, nearly as bad
as Barton. Him I could hardly keep my hands off—but I
did. Gannett didn't look as if he'd ever been near a
church, but he was on the list. Pybus was dead, I found.
There were two Vintons; Auntie hadn't said which, so I

had to take both, to make sure. Because, you see, by that time I'd decided to make a job of it—an artistic job—and rub out the lot of them."

Benbow laughed harshly, and Myrtle felt a shudder go down his spine.

" And did I start on them right away? No, I did not. This was a planned job. It was going to be a perfect job; all the rest of my life I was ready to give to it. I planned to wait seven years before I started, so as to get people accustomed to me—to Blake, Crooky Blake. I'd got to find my way about, find out all about the habits of the people I was going to kill. I soon realised that a roadman's job wouldn't do for that. I had to stick too close to the road, and there was no excuse for asking questions. I had an idea. I'd been working near the station, and I saw people carrying their own luggage away—people who couldn't afford a cab. I thought, why not a sort of porter, get to know people, get into their houses, get all over the place, my own master, come and go when I liked? So I fixed myself up with a barrow, painted my name on it—the name I'd taken—and set about working up a connection. It went with a bang from the start. People were glad to pay a tanner to save themselves lugging a heavy bag through the streets; two bags, two tanners; you'd be surprised how quickly that totted up into money. And the smaller tradesmen used me as a carrier, and the bigger ones for odd jobs. After that I became a handy-man, too—all sailors are that—and fixed things in people's houses, things they couldn't do for themselves but weren't big enough to call in a builder for. I was getting into people's houses now—Cherrington's house, Vinton's house, Gannett's farm, even; not Barton's house, of course—I realised that that would be an outside job.

" I'd found out where Ellen was buried, and every now and then I'd go and have a look at her grave; it kept me keyed up. I got a shock one night, though, when I realised the Vicar was watching me. I don't think he can have seen who I was, but it made me realise that it was time to get started.

" I began with him because he would be easy money and it would get my hand in. He went every week, on Thursday, to the Men's Club down by the harbour. There was always liable to be a sea mist in the early winter, and one Thursday when that happened I lay for him and smashed the back of his head in with a bit of lead piping. Then I laid him head down on the steps of the quay and fixed a rope round his legs. That had two purposes—to make it look as if he'd tripped over it, and to stop him slipping down into the water; because the water would have washed away the evidence."

" Exactly. The whisky," said Myrtle quietly.

Crooky grinned.

" Ah, so they did spot it, did they? Mighty quiet they kept about it. A great disappointment to me, that was. I meant to shame him, shame the whole lot of them, as they'd shamed Ellen. But all hushed up for the quality, of course," said Benbow bitterly. " If it had been . . ."

A sudden cough shook him. He sat up gasping. The nurse was quickly at his side, and her hand on his shoulder gently pushed him back on to the pillow. Looking steadily at the detective, she shook her head.

Myrtle took a quick decision.

" Take it easy, Benbow," he said. " I can save you a bit of talking. We spotted that shamming lay of yours—helped to lead us to you, it did. Whisky for the Vicar, blackmailing letter for the Colonel, a dirty book for the old lady. Where did you get that, by the way? "

Myrtle had for the moment forgotten his pious intention to ask no questions. Crooky leered at him.

" Liverpool. There's always some funny shops where seamen are."

" I daresay. Well, so the Colonel came next. You'd been in his house, of course, learnt the family habits from the maids talking. Spotted that convenient cupboard under the staircase, no doubt. So one night, when he'd be full of beer from the British Legion dinner and likely to doze off, you slipped in through that first-floor window and down into the cupboard. When they came back and the Captain had gone upstairs, all you'd got to do was to peep in at the study door. There he was asleep in the armchair with his back to you. What was it that you slugged him with? A lump of putty in a sock—something of that sort? Oh, yes, that's all clear enough, but what about his gun? How did you get hold of that? "

" Spotted it on a recce. Went in one night specially to look for it—a pistol or a shot-gun. Found it straight away in the top right-hand drawer of his writing-table; he only locked one drawer, and that wasn't it."

" Too easy. Then you burnt some papers, put your bit of blackmail letter among the ashes . . . and shot him in the temple you'd slugged. Back into the cupboard, I suppose, and lay low while the rush was on. When did you get away? "

" After the women had gone back upstairs. I heard the Captain telephoning in the study and that seemed my chance. I was clear away before any police reached the house."

" Neat timing, but you had luck, Benbow; you had luck. Of course, you need it for a game like you were playing. And so, while your luck was in, you went on with it."

"I'd tasted blood. It was too exciting to stop. Besides, when you Scotland Yard chaps came I knew they'd smelt a rat about the Colonel and weren't satisfied it was suicide. There was a risk of my being taken before I'd finished my job."

Myrtle realised with shame that, so far as he was concerned, Blake—Benbow—had been in little danger. Three, four more deaths had followed before, almost by chance, he had been led to the killer.

"No difficulty about Gannett, of course," he said. "No doubt you found him sodden drunk, slugged him, too, and set him alight. But your alibi was pretty tight."

Benbow chuckled.

"Your Mr. Plett helped me there," he said. "Didn't take me long to cotton on to what he was. When he started coming to the 'Herring' I made up my mind I'd use him for my alibi; what better than a dick for that? So one night when he was in the 'Herring' I got them talking about the inquest on the Colonel and a good deal of booze going, and I let him see that I'd got a skinful myself; I got Blossom to fill my gin-flask, so that Plett could see, and then I staggered out. I'd got my old bike tucked away outside; I'd had it a long time, but no one had ever seen me ride it; there's nothing like a push-bike for covering the ground without noise and without a light."

Myrtle nodded. He realised that he had left a good deal of thinking undone in this case.

"I did the job as you said, and it took next to no time," continued Benbow. "I was back outside the 'Herring' not half an hour after I left it, and the flames just beginning to show from there. There are always fellows coming in and out of the 'Herring', and I meant someone to find me asleep in my old barrow, as I'd done many a time before when I was pretending to be three sheets."

" Pretending? "

Crooky laughed.

" Sucked them all in, I did. I never really drank any-thing but beer, but I was always getting my flask filled up with gin, and every now and then I'd spill some over me and let folks find me sleeping it off. It was Ma here that had the gin. Didn't you, Ma? "

The old woman, who had been sitting silently on one side of the fireplace, nodded her head, and two big tears trickled down her wrinkled cheeks. She couldn't under-stand all that was going on, but she knew that her friend Nat was ill and in trouble, and she had a shrewd suspicion that there would be no more of the comforting gin coming her way in the future.

" And it was Plett who found you and fell into your trap, eh? " said Myrtle. " That was luck for you."

" Not so much luck. Evening before, when he came to the ' Herring ', he left at a quarter to eight to get back to his dinner at the ' George ', and I hoped he'd do it again. Sure enough he did; out he came and bumped right into me. He had a good smell at me, and I reckoned I could count on him for an alibi."

And that was exactly what the damn-fool Plett had given him, thought the detective bitterly. A half-crazed sailor successfully hoodwinking a trained policeman.

" And that brought you to the Miss Vintons; not so easy, eh? But, of course, you knew which was the maid's afternoon out, and you knew about the party at the doctor's. So you waited about till you'd seen the maid and the sister go out, and then in you went through a first-floor window, same as at Colonel Cherrington's."

" Not till I'd made my alibi," interposed Benbow quietly. " Went down to the station and showed myself there—asked about a parcel Coote had been fussing about;

it hadn't come, but it made the clerk remember me asking.

"At half-past four I was back; nearly dark it was when I slipped into the garden. I was just getting up to the house when the back-door opened and out came the girl! That was a shock; I'd thought she was gone for the day. I tucked up against the wall, and she came right past me; coming out from the bright lights, she was blind. Nothing was going to stop me, I thought then. I was meant to win!"

Myrtle noticed that the man's colour was rising again, the glitter coming back into his eyes. It might not be possible to get much more coherent information from him. Still, he had got most of what he wanted. He could not, of course, use the statement, because it was not written down and signed. But there would be no difficulty about building a case against him now—if any case were needed. Myrtle had no doubt that this cold-blooded murderer was himself hovering very near the border line between life and death. It had been an incongruous conversation, not easily reconcilable with the regulations, but it was doing the 'tidying-up' that the Chief Constable had asked for.

"Well, anyway, you went in and found the paralysed old woman alone and at your mercy. That was easy for you, Benbow."

The sailor stared at him for a minute without speaking.

"Not so easy," he muttered at last. "Not so easy as I thought. It was her eyes. She looked at me. Her eyes followed me about. Even when I was behind her I felt she was looking at me. I walked to a window and cut off a blind-cord—and she watched me. I told her who I was and why I was there; what I'd done and what I was going to do. I thought I should enjoy that, but I didn't.

I knew she was dumb and helpless . . . but she scared me, more than all the others. Her eyes watching me . . .''

Sister Newling walked up to the bedside and looked at her patient.

" You'd better go now," she said curtly.

Myrtle nodded.

But the voice of the murderer went on:

" I saw the rug on her lap was moving; she'd got her hands under the rug, and I thought maybe she'd got a gun. I snatched the rug away. It wasn't a gun, but a sort of pad—waxed paper. She'd written on it: BLAKE. She had guts, that old woman. I laughed and lifted the wax paper, and the name disappeared. I laughed, I tell you . . . but I was scared. Ha, ha! Scared of an old, dumb, helpless woman. Me, Nat Benbow, of the Royal Navy, been through the war, knocked round the world, killed three men and ready to kill another . . . scared of that old dame!''

Again the nurse urged Myrtle to go, but he could not tear himself away till he had heard the end of the story. Staring straight in front of him now, his gnarled fingers clutching the bed-clothes, Benbow continued:

" I went behind her and put the cord round her neck. ' This is what Ellen felt,' I said. At that she suddenly let out a scream that would have lifted the roof if I hadn't pulled the cord quick and choked it. God! I'll not forget that scream. I was dripping sweat when I'd finished— cold sweat. When she was dead I put the rug back and the book under it. Then I turned out the gas, but I made up the fire so as to have a little light to see movement. I had to wait . . . for the other. Wait . . . with those eyes looking at me! The fire-light shone on them. I watched her . . . and she watched me! Behind the door I stood, waiting . . . waiting . . . she's coming! Now!

The door's opening . . . choke her before she can yell! Aah . . . ! "

Benbow's voice rose almost to a scream. He sat up, struggling to push the bedclothes off him.

" Hold him," snapped Sister Newling.

Swiftly she bared his arm, wiped it with a swab and thrust her glittering needle into the dry, hot flesh. For a moment more Crooky struggled, then slowly relaxed on to the pillow. His harsh features softened almost to a smile.

" Done it," he murmured, " a good job."